STARBORN

STEALING THE SUN: BOOK 9

RON COLLINS

SKYFOX
PUBLISHING
Science Fiction

STARBORN

STEALING THE SUN: BOOK 9

Cover Design: © Ron Collins
All rights reserved

Cover Image
© Alteraposto | Dreamstime.com

Skyfox Publishing

ISBN-10: 1-946176-40-0
ISBN-13: 978-1-946176-40-0

STEALING THE SUN

includes

STARFLIGHT

STARBURST

STARFALL

STARCLASH

STARBOUND

STARCRASH

STARGAMES

STARDUST

STARBORN

Other Work by Ron Collins

Wakers

The Knight Deception

A Trevin Knight Thriller

Saga of the God-Touched Mage

Glamour of the God-Touched
Target of the Orders
Trail of the Torean
Gathering of the God-Touched
Pawn of the Planewalker
Changing of the Guard
Lord of the Freeborn
Lords of Existence

Picasso's Cat & Other Stories

Five Magics

Seven Days in May

Tomorrow in All the Worlds

Follow Ron at:
http://www.typosphere.com
Twitter: @roncollins13

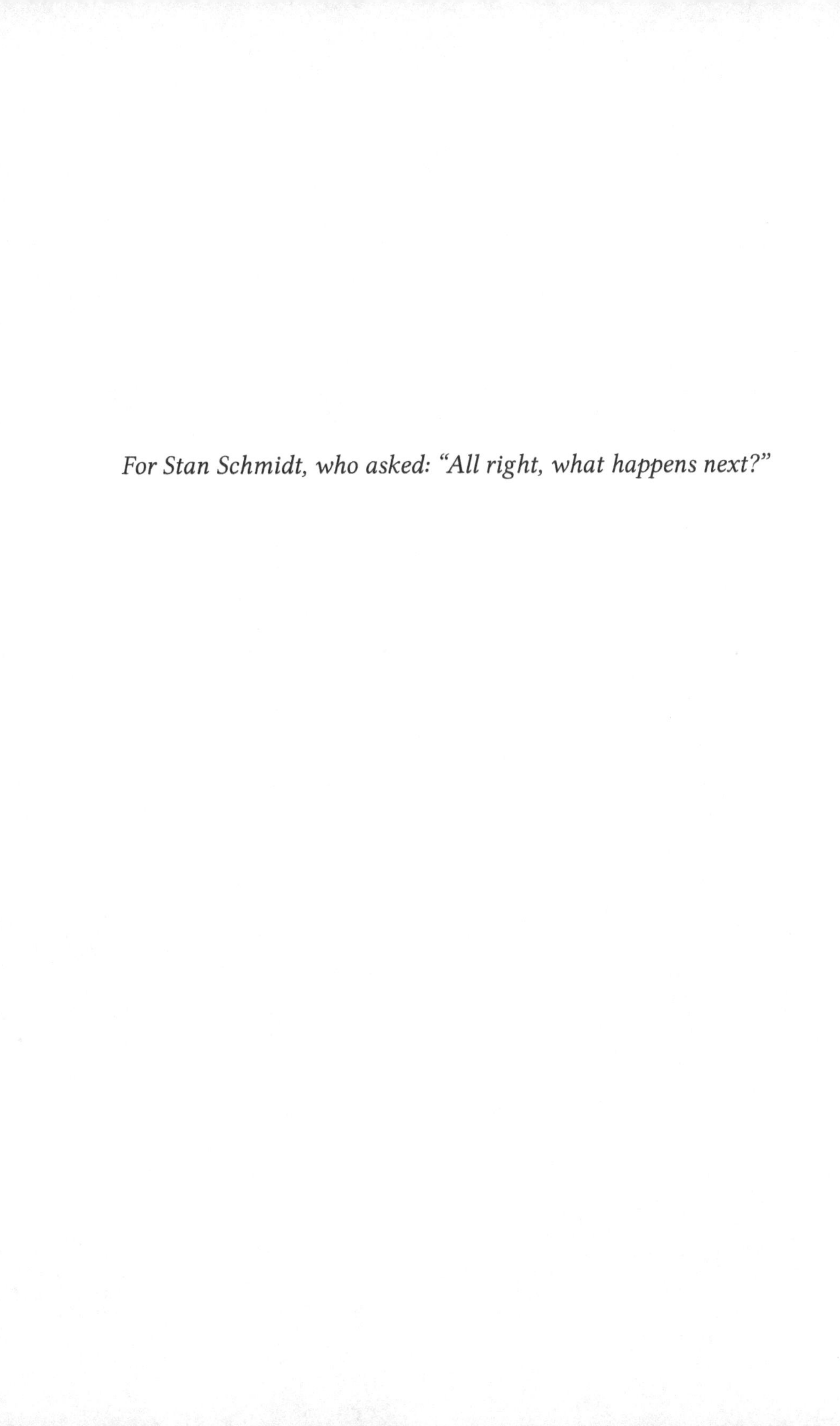

For Stan Schmidt, who asked: "All right, what happens next?"

When a big institution commits a crime, there may be little that an individual can do about it. But does that mean he must do nothing?

Stanley Schmidt

CONTENTS

INTRODUCTION

What is time, right?

We spend it. We save it. We watch it as it flies past.

It's been six years since I published *Starflight*, the first book in this series. Now comes *Starborn*, which is the ninth and last book of the series. Six years that I've had my life touched by writing and publishing this story. Unless, of course, you start counting from when the short story this series came from was published — which was twenty-three years ago. If you count from when I sat down to write the first draft of that story, you'd have to say twenty-four years.

I finished that draft on September 27, 1998.

I know that because I was blogging at the time, and I wrote it down. If things go as planned, I'll release this one September 30, 2022. *[Editor's note: Hah! You think life will go as planned?]*

So, yes, twenty-four years.

The last few days have been a weird mix. I've been going through the last pass at this book, and at points stepping into that time machine to skim through parts of the earlier material. Remembering how I chose to move parts of the story around, remembering how I came upon decisions of how to present the parts that had been in those three shorter stories that were first published in *Analog*. Writing this has felt like visiting old friends. I remember almost everything, but on occasion I run into something I'd forgotten I'd written.

Weird.

A lot has happened in the world since I first started writing these stories back in 1998. For example, the events of 9/11 had not yet occurred as I wrote those first drafts, so neither had the subsequent actions in Iraq and Afghanistan. Climate change was looming, but not looming so close that you couldn't find a way to ignore it without seeming purposeful. We had not seen Barack Obama (which I subsequently found fun due, of course, to one of the main characters in this sprawling little story having been named Baraq), better yet the pandemic, nor Trump and the chaos that he brought us.

We are all different people now than we were when the first inklings of this story began to form in my head. Some of us were not even born then!

When I started this story, I had envisioned it as a piece that would carry forward a sense of hope amid devastation. We'll see whether I've achieved that or not. Hope, after all, is an ephemeral sensation. I am the kind of person who sees hope in many things and in many ways. Despite time wearing things a little thin, I remain at my threadbare core an optimist. But you will carry away your own messages built through your own frames of mind.

That's the gig I signed up for.

All those many years ago.

Even before I wrote that first draft of "Stealing the Sun" that Algis Budrys so curmudgeonly critiqued as "pretty good." Before I published my first story in a now-defunct place called *Radius Magazine.* From the moment I clacked my first words onto a keyboard, knowing I was going to try this life on for size. When I wrote those first few words, and when I looked out into the world of publishing with a sense that was a mixture of bravado and fear.

I was hopeful, then, too. Yes, even then.

This ninth book comes to a world different than that first one. I think it's a more dangerous world. One that might well require tough decisions by bodies of people not used to making them.

Still, as I end, I remember hope.

Ron Collins
2022

PROLOGUE

Local Season: Eldoro Leading, Year of Second *Piela*, Cycle 57

WAR

All of Esgarat

And so it came that — in the dry and dusty lands known as All of Esgarat, which was a planet known to human beings as Eden, and which orbited in its path around Eldoro (the larger Alpha Centauri A) and Katon (the lesser Alpha Centauri B) and tiny Eterdane (Proxima) — the quadars who lived in lands ringed by the great ranges of the Esgarat mountains engaged in a bloody civil war.

Family against Family, clan against clan, innocent against innocent — all combatants paid in blood and suffering.

As with all wars, the humblest among them paid the steepest prices, the independent *hedgie* and those of the lesser families who became conscripted against their will and were sent to face their annihilations. Others became simply lost in the confusion, left to fend for themselves in a world bereft of food and shelter, scurrying from heat to heat in search of a life that no longer existed.

A few, the lucky, managed to escape up into the mountains that ringed that wide city plain. And of those few, a fewer still found refuge with a sect of those same quadars that were once led by a legendary professor of science, and by one human being who also strove to find another path.

In the realm of deep space above, as quadars fought their war below, time ticked away.

Winds grew bolder, racing down the cliffs and the rocky peaks that formed the city itself.

Temperatures, once rocketing upward, now fell.

Skies, having been cloudless and expansive for several cycles, clouded again.

And, for the first time known to any quadarti scholar, a veil of ice and snow fell on upper peaks of that towering ring.

For time is a beast endlessly hungry, a shark that swims forever through the gravity wells of space, never halting, always pressing ahead, forward, relentlessly forward.

As All of Esgarat fought, and as its skies grew cold, this shark that is time, inside the core of the star known to them as Eldoro, fused hydrogen and helium that was still being fed into a dimensional warp to burn in engines attached to fleets of starships that carried human beings from place to place as if having simply folded space-time upon itself again and again.

SUN DRAIN

Chapter 1

Mars Colony Kasbian, Jagger's Field
Local Date: August 8, 2252
Local Time: 0925 (Earth Standard)

Sitting in the shuttle's comfortable passenger bay, and glancing out the viewport as they descended, Marisa Harthing, Captain, Interstellar Command, Navigation section, was worried.

She gripped her armrest, taking in the sight of the clear dome that covered Mars Colony Kasbian, and then the outpost sprawled below. Dim sunlight reflected and refracted from the dome's surface in a prismatic flare. The community inside was thriving, the first ever to be successful at such a scale, but still the harsh, barren Martian landscape sprawled away in every direction around it, making the research colony feel like a tiny island in a desert sea.

The sense of isolation in the image just added to her discomfort.

For all its novelty, Kasbian was a run-of-the-mill science station, so normally she wouldn't have diverted her itinerary to come here. Her duties at Interstellar gave her other places to be, after all — she had projects to oversee, new guidance concepts to explore. Her next formal assignment would be three standard weeks on *Magellan* to oversee the upgrade to that ship's multidimensional Star Drive guidance array.

But she wanted to see Thomas Kitchell — or "the kid" as she and

Torrance had called him back in the years when the two of them had been together.

Thomas Kitchell was the third wheel of what all three called the *Everguard* trio: Torrance Black, Thomas Kitchell, and Marisa Harthing. They had all been tokens for the United Government after the *Everguard* disaster, and each of them had been taken care of to a greater degree — Torrance picking up an assignment that led to his ambassadorship, Kitchell taking a slot in the Academy that he'd used as a springboard to a high-profile life as a renowned scientist, albeit in the wonderfully niche category of signal processing and space communications.

For Marisa's part, the UG gave her a path to what eventually became this role with Interstellar Command.

With recent events, she'd been looking at the timeline more closely, and that examination showed her another truth in each of these assignments. The command had taken care of all three, yet none of them were positions of public consequence. The *Everguard* trio had become a forgettable footnote in history. Except now, of course. Now Torrance Black had become a concern.

She didn't believe for even one minute the crap the UG Intelligence Office was spouting about Torrance being an agent of Universe Three.

Torrance Black was no traitor — and she'd seen Ragnath Gavarian's exclusive in which he stated that a "person close to Black" had disputed the UG's claims. That "person close to Black" had to be Thomas Kitchell because, beyond her and the kid, there were no people "close to Black," and obviously Gavarian hadn't talked to her.

Now Thomas wasn't responding to her calls, and she was getting pressure from her own superiors to put distance between herself and Torrance *just for appearances' sake.*

Coincidences like that annoyed her.

They set her senses tingling.

She needed to know what was going on.

So, she'd twisted a few arms, and now here she was — flying to Mars Colony Kasbian to take a meeting with the station's director, who was also assigned to the UG Sensor Command that Kitchell worked for. The conversation would revolve around Kitchell's project, but she could care less about that.

The shuttle made its way through the dome's air-lock chambers.

A few moments later Marisa stepped through the open portal and onto the tarmac.

She couldn't help but gape at the dome looming above her, how standing in the enormous, self-controlled environment felt. The arching dome was dynamically tinted by a feedback system that controlled how much sunlight it let through and hence regulated how much the thermal gradient needed to be managed.

"Welcome to MC Kas, Captain," an attendant, dressed in a crisp red uniform, said as she approached. "I'm Flight Assistant Ann Rennie. I'll be seeing to your needs while you're on station. Can I take your luggage?"

"Thank you," Marisa said, pointing up to the dome. "When will the tinting fade?"

"It's already thinning, Captain. The shell hits peak opacity between local noon and thirteen hundred this time of the year."

"Fascinating."

"Yes, Captain, it is. It's a long way from the old Ant Farm."

Marisa chuckled. "You can say that again."

She'd read all the briefings. The dome's environmental management system controlled both the air handling equipment and the water cycles that drove the entire facility. *Torrance would love this,* she thought as she absently took in the full surroundings. The flight attendant's use of *local noon* tripped the idea of time travel inside her mind. Mars's rotation was so close to Earth's that it kept the same fundamental calendar and local times — which left thirty-seven minutes unaccounted for. Locals collected those minutes into buckets at the end of the day, calling it simply Extra, as in *it happened yesterday at 15 Extra*, to describe something that would go down as 2415 military. She'd always loved that. Martian citizens got thirty-seven extra minutes a day. Quite lovely.

She pressed her lips together as she looked closer.

Other than the odd warp to the sky, the landing station seemed like any she'd seen on Earth. The tarmac spread toward the horizon, and several shuttles stood ready along the line. Marisa noted that FA Rennie had arrived in a standard-issue, self-guided skimmer that had been painted with the colony seal. The landscape around the airfield was burnt dry, covered in harsh green and brown vegetation, but there were a lot of dry, dusty places on

Earth, too.

Everything smelled normal, too — fresh air scented with the aroma of the shuttle hangar over a thin backdrop of desert rock. The idea of recycled air had never fazed her on a spacecraft, but before setting down, she just knew the air would be strange here on Mars. She didn't see why it *should* be different, but somehow it seemed like it *would* be.

She'd assumed it would be stuffy or stagnant.

She couldn't feel a difference between this atmosphere and Earth's, though.

Mars Colony Kasbian was growing older now, but when it first became operational it was a cutting-edge step forward — a facility so much more open than the original human outposts on the planet, which had been underground caves excavated for human use, and then later had developed into smaller surface pods connected by radiation-hardened tunnels. As the flight assistant noted, the original, now destroyed, Mars Colony Natim had been nicknamed "The Ant Farm" for just that reason.

Standing here for the first time, Marisa understood why her more excitable friends said Kasbian represented the future. True terraforming would always be a bitch, but the colony here served as proof that if given enough time, human beings could build a city anyplace.

"Shall I have your bags sent to the staff office," Rennie repeated. "I can arrange a pod to take you to Sensor Command."

Marisa glanced at local time. As planned, it was several hours before her session with the director. "A pod, yes," she said. "But since I have some time, I think I'll make another stop first."

"I can arrange that, Captain. Would you like a detail to escort you?"

"No thank you, Flight Assistant. I'm just going to visit with a friend."

"All right, Captain. I'll arrange your transportation."

A fifteen-minute ride later, Marisa stepped from the pod and stood straight before Darsi Research Facility, Building Six.

If his message was correct, this had been where Thomas had been working. Wanting to be careful in the lead-up to this trip, Marisa hadn't asked too many pointed questions. But a search on

Sensor Command and Mars had brought the kid's name up, as well as a list of projects he'd worked on.

Classified stuff mostly.

Which made sense.

And mostly for Sensor Command — for which she most definitely didn't have clearance.

Arching her back, she looked first to an upper floor window, to where fire had charred the brick compound dark.

Her stomach dropped.

She didn't need to be a weapons commander to understand that explosives had blown a concentrated hole through the wall.

Automatic barriers still lined off the ground below, their sensors crackling with energy even from this distance.

She didn't have to go into the building to know the charred brick would mark Thomas Kitchell's office.

Despite her already certain sense of dread, though, Marisa Harthing stepped briskly into the research facility, steeling herself, knowing already that Kitchell was gone, and struggling to put together pieces of the puzzle that was telling her that something here was very much wrong.

Chapter 2

Arlington, Virginia
Local Date: August 8, 2252
Local Time: 1135

The briefing was as terse as it was short.

Willim Pinot, director of the United Government Intelligence Office, stared bullets into Evan Josiah, chair of the UG Solar System Environmental Council. The man stood beside the holoprojector and fidgeted.

Earlier, Pinot had wondered how long he had before news about an anomaly associated with the sun got out. Now he knew.

"You're convinced?" Pinot said.

Josiah pulled at his collar — a nervous tic he'd displayed several times already. He toggled down a data table that included multidimensional graphs that would have brought tears to the eyes of any elite physicist of the past three hundred years.

As the UGSSE council chair, Josiah's usual duties were to provide tepid updates on errant asteroids and milquetoast progress reports on plans for cleaning away the clouds of space junk that clogged commerce channels — which was what Pinot had been hoping to hear in this briefing. Josiah's team was working to pick up after the Mercury debacle in which Interstellar Command had lost the UGIS *Hercules* but had also destroyed a U3 vessel in the process. With any luck, the brief would have been full of information about intermingled debris from both ships, bodies lost, data files discovered, and requests for the ability to add security classification to whatever salvage they had managed to retrieve from the dead U3 spacecraft — hence the Intelligence Office's leverage for being first into the game.

Instead, Josiah dropped this on him.

"You're convinced Universe Three has found a way to drain our sun?"

"Yes, sir, I am. I have no idea how it works, but I'm convinced something inside the sun has changed. Given the events at Mercury, I'm not sure there's any other way to interpret it."

Pinot drew a raspy breath and considered his next move.

The fluctuations inside the sun were — so far — so small that the UGIO's internal study had found them only because Zina Nichols's thought experiment suggested they should go look for it. Monitoring solar output wasn't Josiah's group's job, and he wasn't the caliber of thinker to have been able to follow this lead on his own, which meant Josiah had someone in his organization who was sharper than the usual analyst. If nothing else, Pinot could raid the executive's staff after he had buttoned this exercise up.

Pinot marked that idea into the secure section of his dataclip, then swiveled his chair to take in Zina Nichols, his deputy director, who was sitting across the polished wooden table.

"What do you think, Zina?" Pinot said.

She was tiny in stature, but the crisp, squared shoulders of her green blouse and the clear intensity of her dark gaze added a sharpness to her demeanor.

Otherwise, since the briefing had been for just them, the room was small but comfortable.

She folded her hands together.

"I think Mr. Josiah has done some excellent work, but his conclusions are presumptuous."

Pinot smiled dryly as she played her role without him having scripted it.

"How do you mean?"

"As you're aware, we've known about anomalies in the sun's operations for some time, so I think attributing it to Universe Three — while not hard to fathom if you're unaware of certain details — feels like a fanciful jump."

Pinot nodded, frowning deeply as he put his clasped and pointed fingers to his lips. "You think it's something natural."

"Probably. But all I can say with certainty is that whatever's going on inside our sun was happening prior to the skirmish, so it's unlikely to have anything to do with Universe Three."

"Could Universe Three have done something earlier?"

She grimaced.

"I can't see it. U3 physicists aren't that advanced, and we haven't seen any suggestion that they are jumping into the zones they'd have to get to. They would have had to get lucky."

"And you don't believe in that kind of luck?"

"No. Despite Mr. Josiah's most excellent work, I do not."

Pinot's eyes gave a satisfied glimmer as he took a moment to admire his subordinate. He had chosen well. Zina Nichols was smart and as quick on her feet than any analyst he'd ever known. She had the ability hold her position close to her vest and to twist the truth in directions that suited her goals, all while managing to keep the social sensors in her observer's dataclips from pinging red. Spare moments after the Mercury skirmish she'd helped him deduce the fact that U3 was working to sabotage their sun. But the resulting situation showed no immediate danger. As always, knowledge was power. Power that would grow more valuable as long as they could keep the existence of that oddity inside the sun a secret.

Nichols had just played her part to perfection.

She was going to make a fantastic director someday.

He returned his gaze to Josiah.

The scientist seemed to swallow.

"What do you think of the deputy director's assessment?"

"I. Uh. I was unaware anyone had discovered the leakage earlier."

"That's very good to hear," Pinot said with a rumbly voice and a smile to match. "That means I don't have to make anybody disappear."

Josiah's laughter carried too much bluster to cover his relief. "I'm sorry to have jumped to such conclusions, Director. It just seemed like the natural answer. I thought you should know."

"Not to worry," Pinot said, sitting back. "As my compatriot noted, it's an easy assessment to fall to. I appreciate your office's diligence. Please pass me the names of your analysts and I'll provide them commendations."

"Thank you, Director."

"But given the complexity of the situation, I'm sure you understand why I need you to follow our security directives now?" Pinot waited. "No leaks, right?"

"I understand, Director."

"And I'm going to need your data sets."

"Totally understandable."

Pinot leaned forward and put on his most rigid expression. He paused a perfectly dramatic moment. "Because I would hate to have to hold a second conversation on the subject."

Josiah's nod was strong enough to sprain his spine.

"My assessment was wrong, so I no longer have an assessment to give. I can't imagine why we would need another such meeting."

"That's very good to hear."

Pinot sat back. It would do for now, but a shared glance with Nichols said she was reading the situation the same way as he was. Evan Josiah — and his people — were going to be a problem. And if it wasn't them, the system's top scientists would fall upon the truth soon enough.

Time was running short.

CHAPTER 3

Arlington, Virginia
Local Date: August 8, 2252
Local Time: 1215

"What's the play?" Zina Nichols asked, sitting opposite Willim Pinot's desk in the less comfortable guest chair — its hard shell pressing against her spine.

In the fifteen minutes since Josiah's briefing, its contents still played in her mind. She had a read on Pinot's position but wanted to be sure. As her boss settled into his chair, the dynamically inked lioness on her hip hunched into position.

She was now officially Pinot's second-in-command, Deputy Director of the United Government Intelligence Office — by far the youngest person to hold the post in the agency's history. It had been a big jump, but Pinot hadn't been above taking bold actions throughout his career, and she'd deserved it. Her first "close-in" project had been complex and messy, but also a huge success — she'd managed to save Pinot's reputation by putting the final bow on an operation that resulted in Torrance Black's reputation turning from hero to traitor.

The op had required some sleight-of-hand while paying off a few important people and dealing with a renegade media story that had been fostered by Black's compatriot, Thomas Kitchell. She'd also run an additional double-blind operation to change a few important records to connect Ambassador Black more directly to Deidra Francis — or, more appropriately, to her father *Casmir* Francis, who had been among Universe Three's original founders.

If Kitchell could have been confirmed killed in the last part of the operation, rather than just listed as "missing," she would have considered the whole thing to have been perfect.

Alas, in the real world, *perfect* did not exist.

Technically, she still had Marisa Harthing to deal with — something she'd put off a bit because dealing with high-ranking Interstellar officers was a different game. She had irons in that fire, but hadn't pulled on any of them, yet.

Along the way, after working through details of the Mercury debacle, Zina had pieced together the suggestion that something bigger was afoot there, surmising the existence of the connection to the sun that Josiah had just briefed them on.

After all that, Pinot had jumped her several levels.

Now her boss sat comfortably in his black leather chair, his posture signaling a blazing danger to any subordinate who had worked for him much longer than a week — the chair pushed back, elbows on armrests, fingertips lightly touching in the air before him, the index fingers steepled and pressed against his upper lip.

He was an older man, but still vital enough he could stave off the life extensions he might require later. He kept what hair he still had cut short, but left it streaked with gray because, for whatever reason, he thought it looked regal. His belly displayed the excesses of a life lived in comfort. He had been the United Government Intelligence Officer for long enough to credibly say he understood the game better than any person who had ever played the game. He was also a man who would order his own grandmother tortured if it meant he'd come out further ahead in the end.

Zina Nichols understood that much, and more.

Right now, Zina understood he was unhappy with what Josiah's brief meant. Pinot did not like surprises, and the one Evan Josiah had just dropped on them was one big-assed surprise.

She knew how to play the floor, though.

Even after having worked with Pinot for only a short time, she knew those words *what's the play?* were enough to get him started.

"The science wonks will figure it out soon enough," Pinot said, finally answering Nichols's question.

The idea pained him, but he'd come too far to pretend now.

If something was true it was true.

The good news was that the drain was exceedingly slow. The sun's power spectrum wasn't fading quickly enough to register on standard solar utilities yet, but if you knew exactly what you were looking for you could see it. The bad news was that someone would eventually find it, and when they did, certain systemwide dynamics would change.

The classified report had been clear about this.

Sooner rather than later the solar mass will do something impossible for sensors to miss, the report had projected. *At that point, some scientist somewhere is going to see it.*

It meant he was going to have to move more quickly than he'd wanted.

He watched as Zina Nichols took him in.

She sat in a precise, almost birdlike fashion, back straight, gaze angled gently toward him, dataclip pressed into her ear canal, hands folded in her lap.

Her dark, sharply creased pants and her pressed green blouse radiated an essence of efficiency — as did her hair, which Pinot noted she had cut shorter after her promotion. He thought he understood her, but the intensity of her expression took him back. *Hunter,* that expression said. Pinot wondered if his own gaze had ever carried such raw ambition. *Yes,* he answered his own question. It had. But Sela Matz, the UGIO before him, hadn't been able to see it so clearly.

Like senses like, though.

Someday Zina Nichols would be as dangerous as Willim Pinot was now. He did not want to be opposite her when that time came.

"I agree," Nichols replied. "The scientists will still take time to discover the truth. But what's the play now?"

"We can't keep the news from leaking eventually, but we can prepare for the fallout," Pinot said. "As fractious as this is going to be, it's going to lead to opportunities. So, we leave the scientists to do what they do, and focus on the councils."

"The councils?" Nichols asked, one eyebrow rising a slight notch. "Which ones?"

"All four," Pinot answered, counting off the organizations on his fingers. "Supreme President Mubadid's Cabinet. The Defense Council. Internal Security. Interstellar Command."

He looked at Nichols and enjoyed watching the wheels turn in her head. Her expression reminded him of when he was second-in-command. He had never liked not being able to read Matz well enough to be at least a step beyond her. Now he watched as Nichols tried to find his angle.

"Start with Mubadid's Cabinet and IS?"

"Yes. Those two are the bigger players. I'll take Mubadid's cabinet myself," he said, still taking in his subordinate's expression. "You focus on Internal Security. When the facts come out, we're going to see huge splits in leadership, so we'll want to be ready. I want information on every council member. Where they drink, what extracurriculars they enjoy, who they've been with, what their families are doing. You know the drill."

"Yes," Nichols said. "What about Defense and Interstellar?"

He raised a hand. "They're reactionary. If you can gather the right information to start with, we can give them to Delia. The Supreme Cabinet and Internal are the two most important."

Nichols seemed to relax. Delia Reghat was a sharp principal analyst assigned under her.

"I see that," she said, as if voicing a new standard. "If we control Supreme and Internal, we control the rest."

"Exactly. Pay attention to this over the next few months, Zina. If we play the game right, we will see a gap open for us to run through."

Nichols seemed to calculate again, which made him happy.

If he waited long enough, she'd see it.

The cabinet was, for all purposes, Supreme President Mubadid herself. The woman was getting old enough to be on her last extensions, and she'd already lost a step. Something had to be done. And Internal Security — the core group of systemwide law enforcement — was the primary tool anyone needed to exert real power across the system. Pinot had been itching to break the barrier between his covert operations and those of law enforcement.

The answer fell into her gaze.

"You're going to run an operation on the president," Nichols said, her voice flat.

Pinot smiled. "I knew you'd get there."

Zina created an appreciative smile.

She should have expected it.

Given the frame through which Pinot viewed the world, making a move to control the system now made sense. He would assess things carefully, but conservatively — conservatively in the sense that he held certain truths to be self-evident, anyway. The idea of Universe Three trying to drain the sun, for example, he had assigned into the category of "fixable," despite there not being a solution in sight. Where a normal person might blanch at the idea, it was in Pinot's framework to assume that scientists, or the "wonks," would find a solution.

That's how things worked throughout Pinot's history.

See problem, fix problem.

In Pinot's world, scientists could be molded.

It was a mistake, though, and to Zina an obvious one. Despite trying, the "wonks" hadn't made a breakthrough in interdimensional physics since U3 had stolen Jorge Catazara out from under their noses. Even though U3's attempt to sabotage the sun had not been a total success, the attempt itself meant U3 had capability the United Government did not. And it meant they were working in a specific direction. The Solar System's massive size gave it certain advantages, but Zina did not like the odds that UG scientists would be able to counter Universe Three now. To go all-in on them was a big bet. One she wasn't ready to accept.

"That's going to be quite an operation," she said.

"It will be big enough, I suppose," Pinot said, his dark eyes gleaming with anticipation.

"I appreciate your confidence in me," she replied, keeping her reactions inside herself as, already, she felt plays fall out before her in a network of cause and effects.

"I've left you information regarding the four primary subjects in Internal," Pinot said. "You'll need profiles, assessments, and opinions on them."

Zina checked secure paths through her dataclip and suppressed the urge to smile.

"Timing?"

"Three days max."

She had been studying those four names and several others attached to Internal Security for some time now. The only thing that would take three days was deciding which bits to share with Pinot and which to keep to herself. It left time for her to catch up with, and close a loop on, Captain Harthing, as well as begin to scope out how she might best delve into Defense and Interstellar Command.

"That won't be a problem," she said.

Two minutes later, striding toward her office, Zina's mind raced.

Pinot may well wind up winning this game, but if he did, he'd be controlling a doomed system, which wasn't a game she cared to win. She would help him, of course. She would help Pinot so long as she got to play her own game along the way.

Because she, too, wanted to control something.

The only question that mattered now was whether that something would be in the Solar System, or outside it.

Either way they were going to need to stage a coup.

Chapter 4

Mars Colony Kasbian, Jagger's Field
Local Date: August 10, 2252
Local Time: 2115 (Earth Standard)

Oddly, when she returned to her guest quarters, Marisa Harthing wasn't surprised to find the woman sitting at the wide table in the dining area.

The security on Kasbian was less intense than most places — probably because they relied on the dome's air locks at the top level. "Don't let kooks into the colony in the first place, and issues tend to go away." It was a viewpoint that could cause problems.

The meeting with Director Stilson had been as perfunctory as she'd expected it would be. He briefed her on his team's projects, focusing on work she'd asked about, mostly things Thomas Kitchell had been working on and specifically research regarding the possible use of multidimensional signals as guidance sensors. His progress had been promising. Since she formally represented Navigation Command, she'd entered that conversation with a ginned-up hypothetical in which such capability might improve the efficiency of controlling Star Drive jump locations. The idea was bullshit, but it was one Stilson jumped on like it might well have been the second coming of standard gate theory.

"That could work," he blathered on, tipping a glass of the local rosé he'd been so proud of toward her. "If it does, maybe you'll share in a prize."

"That would be pleasant," she replied.

The chime of their glasses was better than the wine.

She'd gotten what she needed.

Something was definitely wrong here.

It seemed impossible that Stilson could be unaware of the connection between her and Thomas, yet at no time did Stilson mention Thomas — even while directly discussing his work. At one point she considered dropping his name simply to read the expression on the director's face, but she worried that would be going too far.

The visiting dignitary's compartment was roomy and comfortable.

Now — as the door irised shut behind her, and as Marisa saw the woman seated at the table — she laid her staff jacket casually over the chair by the door and took in the visitor.

The woman appeared young, but years had taught Marisa that appearances could deceive. The woman's gaze was sharp. The dim light darkened her blouse to maroon or burgundy. On the table before her, a mobile data system projected a small ID screen into the space above it, complete with a recent photo and a collection of personal data.

The photo was her daughter, Mercedes.

Hackles rising, Marisa crossed the room to sit across the table.

The sturdy piece of furniture, with a marbled top polished to a warm shine, sat between a wall-mounted dispenser system and a wide, comfortable-looking bed.

"Captain Harthing," the woman said. "It is an honor to meet you in person."

"I'm afraid I don't have the privilege of your name," she said.

"Zina Nichols," the woman replied.

The name clicked into place. She'd seen news blocks on the woman earlier, but until now she hadn't connected the dots.

"Intelligence office?"

"Deputy director to Willim Pinot."

"Congratulations on your promotion. I assume this visit has something to do with Thomas's disappearance."

"Not really," Nichols replied. "I'm here to determine what connection you may still have with Torrance Black."

Marisa caught her breath. She glanced at the image of Mercy hovering above the data system. She should have been ready for that.

"I'd say you already know what connection I have with Torrance Black," she said, stalling to add up the figures. "I'm not that close to him now."

Nichols reached for her data system and snapped off the projection.

Mercy disappeared into the ether, and the intelligence officer turned her gaze back on Marisa, rapier-sharp focus drilling into her essence.

"You've no doubt read recent news about Ambassador Black's ties to Universe Three."

"I have. Though I admit I can't say I believe them."

"You can see my problem, then, right? We have all the proof we need to say that Torrance Black *was* a traitor to the entire Solar System. Of that there is no doubt. The question I'm left to answer, then, is whether that label applies to you, too."

"That is insane."

"Perhaps. But if I can't get a story that hangs together here, then I need to progress farther down the line. How deep does this whole thing go? Was Torrance Black simply the tip of a larger iceberg?"

"You've already killed Thomas," Marisa said, seeing a full truth that until a moment ago she'd only felt. "He went to the press, so you shut him up."

Nichols's shrug was almost sad.

"It turned out that Thomas Kitchell, too, was working with the Universe Three terrorists." She edged forward. "I'm sure you can see the dilemma that leaves me in. Black and Kitchell were both heroes of the *Everguard* disaster. And yet they were both U3 moles. Just how far down could this go? Who else could be involved?"

Marisa's throat tightened.

The woman's gaze grew even sharper, then slid to the datapad where Mercy's image had hovered a moment ago.

Marisa understood the threat.

And she understood something else, too. This was a game she couldn't win.

Not now, at least.

But she could wait. She would play the hand she'd been dealt, and she'd find her spot. She'd grown used to that approach while progressing her career.

"What do you want?" Marisa said.

Zina Nichols straightened her back. Her lips formed into a smile. "Nothing too hard for an Interstellar Command officer, I'd say."

Marisa nodded, knowing what Nichols wanted.

Just deflect, that's what she wanted Marisa to do.

Demur.

Pretend that she didn't know Torrance as well as some might think — that they hadn't been together for years, just as she'd already played when Nichols had asked the first time.

She could do that.

For a while, anyway.

"All right," Marisa said, putting on her command voice. "Let's get down to business."

DISCOVERY

Chapter 5

Free Space - Triton Station 12
Local Date: October 12, 2252
Local Time: 0912 (Earth Standard)

Kip Pyle, the midshift supervisor, looked at the tech who had just brought in the report. With the station able to afford barely enough power to drive a single desk lamp, his office was small and dingy to begin with. It felt claustrophobic with another person in it.

"Are you certain?" he said.

"I've run it six times."

"Adjusting the gains?"

"It's not noise, Kip. I've adjusted gains and I've played with the frequency matcher, and I've done every transformation we've got."

"Heterodyne?"

"That was pass four."

Kip sighed. There went another weekend. "I need a vacation," he said.

"Don't we all."

He sighed and ran a hand over the stubble on his skull. He needed another shave as much as he needed a vacation.

The tech was young, as was every tech who came through Triton 12. The place was Kip's home, but for everyone else it was a waypoint — a place to do an internship or just a quick first job out of school. No one else seemed to want to live their lives in a tiny tin can that rotated out in the deepest of deep space — tide-locked to the largest moon that orbited Neptune.

The tech had dyed her hair lime green and wore her faded-green station jacket baggy and unzipped far enough to reveal a white band underneath — a whole package that made her look more like she was going to a friend's party than sitting at work.

It was fine to Kip.

Keeping people here was hard enough without pushing a bunch of dumbass rules made by people who didn't care enough to visit anyway.

He preferred keeping things loose.

He looked at the report.

Triton 12 was the most distant outpost in the Solar System — a place so remote it took light from the sun over four hours to arrive.

Four hours and fifteen minutes and fifty-one seconds. Don't forget the fifty-one seconds!, he'd always say to a recruit.

That distance from home was what mattered here.

As such, staying alive meant Triton 12 needed every photon its receivers could collect. If the tech was right, they were down on power. Not by much, but out here even a percent of a percent mattered.

"All right," he said, clipping on his mag boots, which he grumbled about again as he finished — they were needed here because no one in their right mind would spend for an artificial gravity system on Triton 12. "Let's run the whole thing again."

The tech grimaced but came along.

CHAPTER 6

Sydney, Australia, United Government Parliamentary Chamber
Local Date: October 14, 2252
Local Time: 1025

"We've confirmed the drain, Madame President," Jared Kulpani said.

This was the third time in five months that he'd briefed Supreme President Laney Mubadid and her cabinet. The first two had been more informal, personal conversations — both discussions regarding the disappearance of Torrance Black, who had worked under Kulpani at the Jovian Science Center on Europa Station. This time, however, he was here in his official capacity as a scientist.

He decided he could do with less face time.

Kulpani took in the cabinet, pausing only briefly at Willim Pinot, the UGIO director, who had been his contact for that second briefing. The chamber was open and airy in design, a configuration that in most situations would feel sharp and professional, but right now made him feel untethered and alone, like he was in a lifeboat on a swelling sea, clouds forming on the distant horizon, the rows of faces focused on him circling like sharks below.

"You're saying our sun is dying?" the supreme president said.

"At the risk of being maudlin, our sun has always been dying," Kulpani replied. "But based on reports from several deep-space stations, our sun appears to be losing mass somewhat faster than it should be."

"I don't feel any different," said an aide. "It's eighteen degrees outside."

"The change is slight, but real," Kulpani said, fighting an instinct to roll his eyes. Maybe the aide was joking.

"If the sun is burning fuel too quickly," a different member asked, "does that mean we need to think about climate again?"

"We're not sure," Kulpani said. "It's a different problem from before. When we look closely, we estimate that the sun's mass has declined — again, very gently. However, if the sun were burning material at a faster rate, you would expect its power output to increase. Instead, it's decreasing."

"So, if we have to worry about anything it will be an ice age rather than a warming."

"Right, but with all due respect I don't think that's the key take-away here. At least not yet."

"What is the take-away, then," Mubadid said.

"I said it a moment ago. Something new is draining our sun. Something not natural, or at least something unexpected."

"And what do you think that something is?" Willim Pinot's gravelly voice broke in.

A coldness clung to that question. Kulpani didn't know much about Pinot beyond what was in the press, but it hadn't taken him long to determine that the UGIO director was a dangerous person to be on the wrong side of.

"I'm sorry to deflect, again, but I can't say. We need to explore it further."

"When did it begin?"

"We're going over logs filed from the past several weeks, and while we're not able to pinpoint an exact date yet, power spectrum analysis says not less than two months ago. Probably longer."

Pinot gave a neutral *hmm.*

"Someone has to bring up the elephant in the room." All eyes turned to the supreme president. "Is this the same drain we put in Alpha Centauri A?"

Kulpani hadn't wanted to address this question. In his opinion, the answer would be a resounding yes, but he couldn't prove anything. To be wrong about that kind of sensational proposal would be career death.

"If so, then it's Universe Three," said another cabinet member.

"I don't think they have that capability," replied another.

"You think it's more likely to be someone domestic? That we might have a renegade scientist someplace?"

"I think we had a battle with Universe Three in a remote place behind Mercury for reasons we can't explain. This could explain that."

There was silence.

"I don't think it matters." Pinot again.

Kulpani watched the UGIO director gather attention, then find the right moment to speak further.

"Regardless of who did it, the important fact is that it has been done. We all agree it's unlikely Universe Three has the chops to make something like that happen, but we'll need to open an investigation to know for sure. You have my word that this will be the top issue on my billet until we get answers, and that when we have those answers, I'll be the one standing where Mr. Kulpani is. So, I suggest we leave identifying the culprit to me for a little while and focus on the most important next step."

"Which is?" an adviser asked.

"Direct our top scientists to focus on defining the problem."

That makes sense," Mubadid said.

"It's your call, of course, but this is important enough to seal under your presidential security directives. Nothing good can come from the public hearing news that the sun is draining — infinitesimal or not."

Mubadid nodded.

Everyone in the room understood the politics of the moment. The supreme president was facing a potential confirmation vote several Earth standard weeks from now. If she won that, she would remain in office. Otherwise, she would have to run an actual campaign, and her leadership would be in peril. She was having problems enough in the asteroid belt and with the economy dying over the inner planets. She didn't need a distraction now.

Kulpani saw something more here, too — a sharpness to Pinot's gaze that he would recall for a long time afterward. Willim Pinot, the United Government Intelligence Office director, had something up his sleeve.

"I agree," Mubadid said. "We need to get our best scientists working on this now. And I want all information about this conversation sealed until we're ready with a full story."

With that the briefing was over.

Kulpani had a moment to pick up his equipment before security officials escorted him from the room, which gave him just enough time to note the deep satisfaction etched on Pinot's face.

CHAPTER 7

Sydney, Australia
Local Date: October 14, 2252
Local Time: 1215

Willim Pinot left the chamber and went to his waiting taxi pod.

Once he was inside, and once the door sealed shut and the pod began the trip back to his hotel, he let himself relax. He felt the pod's vibration as it moved through the city that slipped past the unit's tinted windows.

The scientist — Kulpani — was the weak link.

The rest were lifetime politicians that he had dossiers to fall back on. He could twist their arms. Expose their secrets. Threaten their families. But the scientist was a different beast. Kulpani's expression earlier in the session confirmed it for him. The man was a step too smart for his own good.

Which is why, when the time came to release Mubadid's final decision, the story he'd have in place would take Kulpani down, too.

Pinot dropped Nichols a note to get something on Kulpani.

The idea made Pinot happy. Two birds, one stone.

Mubadid had gotten too powerful for her britches.

It was time for a change.

NEWS

SOURCE: INFOWAVE — NEWS for the 23rd century
TRANSMITTED: December 1, 2252, Earth Standard
HEADLINE: Independent Source Claims Sun Is Dying

Kensington Station, Asteroid Belt – Local astronomers released a report today across broadband stations stating that the Solar System's sun is fading much more rapidly than it should be.

The report does not name its sources, but an independent review of the document by local academic officials suggests the methodology used in the claim is sound. "We're going to need to peer review the data," said Professor Lia Mass, who teaches astronomy at LUMI, Kensington.

Officials at the United Government Science Office have not commented publicly beyond a tersely worded statement to say the report was under consideration, and to note that people should always view such sensational claims with care.

Anonymous sources inside the UG hierarchy are blaming renegade factions for the report, suggesting that radical groups within the population are attempting to stir up fear and anger during an already tense period of political unrest.

As news leaks across the system, however, reports of protest are already rising, so officials are expected to comment soon.

SOURCE: INFOWAVE — NEWS for the 23rd century
TRANSMITTED: December 3, 2252, Earth Standard
HEADLINE: UG Scientists Deny Sun Dying

Jovian Science Center (JSC), Europa Station, Jupiter Orbit – JSC President Jared Kulpani said today he could not confirm that recently leaked reporting that the Solar System's sun is dying more rapidly than it should came from scientists at his station.

"My staff is well trained and professionally diligent. We do not release statements on science of such critical nature without extensive peer review. I can say with complete certainty that this leak did not come from our offices."

A trace of information nodes, however, suggests that the last datapoint to process the information was physically inside the JSC memory complex. "It's damning evidence," said investigation spokesperson Evan Abade, who refused to comment further due to having been assigned the case only today. Abade has been recently assigned to gathering evidence regarding the loss of U3 spy Torrance Black, and some are suggesting the assignment means the two cases could be linked.

Black worked last at JSC, and his research was under Dr. Kulpani's control.

SOURCE: INFOWAVE — NEWS for the 23rd century
TRANSMITTED: December 6, 2252, Earth Standard
HEADLINE: Claims Surface, Mubadid Hid News of Sun Death

Sydney, Australia – Reports have come today that Supreme President Laney Mubadid and her staff received information that suggested the Solar System's source of energy was failing months prior to original reports. Reporters are now saying that the first briefing could have been as early as last October, and Mubadid gave an order to keep the information classified to avoid compounding problems with her domestic agenda.

Mubadid, who is facing intense pressure as she undergoes a confirmation vote of the people, does not deny she received a brief but says that the report held no suggestion of the sun's imminent failure. She stated strongly that she would not have withheld this information from the public.

"I have nothing to gain from hiding that information, so clearly someone is playing a political game. It is game I expect they will lose. There is nothing here."

SOURCE: INFOWAVE — NEWS for the 23rd century
TRANSMITTED: March 5, 2253, Earth Standard
HEADLINE: Jihansen Claims Supreme Presidential Race

Buenos Aires, Argentina – In a stunning turn, solar mining magnate Ils Jihansen has claimed victory over Supreme President Laney Mubadid today, ending Mubadid's decades-long control of the United Government.

Mubadid's opposition pointed to issues with the incumbent's performance over the past several years, including a weak response to labor uprisings in the asteroid belt, an inability to put an end to terrorist strikes from Universe Three, and a lack of transparency regarding corruption within her administration. Still, few expected Jihansen's victory, and even fewer expected that victory to come in such a resounding fashion.

Recent news regarding the current administration's handling of a flaw in the Solar System's sun provided the killing blow.

Until that time polls showed Mubadid's public support, while flagging, would still be strong enough to hold on to her position. In the months since the news leaked, however, Jihansen used Mubadid's secrecy as a cudgel to suggest that her continued insistence on her position — that the sun's rate of deterioration was still too low to be of concern — showed disregard for the common people.

"We're still building Star Drive spacecraft," he would often say in counter to Mubadid's assurances that if such a time came they had options, including such radical ideas as finding homes in other systems. "But more than a hundred billion people live throughout the Solar System today. We have six such ships and a flotilla of smaller, independently owned jump craft. If the sun dies tomorrow, who do you think will get the golden tickets? If the current supreme president had succeeded in keeping the problem secret, would we have simply woken up one morning to find those golden ticket holders all gone?"

The scientific community is still divided on their position regarding the sun, but the majority opinion seems to be that our power source will continue to support life for millennia at the current rate of decay. Since the cause of this new acceleration is unknown, however, any such predictions should come with severe caveats.

Though he will use Buenos Aires as his capital city, Jihansen, born and raised on Mars, becomes the first supreme president not born on Earth in UG history.

"This is the beginning of a new chapter in our existence," Jihansen said in a prepared statement. "People can rest assured that we will work hard to ensure their safety and their prosperity for generations to come. We will get to work immediately."

SUN BLIND

CHAPTER 8

Apogee: 37 Gem System
Local Date: C15/D84
Local Time: 1/13:15

Everyone said he'd adjust, but Thomas Kitchell had been here for almost a standard earth year, and Apogee was still too hot for him.

Gem was like Sol in composition and Apogee's landscape felt quite close to Earth's, but that didn't matter. Winter or summer, the planet's positioning and atmosphere were different enough to make for a climate that ran on the hot side.

It wasn't the heat, though, it was the humidity.

The planet's air currents were always damp.

So now he sat here on his midday lunch break, on this strange little planet that was home to Universe Three, baking in the heat, sprawled in the shade of the stiff, umbrella-like covering he'd strung out over the balcony of the private quarters Deidra Francis had posted for him. He wore one of the gauzy thin shirts that were fashionable among the U3 community — undyed and pale yellow in color due to the textile's natural origin. Lifting the fabric, he pumped it to help ventilation.

It didn't work.

His frustration boiled over.

What was he doing here?

He'd been asking himself this question at least twice a day lately.

While he never agreed to fully join the Universe Three rebels, the events of his last few months in the Solar System — in which his own government had accused both him and his friend Torrance Black of being double agents, and in which an agent of Universe Three had literally saved his life — led him to almost look forward to developing signal jamming technology that could thwart the United Government's efforts to find them.

Working with U3 had made it easy to get even more comfortable with the situation.

The people serving under Universe Three's banner weren't any different from those living under United Government flags. They were just as intelligent, just as irksome, and just as interested in simply living their own lives as anyone else.

Sure, parts of U3 ideology still made him clench up inside.

That they'd decided to drop a wormhole connection into the sun said everything he needed to know about their leaders' viewpoint, but he'd seen enough of UG operations to know better than to think his own "side" was any more pristine. He knew for certain that the United Government would have done the same thing.

So, he met with U3 engineers, and they showed him their lab and the tools they'd created so far.

The facility was more advanced than he'd expected — filled with the basic equipment he needed, sensors and computer systems with signal filters and data processing capability that was only a generation or two behind what his cohorts with the United Government had.

He'd been on teams that designed the systems UG scientists were using to hunt for U3's presence. He knew how those systems functioned, understood the mixtures of bioengineering and signal scanning patterns the UG were using, as well as their pattern matching algorithms. Add it up and Kitchell assumed it wouldn't be too hard to develop a system that would protect U3's outpost from discovery.

That's how he felt until he got into it, anyway.

Until he realized he couldn't get the feel for U3's tools.

The equipment here was different, and if he were being direct, the signal processing engineers were out of step with practices he was familiar with. Bottom line, getting familiar with U3 equipment had been harder than getting familiar with U3 people as human beings, and now — after weeks and weeks of flailing, he was simply angry.

He did not like feeling stupid.

That's what he was thinking as he retreated to sit alone on his patio this midday.

His quarters were on the top of a two-story building.

The thin whine of hover carts rose from the streets below. Grunts and heavy footsteps from people and animals pulling loads themselves played a lead, while other citizens moving around in the mire, oblivious to the heat and busy with the effort of building the city, completed the ensemble.

Kitchell took a big tug on the decanter of chilled water he kept beside him.

"Are you okay?"

He jumped at the voice, spilling a cold dribble down his chest, then standing to brush it away.

"I'm so sorry." Allie Feder stood in the open doorway that led to his living space.

"Not a problem," Kitchell said, kicking his lounge chair backward with the shuddering of wood on wood, and holding the decanter up over his head like that might help. His other hand ran down his shirt in a vain attempt to dry the liquid stain.

Feder put her hand on Kitchell's shoulder to help him balance.

"Thanks," he said. His grin was sheepish.

"I looked for you at your station, but everyone said you'd left for lunch and said I should check here."

"I thought I'd try to enjoy the breeze," Kitchell said.

"Good luck with that," Feder replied.

He grinned. "Maybe the shower will help."

Feder chuckled. "It gets better after you get used to it."

No longer shaded, Kitchell shielded his eyes and glanced up at 37 Gem. "I hope so. This place is a helluva lot different from the tin cans I've lived in most of my life."

"I'm sure that's a pretty big change of pace." She shielded her eyes against 37 Gem, too. "Yamada says she'll be working on automated cooling in the next season."

"Not too soon for me."

Allie Feder was the number two ranking physicist on the planet but, to Kitchell's admittedly limited exposure, was the better of the two. She was younger than Kitchell by at least twenty standard years, but clearly one of the brightest people he'd ever met. In a just world, it wouldn't be long before Allie Feder oversaw the outpost's science operations.

She stood here now, tall and slight, dressed professionally in loose-fitting dark shorts that fell to her knees, and an equally loose-fitting top with a Universe Three logo sewn onto the left shoulder.

"What can I do for you?" he said.

"I think the right question is what can *I* do for *you*?"

"Come again?"

"I understand you're struggling to get into the flow of things in your lab. I thought it might help if you had someone to bounce ideas around with."

Kitchell gave an involuntary step back, then leaned against the balcony rail. Heat radiating from the composite was warm against his backside.

"I see," he said coming to his conclusion. "You mean Director Francis has asked you to come talk with me?"

"No. Not at all." The hurt on her expression seemed genuine.

"I'm sorry," Kitchell said too quickly. "I didn't mean to offend."

Feder ran her hand through her hair, which blazed a metallic bronzy-red in the sunlight. It cascaded down one side of her face to touch on her shoulder. "No, it's all right. I should have understood where your mind would be."

"Well," he said. "Good luck with that, too."

He laughed then. What chance did she have in understanding a gently aging scientist who'd been a cog in the United Government machine for so long he'd forgotten how to think for himself?

"Don't kick yourself too hard, Thomas. And don't kid yourself either. Frustrated scientists can sense other frustrated scientists from kilometers away. I see what's happening."

"Please tell on," Kitchell said, taking another pull on the water and motioning for her to continue.

"Everyone knows me for the wormhole theory Dr. Catazara and I are developing, but I'm not just one-dimensional. I understand where you're at — our systems aren't as advanced as the ones you're used to, and the progression path of those tools branched off differently from the one you're used to."

Kitchell nodded. "Yeah. One signal splitter isn't exactly like the next."

She leaned against the door frame and crossed her arms, movement that gave her a more pensive delivery. "For most people that wouldn't matter. Hell, most of them may not even see a difference. But I see you. Signal processing isn't my primary expertise, but I know what it looks like to be better than your equipment." She twisted her lips into an expression that conveyed the unique sense of frustration she was defining better than any words could. "It sucks to have to play at the edge of your tools' capabilities. Even tiny differences break your back, and since you're the only person who understands what you're doing it's always faster to do something yourself than to bring other people up to speed — but there's so much to do."

Kitchell reveled in the relief that welled through his body.

She continued.

"And I'd guess that doesn't even touch on what it takes to work with new people and on a planet that until a handful of standard months ago you never knew existed."

A grin creased his face, and he waved his free hand in surrender. "All right. I give up. I'm sorry. You *do* understand."

Her chuckle was soft in the open air.

The distant ring of hammer blows filtered up from the road below. Saws screeched. A generator hummed.

Feder sat on a shaded chair. "The breeze is nicer here," she said. "I can see why you like it."

Kitchell smiled and pushed his lounge seat back into the shade, then sat down too, breathing in the aroma redolent of growing trees nearby.

"So, talk to me," she said, "tell me what the problem is. Maybe you'll talk yourself to the answer."

"All right," he said. "But can I get you something to drink first?"

"That would be great."

"Excellent."

Taking his own decanter with him, he stepped into his living quarters and poured them both a cold glass of something he'd taken to calling lemonade. Returning to the balcony, he handed Allie Feder a glass, then used a foot to position the lounge chair again

before sitting down.
    Suddenly, the heat didn't feel so oppressive.

CHAPTER 9

Apogee: 37 Gem System
Local Date: C16/D2
Local Time: 2/09:20

If she was being honest with herself, Allie Feder had to admit that — at the beginning — she looked forward to working closely with Thomas Kitchell mostly because she had long ago come to understand how her brain worked. Being blunt, she needed a break. She thought that time spent focusing on Kitchell's problem with his signal processing issues would help consume her conscious brainwaves enough that her subconscious mind could be free to work on its own tangled webs — of which she had plenty.

As days passed, though, she found him to be interesting.

Funny.

Insanely smart.

Not in her field, of course, but by simply watching him think through issues she could see why his reputation had been so bold within the Solar System. The man understood information, coding, and cross-dimensional wave flow. He had an intuitive knack for seeing how patterns fell together. Helping him think through new algorithms stretched her mind. Helping him translate what he knew about equipment he was familiar with into ideas that would work with U3 machines made her happy. She could learn things from him.

He was older than her, but his complete dedication to his work at the expense of many of the simple things it took to make it through a day made him feel so much younger than her.

She was surprised to find those things mattered to her.

Watching him curse — fluently and profusely — while trying to use a laundry wand had cracked her up. Then, after she'd shown him how it operated, his animated act of pretending to wash his mouth out with it had put her into stitches.

His expressions could be hilarious.

And, like her, he was also not comfortable with what they had taken to calling NP — normal people, people who didn't enjoy spending time pondering scientific work. Something they discussed during evenings on his balcony or sitting out on the patio outside her quarters.

The fact that he seemed to look forward to their sessions, too, had begun to make her see him in ways she hadn't before.

As the days passed, Allie realized that Thomas Kitchell was someone she could be herself with, and that made her both happy and anxious in similar degrees.

Chapter 10

Apogee: 37 Gem System
Local Date: C16/D93
Local Time: 2/00:30

In the end, something Allie said triggered the thought that made the difference for Thomas Kitchell.

They were eating lunch at her hut — or, more correctly, on the expansive community patio built outside her hut. It was one of Allie's favorite spots, and it was central to their workstations. They came here often. He'd barely touched his food — a wrapped combination of local walnuts and rice that he usually loved.

"What's wrong?" she said. "Walnuts gone bad?"

That was a thing about their relationship, whatever their relationship was.

A given — for both of them — was that no one else on the planet could ask the right question that needed to be asked, but it went deeper than that, too. Among the reasons he'd come to feel so comfortable with her was that she also knew the right *time* to ask that right question.

He laughed at her timing now.

He had just thought those exact words to himself.

"I understand the equipment well enough now," he said. "I just don't see why it's not working."

"Tell me about it," Allie said.

He grumbled.

"Seriously. Have at it. I could use a diversion."

He sighed, then jumped in, ignoring for the moment that he didn't know how he felt about the problem Allie was working on — trying to understand exactly why the black hole connection they had put into the Solar System's sun wasn't working as quickly as they expected. If he pretended that she could never make it work, he could ignore that question.

"Basically, I think it's a driver problem."

"And non-basically?"

He fluttered his lips as he let out a long sigh. "I'm trying to create a signal blind that spans dimensions."

"I see."

He explained his process. How he was trying to expand upon existing jammers by creating an active array of receptors that could, in theory, receive radio signals, rapidly calculate the wave forms that needed to be added to any reflected signals to damp them out, then release them into a multidimensional path that would let them jump ahead of the return signal and effectively cancel them out.

Call it jump drive tech in a quantum foam casing.

To his knowledge, no one had fully accomplished it, but the idea was nowhere near new. The concept of actively eating a signal — rather than just avoiding one altogether or scattering it — would render a ship, or in this case a planet, truly invisible to any sensor looking for it.

JSC had used the concept to create a noise profile that "hid" details of the subject, but that wasn't a blind.

And no one had been able to make it work in multiple dimensions — which was the key to making the device stronger.

"What I think you're saying," Allie replied, "is that if you can extend your shield across the dimensions, we should be essentially invisible for a long, long time."

"Exactly. If we can sense the incoming signal, anyway. UG is working to extend sensor readings into deeper dimensions, too. If we can get there faster, they'll never see us."

"So, what's wrong?"

Kitchell explained.

Using a sudden inspiration, he had built a system he thought should do the trick. And he'd been successful. Almost. The processing time was so short that he *should* be able to create and send the blinding signal in less than one wavelength — especially down in the lower ranges of multidimensional space. Unfortunately, the thing was hanging up.

He was so close, but so far.

He tore into his wrap, chewing with anger.

"The code should work," he said. "But I got bubkes."

Allie, who had finished her own lunch during the time he'd been rambling, stared off into the distance.

"What happens if you match gains?"

"It's not a gain match issue."

Allie raised her eyebrows.

Kitchell paused in mid chew then.

His heart froze.

No. The issue wasn't the strength of the two signals — though he had already considered the fact that he was going to have to ramp up the return when he was fine-tuning the final system. The problem was that the signal he was trying to add was disappearing completely.

It wasn't a gain match issue.

It was frequencies. But not just frequencies. It was frequencies *and* power spectrums — and specifically power spectrums down through the dimensions.

Of course.

He'd missed it because the primary domain frequencies and their power spectrums — meaning the waveforms in normal space-time — *were* matched. The problem, he was suddenly sure, was in the subspace domains under the quantum foam. *They* would be mismatched. He'd have to do more coding. Difficult, but doable.

"What is it?" Allie said.

Kitchell finished chewing, then swallowed, and then looked directly into Allie Feder's eyes and said the only thing he could possibly say.

"I think I love you."

Three weeks later he'd built the small prototype device.

It worked. Almost, anyway.

He had more ideas that would tweak performance, but when he focused on the problem now, he knew it had gone from one of invention to one of engineering.

The only variable was time.

He made her dinner that night. She stayed at his place. He stayed at hers the next.

Chapter 11

Apogee: 37 Gem System
Local Date: C16/D91
Local Time: 2/11:45

Having someone in her life was strange.

Exhilarating, but strange.

Strange to wake up thinking about another person rather than ruminating on tensors and systems of equations or dwelling on a multidimensional gravity map, hoping to find a new way to address a sink.

On the whole Allie liked it.

Looking back, she supposed it was only natural that things progressed.

Thomas Kitchell was a kind man. Despite his age, he had been as reserved physically as he had been in sharing his math and his system thinking at first. But he loosened up quickly.

As they grew closer, she found working with him refreshing. All *her* efforts were focused on theory and, therefore, consisted of mind games and thought exercises that got implemented in code and then tested in simulations. It was the rare idea that made it to any physical manifestation.

And, if she were being open to herself, she was now Officially Stuck.

Catazara had asked her to determine why the wormhole pod they had affixed to the Solar System's sun wasn't pulling material as fast as their physics had expected. The answer was obvious in one fashion: Their physics had been wrong. That was how science works. If something doesn't follow the theory like the theory said it should, the theory was wrong. Or at least lacking. But the challenge of discovering *why* she was wrong — or what she was wrong about — was going to kill her.

Try as she might, that nut was just not cracking.

The wormhole throat tensors they had injected into the Solar System's sun were stable, as they should be. And the controllers for flow rates were in the right places down into the foam and layers of D-space.

Still, the damned thing wasn't working.

She was only marginally surprised to find that working on Thomas's problems was better than she'd expected.

His work manifested itself in real things — physical boxes and electronic compounds that reacted in predictable ways. To examine a schematic was to read a book. Her mind could follow logic, link traces, and discover results.

This worked. That did not.

Here was why.

Not that Thomas's work was simple.

Thomas Kitchell, she realized, was a brilliant engineer — able to see things two and three steps farther down the path than anyone else could. But his work was more solid than hers. Less theoretical. Helping him develop the rebound accelerator — a device he would use to catch a return signal up to its original waveform — served to fill her head up and block the essence of defeat she felt whenever she focused on the subquantum gravity profiles she was stuck on.

His desire to protect her people had been as noble as hers, too.

Moreso, really.

Thomas Kitchell's method would save UG lives as well as those on Apogee.

Allie Feder's project would take them.

Perhaps that was another reason, as time went by, she spent more time and more brain cycles on Thomas Kitchell's problems and less on hers.

Coordinating manufacturing techniques. Adjusting machines.

Running algorithms to simulate launch points and satellite positions.

She liked that the work kept them close.

It was, she realized, just easier this way.

Late one evening, in Thomas's quarters, he was teaching Allie how to understand the ways radio waves propagated through dimensional space when the whole thing came together for her.

He used a small holoprojector to convey waves propagating through something he called Michin fields.

"The waveform splits here," Thomas said. "If you follow old Heisenberg logic, all the probability waves would collapse into a single result at that point. And, as far as this dimension is concerned, it does."

She was catching on. "You're saying that the wave dies here, but it carries on under the next dimensional surface."

"Yes. But it's dicey. Or I guess flakey is a better word for it."

"The collapse itself is probabilistic?"

"Right. You can't say definitively how it will collapse down under a specific D-surface, but you can point to states and stages." He flipped a switch to alter the display, then pointed at a purple plane that represented the barrier to extradimensional space. "Standard theory says that the wave would propagate here."

"Right."

"But Michin proved that a wave that moves through the quantum foam to emerge in extradimensional space can split into multiple component parts. So, we have to look at every level at the same time."

"I see," Allie said, suddenly catching on. "The quantum foam works more like a prism than a mirror."

"Exactly," Thomas said, his cheeks rosy now, his eyes glittering with excitement. "And each split finds its own home space."

Allie stood bolt upright, her heart pounding with the chilled energy she got when everything came together. Adrenaline hit then, and for an instant she wasn't sure she could breathe. Suddenly so much made sense.

"Are you okay?" Thomas said.

She grabbed him by the shoulders then, clamping them so hard he winced.

"Oh, I am so much more than okay," she said.

Then she kissed him hard and left.

She had to get this down now. Had to get to her lab. Had to let herself lay it all out.

If she was right, Allie understood *exactly* what was happening.

If she was right, it changed everything she understood about wormhole physics.

If she was right, she could change the world.

Chapter 12

Apogee: 37 Gem System
Local Date: C18/D12
Local Time: 1/09:45

"The goal would be to build it into a satellite, and then put it into orbit," Kitchell said as he finished briefing the Universe Three leadership staff about his new device. "If we can get it placed properly, UG sensors will never be able to find us."

Facing the director and her leadership staff who, months before, had been dead set on killing him was an awkward thing. And more awkward because Allie hadn't attended. Too busy, she'd said. Too distracted was more like it. She'd run off to her lab like a shot of lightning a day ago and hadn't emerged since.

The staff knew who he was. He'd been in this rounded assembly room in an earlier session where Deidra Francis introduced him and the gathering discussed his work — or, more specifically discussed who should oversee his work.

Still, it would have been nice to have Allie's familiar face here, if nothing else for emotional support.

Despite his goal, he could feel resistance in the room.

Not that he could blame them.

He was from the Solar System, and even if he'd never officially been inside the full construct of the United Government, he'd worked against U3. Also, Captain Timmon Keyes — who, Allie had informed him earlier, had been on *Vengeance* — and Kazima Yamada, who was his partner, had become a power pair in the U3 structure. In a distant way, he saw Torrance and Marisa in them, though neither Torrance nor Marisa ever had the power Keyes and Yamada seemed to pull.

He didn't know how he felt about that.

Technically, Kitchell's work fell under Yamada's umbrella as she was the engineering leader, but his expertise wasn't her strength, which was among the reasons U3 signal processing technology had been lagging the UG's. She had her fingers in a lot of pots, too, something that split her focus too far. Still, she understood fully that becoming hidden from UG was important, too.

He pondered what line she was walking, and how much her relationship with Keyes might sway her opinion.

The cloudy skies didn't relieve his sense of unease. The roofing had been extended, sealing the room, and giving it a sense of claustrophobia that pressed in on him. The random patter of rain played against the composite tiling above, giving his presentation an oddly eerie sensation.

Kitchell held up the physical model he'd been using to show people what he meant — which was something he still enjoyed creating — and placed it into the holographic display that indicated the position of various stars, and in this case Sol and 37 Gem.

"We put it into orbit here," he said. "And then arrange it so the system is always between the Solar System and us. With the receiver pointed at the Solar System, we should be invisible across the dimensions."

"You're certain about that," Yamada said.

"I've tested a small system. It works at that scale. But I know better than to make guarantees. The only way to be certain beyond all doubt is to build it, then run a quick jump to evaluate it ourselves. I'd say the only thing that seems dicey would be whether we'd want to put more than one unit up just to cover space. My guess is you'd really want to do three, both to give a more full-throated coverage as well as to ensure redundancy in case of failure."

"That could be done," Yamada said. "The testing, anyway. But it would divert resources we're focusing on *Perigee*. With the loss of *Vengeance*, a second Star Drive ship is an imperative."

"How long will it take to build the shields?" Director Francis asked.

She'd been quiet through the conversation — introducing him first, and then stepping back to watch the gathering work. It gave Kitchell a certain appreciation for her style, despite the weight in her assessing gaze that left him cold at times.

Kitchell felt the engineering leader's gaze on him even on the periphery. He remembered the confusion he'd felt in deciding to leave the Solar System, remembered the term *pawn* from a conversation he'd held with Deidra Francis.

He braced against Yamada's concern.

He might lose, but he wasn't going to back down.

"I'd say a few months," he replied.

"Two? Three?"

"It depends on our ability to manufacture the sensors," he replied. "I can work with Leader Yamada to develop a full schedule. But regarding any concern on the timeline, I'll note that if this project is successful, it removes the pressure on *Perigee*'s production team. And it also means that you could execute your plans to expand into 37 Gem's system without concern that UG fighters might suddenly appear in your airspaces."

Yamada nodded. She glanced at Keyes, who almost managed to stifle his frown. "I can work with him," Yamada said.

Their reactions confirmed rumors that said something was going on between them, but Kitchell didn't understand what it was. Allie had suggested Keyes was becoming more aggressive, and that Yamada was helping make his points, but he hadn't seen it that way — and in this case it was clear the two were, at least now, on opposite ends of the play.

He wondered what Keyes was thinking.

"We can have missions ready in a few days," said Henri Shudar, *Defender*'s captain.

He went on to describe the steps he'd need to prepare the ship.

"It's also possible we could use a Star Drive skimmer rather than jump *Defender*," Yamada said. "We have three on station now and those could be made ready at almost any time."

Francis turned to Kitchell. "Is that right?"

"I'm not sure. It would depend on the size of the system."

"All right," Francis said, having obviously gotten the answer she'd expected. "It all seems doable. And if we're talking a couple of months in return for ultimate safety, I think we should do it."

She gazed around the room.

"Anyone against?"

No one moved.

"Then we approve. We'll use a skimmer if it works, but *Defender* can make the jump otherwise."

Francis turned back to Kitchell. "Thank you for your work, Thomas. We'll make a full-fledged member of you, yet."

He missed Allie's presence the most then.

He wanted her to be here.

"Well," he said to the director. "You might just do that."

Francis noted his glance and raised an eyebrow but didn't respond.

"All right," she said. "This meeting is adjourned. Let's get to work."

Chapter 13

Apogee: 37 Gem System
Local Date: C18/D12
Local Time: 2/04:00

Allie had to kick Thomas out of the room.

Yes, his first test had been successful.

Yes, he wanted her to come to the leadership staff meeting.

But she had her own work to do, and she needed to concentrate.

She'd even turned him down when he offered to be a sounding board for her work.

"You can't help me," she said with enough energy that she knew she'd hurt his feelings. But it was the truth. Since his world was physical, she could scale her skills to it, but he could not expand his framework to hers — and she didn't have time to let him down softly.

The ideas were burning in her head.

Code flew off her fingers and voice commands crackled like they were coated in lighting.

The throat tensors that kept a wormhole gate open to begin with worked down through the dimensions. Both she and Catazara understood that part of classic theory as well as any of the original developers of it did. It was the concept she'd used in inventing the guidepost locators that had allowed them to accurately remote-cast gates in the first place.

Flow rate was different, though.

The gate that *Everguard* had created in Alpha Centauri A was keyed to a specifically designated engine structure — and that key had the same multidimensional existence as the gate itself.

A connection to a black hole would be different.

Of course, it would.

A black hole warped everything around it. Brought time to a halt, spread space into infinity. In other words, a black hole broke dimensions into infinite subdimensions — just as a prism broke light into infinite subfrequencies. And, like prisms, each one could be different.

The second time she chased Kitchell from her office, she locked the door.

At least he brought her food.

And coffee.

Leaving them both in the hallway when she refused to open the door.

Thank God for the coffee.

Thomas was a saint, she realized, but even that wasn't enough to give him access to her office now.

She went back to work, and time seemed to compress into something that did not exist. When, finally, 37 Gem rose to bathe Apogee in its new dawn light, Allie went to the bay window that opened to the city around her.

The sky was clear.

She would remember that.

The sky was clear. Sounds of the waking city came softly through panes of glass. She pushed the window open and breathed the clean scent of a breeze that carried the aromas of baking bread and freshly turned soil.

She would remember it all.

She shaded her gaze from the silver-orange light at the horizon as 37 Gem came over the distant mountain peak. Wheels creaked. An insect she'd taken to calling a dragonfly buzzed in the brush that grew at the corner of the building.

The model was working.

She understood why the black hole had taken hold but wasn't moving material through the gate in the way classic theory said it would.

The world outside was moving as if nothing had changed, but this morning was different. Allie Feder stood at her window watching her own sun appear and realizing that she was the only person in the entire universe who understood this piece of how the universe worked.

She would remember this feeling forever.

Chapter 14

Apogee: 37 Gem System
Local Date: C18/D15
Local Time: 2/01:15

"What does it mean?" Deidra asked, already knowing the answer in her bones.

"Isn't it obvious?" Professor Catazara replied before Feder could. "It means we can finish the job. We can drain that sun much more rapidly." He paused for effect. "And it means also that our scientists are ahead of theirs again."

Deidra looked toward Feder, whose cheekbones now glowed with the reflection from the model.

Feder nodded. "That's what it means."

They were in Allie Feder's science lab because Feder had been so insistent that Deidra would need to see the display here.

Deidra nodded, letting the situation fill her. The room constricted into a silent hum of the equipment that ran here. The familiar tension that came with big issues crawled up her neck.

She stood up, then stepped into the model of the Solar System that spun silently in midair, orange swirls mixing with dark patches. The model felt bigger now, yet distant. It felt cold, too. It was almost vaporous, yet still more than she could digest.

With news that Kitchell's planetary blind was working, her calendar said she was supposed to be attending a session in which the staff was to finalize plans with the agricultural director for seeding the three expansion sites. That would happen immediately after *Perigee* was available, and no one wanted to waste another minute. Instead, Professor Feder had called her in to something she had called a "special session" and proceeded to lay this information out as if it was simply another technical conversation — which it most certainly was *not*.

Feder could enable the full black hole inside the Solar System.

This changed everything.

"You're sure this will work?" Deidra said.

"You can never be certain on a model," Feder replied, "but the math is solid."

Catazara sat beside Feder, nodding his head in the way he did whenever Feder spoke anymore. "I've reviewed it all," he said. "I can't see a flaw in the theory, and the code Allie created holds together."

Deidra looked at the image.

The rush of anger she'd felt on *Defender*'s bridge came back to her, the conviction she felt at having finally commanded her crew to embed the black hole connection into the sun. The sense of dread. The gaping absence left behind after the loss of *Vengeance*.

In the time since giving that command, Deidra had had ample moments to consider the ramifications of her action. The deaths she had commanded weighed on her at certain times when she was alone with her thoughts.

The opportunity was here again.

Save her people. Stop the war.

She wasn't sure what to do.

Her first decision to kill off the Solar System had been a last-gasp moment, something she saw as the only way to protect her people against the United Government.

Now the situation had changed.

Time had passed.

Kitchell's blind was working.

For the first time since Universe Three had arrived at Apogee, she had been starting to feel safe. Her team felt that, too. She could tell because for the first time they had made real progress toward their plans to expand U3 outposts to three more planets in the system. With *Perigee*, their new Star Drive spacecraft, being months from completion, a jaunty feeling of expectation seemed to radiate from the staff in ways she never felt before.

It all added up to say she'd become comfortable. In those quiet moments she admitted she was happy about the technical issues that had reduced the black hole's appetite and thereby saved the Solar System from her wrath. In those quiet moments she could admit to herself that she did not want to go down in history as the woman who had killed a hundred billion people.

Now?

Deidra gave a weary grin.

She wished she knew more about where UG's scientists were.

In the past she'd had considerable confidence that her vast network of moles and spies was able to keep her up to date. Now, with only one Star Drive spacecraft in service, she and her staff were less inclined to jump into UG territory — which limited their ability to make direct contact with their network. All they had to go on was a thin trickle of multicrypted messages that would come in sporadic bursts. The bottom line was that losing people like Oscar Pentabill as doubles was a bigger blow than she'd wanted to admit.

"Do we need to attach to a new black hole?" Deidra asked. "Or do we use the existing connection as its base?"

Feder ran her hand through her short hair.

The cut made the scientist's face stronger. Gave her a bolder presence. It was that, or simply that Feder had finally grown into the force Deidra had been expecting when she took Feder on the joyride around Mercury.

Feder looked at Catazara.

Lines deepened down to his jawline, but he didn't say anything.

"I haven't run that study yet," Feder responded. "But I expect we could simply use the current gate and essentially go deeper."

"So, no new gates?"

Feder chewed a corner of her lip, thinking. "I'm not sure, yet. But, yes. I think we can use what we have. We'll need to remote-cast about a bit on the black hole side until we get the connection right, but that's not a problem."

"Remote-cast that link?"

"Yes. *Vengeance*'s mission created waypoints in Sol that we can still use. But the black hole side was manually set," she said, turning to Catazara again. "What do you think, Jorge?"

"It's certainly possible we could use the existing construct."

"Possible?" Deidra said.

Catazara shrugged. "Like Allie said, we won't know until we do it, but the theory holds. And I can't see any damage that could come by trying. All the constructs are virtual in this dimension."

Deidra looked to Feder.

"Hate to say it, but Jorge is right," the young scientist said. "It's always dangerous to predict something we don't have any real-world experience with, but the model holds up. If we *can* use the existing gate posts, the only way to test it is to try it."

"All right, then," Deidra said. "Once you've decided how to progress, bring me a plan and I'll put it in front of the staff for confirmation."

"We can do that," Feder replied.

As she walked away, Deidra Francis felt relieved.

At least she hadn't had to make that decision today.

Chapter 15

Apogee: 37 Gem System
Local Date: C19/D47
Local Time: 2/07:45

The shield was up and working now. Universe Three was as safe as he could make them, and Kitchell could already see Deidra Francis's staff refocusing their efforts on expansion into three other planets in the 37 Gem system.

He was feeling good.

Kitchell checked the time. Allie was late again, like she'd been for the past couple of days.

He'd made her dinner by hand — a casserole he was quite proud of, filled with sweet nuts and corn mash. The sauce was a probiotic cheese. Very tasty. The aroma made him even more anxious for her arrival. Another five minutes and it would be past its peak flavor. He hoped it wouldn't be ruined.

The door opened and Allie stepped in.

"There she is!" he said, his smile widening.

"Everything smells amazing."

"I had some time on my hands."

"I'm a lucky girl, then."

"Who am I to argue with the expert?"

He escorted her to her seat, served the meal up, then stepped behind her to rub her neck and back — pleased when she melted into his hands.

"You have exactly three light years to stop that."

"I know you know that's a distance, not a time." He pressed fingers into her neck.

"Yes." She sighed. "Start now and don't stop until we've traveled three light years."

"Hard day?"

"The opposite, actually."

When she didn't continue, Kitchell prodded. "Breakthrough?"

Between a forkful of casserole, Allie explained, finishing with her conversation with Director Francis. "Now we need to come up with a plan," she said.

Kitchell had stopped rubbing her back as she'd spoken, but still had his palms cupped over her deltoids. He felt numb. "I don't understand," he said.

"It works, Thomas."

"Yeah," he replied, voice trailing away as he absently kneaded her shoulders and tried to form the right question. "I get that."

"Then what do you not understand?"

"Why would you do this now?"

"What do you mean?" Allie said.

He knew it had been the wrong thing to say even as he was saying it but stopping his mouth from voicing a question after he'd thought it had never been in his skillset. He rubbed her neck again, but she moved away.

"Seriously, Thomas. What do you mean?"

He took a seat at the table.

"I mean, the satellite jammer is protecting the colony. Why would U3 drop the black hole into the Solar System now when we know it will kill the entire population?"

The temperature of her gaze dropped a couple hundred degrees centigrade.

"So, you're saying I should stop my work?"

"It's not like that."

"Then what is it like?"

"It's ... I don't know. It's just ... are we *really* ready to kill everyone in the Solar System?"

"I don't know, Thomas. Are the UG leaders *really* willing to wipe out Apogee?"

He shut up.

Too late, he knew, but at least he got there eventually.

When Allie spoke next, it was in low, dangerous tones.

"You've been here long enough to understand, Thomas. Every member of this community has lost family. Everyone here. Your United Government has chased us into this little nook of the universe and has made us hide like kids in a bomb shelter as the shadows of their spaceships cross over our airspace." She looked directly at him. "Your shield is amazing, but it's not permanent. Someone, sometime, is going to create a process that your system isn't designed to deal with."

Unable to disagree, he nodded.

"It could be decades," he said.

"Or days."

He put his hands together, thinking about people he knew back home. That was in the equation he often ran through his mind. He'd counted their lives among those his blind had saved.

"I understand what's at stake," she added.

"I'm not sure you do."

"Believe me, Thomas, I understand exactly what I'm working on," she replied, bitter now. "And I understand exactly what we're talking about doing with the tools I'm creating. Don't you know I think about that every night when I go to bed and wake up with it every morning?"

"I'm sorry," he said, knowing she was right.

"What are we supposed to do, Thomas? Sit silently while the UG maneuvers around to destroy us?"

"I said I was sorry."

She sat in silence for an uncomfortable moment. Then sighed and picked up her fork to eat again.

"This is good," she said.

He smiled but didn't feel better.

He took his own bite. It was cold.

She was right, he thought as he chewed. As much as he hated to think about it, Kitchell was more than aware how far United Government leadership could go if it meant maintaining its power — and destroying U3 would play to that point.

"I'm sorry," he said. "You were right. I was wrong. I just wish things were different."

"I know. I wish they were, too."

After they had cleaned up dinner, Allie ran her hand through her hair and announced she wanted to stay at her place, alone.

"I'm dead on my feet," she said. "I'll probably just wake you up snoring."

"You haven't slept in two days, so I guess that makes sense," Thomas replied.

There was something more in her words, though.

He could feel it.

He'd called her on the most important thing she'd been working on. Questioned her very purpose of being. He felt a new distance between them tonight, even if — at least on the surface — she'd accepted his apology.

When the door shut behind her, he was as alone as he'd felt since long before he'd come to Apogee.

That night, Allie woke up with a jolt.

Her heart pounded and her head ricocheted with thoughts. Croaking lizards belched from somewhere around the pitch dark patio.

Kitchell was right — or at least not wrong.

There *was* another way.

If she could key another link. If she could drop a new core wormhole. Deidre Francis had been willing to do it before. That had been the entire point of the *Icarus* mission at Alpha Centauri A. And Allie had seen the darkness in the director's expression when she briefed her success.

Deidra Francis didn't want to butcher a hundred billion or more people if she didn't have to. Allie didn't either.

Maybe they didn't have to.

Chapter 16

Apogee: 37 Gem System
Local Date: C19/D48
Local Time: 2/06:12

"I think that's a bad idea," Thomas said to Allie the next day as he was finishing dinner preparations.

"Let's not do this again," Allie said.

She sat in the small dining nook across from the kitchen. The last of the early evening sunlight fell over her shoulder. She didn't know why Thomas liked cooking so much, but she wasn't going to complain. His concoctions were always better than what the dispenser system made, and the sound and smell of sizzling onions as he dropped them onto a lightly oiled skillet was a sensation no dispenser could duplicate. Raw peppers added a fresh scent.

If Allie had been thinking ahead, she would have foreseen his reaction, but she was physically and mentally drained, and to be honest, not up for a fight over the concept.

She'd spent all day getting her ideas into a form she could use to explain them. Twelve excruciating hours during which she bounced her earliest weird little models off Catazara, and then bounced her even more arcane thoughts off her own apprentices. No one could find flaws, though to be certain Allie didn't think anyone else understood the depths of the exercise.

The idea was simple in concept: Strip the link between *Defender* and Alpha Centauri A, and attach it to another star, then drop the black hole link into Alpha Centauri A. It would keep Universe Three Star Drives jumping while strangling UG's equipment.

"I don't see how you can think this is a bad idea," she said. "It solves all our problems. I mean, if we break the connection between our Star Drive and Alpha Centauri A, then forge a new one with a different star, we maintain our own ability to jump, save lives in the Solar System, and system-lock the entire UG fleet. Seems perfect to me."

Thomas pulled the pan off a burner.

"I see that logic, but you can't just kill Alpha Centauri A."

"Sure, we can."

"You know what I mean."

Yes. She knew what he meant.

She'd heard him talk about life on Eden so many times now she could recite the speech. All his thoughts on the subject were theoretical, though — or at least based on indirect information.

"I know you're attached to that star, but the system is already doomed."

"It doesn't have to be."

"There's nothing there, Thomas."

"We don't *know* that. We won't know *anything* until we go there."

Allie put her hand through her hair and gazed to the view outside Thomas's window. A scattering of buildings lined the street. The green ridge of a distant mountain rose to the left.

"Tell me about him," she said, hoping to change the subject.

"Who?"

"Your friend. Tell me about him."

"Torrance?" He'd returned to the skillet and was now rolling in peppers and a new base of oil and herbs.

"That's who you're thinking of, right?"

She knew about Torrance Black — the man who had been whisked to the Alpha Centauri A system during the *Icarus* disaster. He was dead, of course. Had to be. As was Katriana Martinez and another twelve U3 heroes who had volunteered for that mission. Allie understood the ironic tragedy inherent in Black's demise coming in the system he'd championed visiting for so long.

Thomas's stories brought that pathos down further.

He needed to talk about it now. That was obvious. Killing Alpha Centauri A meant the end of a lifelong dream for Thomas, and even if that dream was farfetched, he would need time to mourn. She'd prefer to hear Thomas's memories again rather than fight over whether it was a good thing to give a death blow to an already dying star.

"He was a good man," Thomas said as he seasoned the sizzling vegetables. "I knew it from the minute he took a brainless halfwit teenager and gave him a place on his Systems Command."

As Thomas spun his yarns, Allie's mind wandered. Killing Alpha Centauri A outright *would* solve a major problem, but the full process wasn't going to be as easy as she'd first thought.

Remote connection to another star should work fine.

Catazara had already done it once when he lassoed the black hole to begin with. Since they had, in theory, infinite tries, that part would be trial and error — or, if they wanted to speed up the process, they could jump to new locations and plant guideposts as they had done in the Mercury mission.

Establishing a new link to an existing Star Drive was the dicey part.

She had made the rounds earlier in the day.

Everyone she spoke with understood the multidimensional complexities associated with making links and breaking them, but it seemed clear they had vastly underestimated the very real problems entailed with connecting an existing Star Drive engine — one already keyed to an existing gate — to a new source.

There were basic math issues to settle, and the physical dynamics required to control intense flows of fusing material as they jumped the dimensions was not for the faint of heart.

Explaining things to colleagues helped because it made her think both harder and from different directions.

"I just don't think you should do it," Thomas finally said as he slid a dinner plate onto the table in front of her.

Allie's stomach did little leaps of joy. "That looks fantastic," she said, digging in.

Thomas took a chair beside her but left his food untouched.

Finally, Allie looked up at him.

"You haven't heard a word I've said, have you?"

"Torrance was a great friend. He saved your life."

"I was talking about the mission."

She grimaced. "I'm sorry."

"And I'd appreciate it if you didn't patronize me. I know Torrance is dead. But I can't support killing a planet when there's still a chance that sentient life exists there."

"Perhaps you should have told that to the United Government before the *Everguard* mission put it there in the first place."

She knew it was the wrong thing to say, but she was tired and a bit more than fed up. Yes. Blame it on the tired. She didn't have the energy to stop the words before they appeared, and now that they were out, she clamped her lips shut, and glanced back out the window.

A few seconds of silence later, she turned back.

"I'm sorry," she said. "I shouldn't have said that — and definitely shouldn't have said it that way — but I think you might be too close to this one to see the details for what they are."

He stared at her.

She wanted to reach a hand to him but didn't feel she should.

"Whether life exists there or not, Alpha Centauri A is dying. We're adding new spacecraft to the drain every year, so it's going to happen even faster than anyone predicted. Like it or not, Thomas, that is the truth we're living in."

He sighed. "I hate this."

"Do you have a better idea?"

He was motionless for a moment, then picked up his fork. "No," he said. "I don't."

She watched him shovel forkfuls into his mouth.

When they finished dinner, Allie returned to her own hut, and once again Thomas stayed in his own quarters.

Chapter 17

Apogee: 37 Gem System
Local Date: C24/D13
Local Time: 1/08:35

Allie Feder was good. That was the main thought Deidra Francis had as she watched the still-young physicist work the Universe Three staff. She was growing into her powers as a communicator as the cycles passed and her technical expertise grew, and Deidra, having already heard the core message — that Feder, with help, had been successful in determining an approach that *should* work to link *Defender* to a new source — took in the expressions of her cohorts as the story played out.

They were in the usual assembly room for this early morning briefing.

Deidra preferred the open roof and the air flowing freely from the breeze the room's depth and rounded shape helped to create, but the world gives what the world gives. Since rainy weather was expected, the briefing center's roof was fully closed, a configuration that gave the assembly room a more damped echo and made the air more dense than usual. It added up to a less-than-natural aura that would normally make the collective less open to ideas.

Still, the aura of interest grew more obvious around the room the longer Feder spoke.

If the approach worked, it would be possible to avoid wiping out the whole Solar System.

Deidra wanted to know what her staff thought.

Timmon Keyes was growing more active each day, and her feelers said he was out to gather support among the staff — support that might even have gone as far as to suggest an actual coup. She wanted to know how far he'd gotten.

Knowing the brief's content in advance helped her read the room.

It was a tactic very much unlike her father, she realized.

Casmir Francis preferred to hear news at the same time as his staff, which he thought gave the organization an egalitarian sense of sharing. She supposed that was true, but her father had always been better at analyzing things in public and in real time. Deidra had never been good at reining in her worse instincts, so she was better when she could put distance between the problem and a response.

Watching her staff work also made her feel closer to them, which was something that she'd appreciated more as she'd grown older.

They were her family now.

If her family was going to turn on her, she wanted them to do it up front.

That's why Keyes's efforts hurt her so bad.

Watching them work said that Deego Larsi may be slanting Keyes's way. Henri Shudar, *Defender*'s captain, seemed on a balance point, but that could simply be due to a desire to protect his ship at all costs. Three others, lesser or younger officers in various organizations, seemed to harbor leanings toward Timmon Keyes's absolutist framework.

"So," Feder said in conclusion. "It turns out we have two viable options. First, simply deepen the black hole gate we already have — which kills the Solar System outright. The second is to reposition our own source, and then kill Alpha Centauri A, which would serve to system-lock the UG, thereby making them harmless as far as we're concerned."

Silence fell while the group digested the information.

"If it can be done, I think connecting to a new star is brilliant," Martin Scalese said.

"I don't see the point," Captain Keyes snapped. "And if I read the report right, mistakes in the transition between sources could result in existential damage to the spaceship. I don't see how we can do anything that risks *Defender* right now. I say we stop dancing around the moment. Just drop the damned black hole into the Solar System and be done with it. It's a simple solution, and it solves our problems. It's what they would do."

"It would certainly shorten the cycle time," Kazima Yamada said. "To adjust the link would mean we have to determine which new star we want to use, then ensure the conversion is right before we crash Alpha Cen A. And, while I'm sure Professor Feder's models are solid, the framework is still a big theoretical jump. Is it smart to delay action if we're not convinced this is real?"

"Are you suggesting that sparing a hundred billion innocent lives isn't reason enough?" Scalese asked.

"Would it be enough if the shoe was on the other foot?" Captain Keyes said. The edge to his voice made his answer obvious.

"I'm suggesting the question isn't as clear-cut as you might think," Yamada replied. "For example, how hard will it be to find another star system that doesn't already house life of *some* kind? Either choice could well wind up killing something."

Scalese considered the comment. "I see what you mean, but it seems doable. With time, anyway. And we do have access to data on several systems that the UG has gone to. That data might help us choose a star. I can see if we can scrounge some more."

Yamada's eyebrows rosed in animation. "Time. Always more time. In the meantime, we're talking about delaying our own expansion efforts. Again."

Deidra felt the underlying positions in the room.

"You are aware that *we* still have people in the Solar System, right?" Scalese said.

"Yes," Yamada replied. "I am aware of that. Nothing about this is easy."

Scalese was the closest thing the U3 had to an intelligence officer. He'd liked the concept Allie was proposing because he still had moles embedded in the Solar System. As such, he'd already been arguing for rescue sweeps to get his people out of harm's way

— missions that the staff worried might expose *Defender,* again, the only primary asset the U3 leadership staff still had left.

They had put a new ship into production after the Mercury skirmish, but their cycle time was long. *Perigee*'s readiness was still a few standard months away.

Changing Star Drive sources and killing the link to Alpha Centauri A would save Scalese's people, so he was for it. Add in the fact that Thomas Kitchell's work in creating the signal blind fell under both Scalese's and Yamada's direction, that Kitchell and Feder still seemed to be paired up, and that it was Scalese's operation who brought Kitchell here in the first place, well, Deidra could come up with a tangled web of reasons Scalese would back the concept.

Bottom line, Deidra had already known he'd love it.

Keyes and Yamada had different needs.

Without a ship to command, Keyes had been relegated to logistical activities — hence his connection with Larsi. Beyond that, he had to be reading the future. When *Perigee* was ready, Deidra would need to decide who would captain it. Keyes's experience would be a benefit, but his struggles to put aside his anger made him a liability, and Deidra had Jessamine Mikayla, who was younger, but now considerably experienced, too, coming along behind him. Bottom line, Timmon Keyes was looking to make a move.

One problem at a time, though.

Yamada's interest in the shorter route — dropping the full depth of the black hole — was for more pragmatic reasons than political. The U3's chief engineering director was impatient to begin enacting expansion — plans which the staff had now halted and restarted more times than either one of them wanted to count, the last being the loss of *Vengeance,* which made the logistics required to execute the original plan impossible.

They had three Star Drive skimmers that could lessen the burden, but they would never be enough to make the original plan work.

Yamada wanted *Perigee* ready now.

Any effort that delayed that was something Deidra would rather avoid, and if the group decided to pursue Feder's plan, she knew something would have to give.

The others had distinct reasons for holding different positions.

The conversation went on until voices rose into such a tumultuous buzz that Deidra had to calm them down.

She called out in a loud enough voice to eventually bring the focus to her, "I have a proposal."

Standing, she cleared her throat to give emotions around the room an extra moment to recede.

"We've all been making hard calculations in our minds, but I know there isn't a person around this table who genuinely, at their core, wants to kill every person in the Solar System. I know I don't."

She held up her hand when Keyes prepared to break in.

"And, yes, Timmon, you can trust me when I say that I'm certain that UG leadership would have no problem wiping us all out. But that's a difference between us. They will do it because they *want* to. We will do it, too, but only if we *have* to."

The room settled.

"Thanks to Thomas Kitchell and our signal engineers, we have a signal blinder now that we know works — at least against the tools UG has today. I hate delays as much as anyone, but we have at least a little time to play with. What I don't think we can afford at this point, though, is to risk *Defender*. Henri and Timmon are right to point that out. That's our only Star Drive cruiser. So, we just can't do that."

She turned to Feder.

"Can you use a Star Drive skimmer to test the process in a real-world setting?"

Feder pressed her lips together. "I considered it, but the scale is quite different."

"It would prove concept?"

"Of course."

"And if something went wrong it would cost us only a skimmer."

"I..." Feder paused, thinking. "Yes. That's right."

"How long will that take?"

Feder shrugged. "It's a smaller lift. I don't know. We'd have to extract its current key, then run all our transformations again. Then get things reloaded." She looked at Professor Catazara. "Two weeks? Maybe four?"

Catazara both shrugged and nodded. He seemed suddenly ancient.

Feder continued. "I'd have to do some work to answer the question for sure, but that seems about right."

Deidra turned back to the gathering.

"Then that's what I suggest we do. Delay dropping the black hole gate extension on the Solar System to give Professor Feder and her team time to create a link in another star and connect it to the skimmer. If the proof of concept works, we spend time finding the right donor star. Otherwise, the plan proceeds as originally designed, and the bigger, more functional black hole gate goes into the Solar System."

It was a middle-ground proposal that kicked the can farther down the road.

She could tell it made them happy.

When Timmons realized he'd lost, he sat back in his chair with his gaze darkened.

"History will at least say we tried," he said.

Yamada nodded.

Chapter 18

Apogee: 37 Gem System
Local Date: C24/D78
Local Time: 2/12:15

Allie sat alone in her office, unable to let it go for the night.

The problem was harder than she had expected, and the fact that Jorge Catazara had gotten his ire up and was pursuing his own thing now, and that Thomas was still being prissy about the whole thing, wasn't helping.

Sitting in the stale, darktime quiet of her office, the pressure felt like a fist clamping down over her heart.

Or her chest. Or brain.

The wormhole pods the UG had used to create the original gate in Alpha Centauri A all carried the same characteristics. *"Think of it as a shared account,"* she'd say to people who needed a base understanding. *"Every ship we jump today accesses the power of Alpha Centauri A through the same throat tensor — which works because it's a fixed entry."* This behavior was why every new ship had to carry the same engine port. It was why, if the original *Icarus* mission had been successful, it would have severed jumping for everyone, but it was also why every ship needed a unique key on the receiving side. Otherwise, every ship would be exposed to power anytime another jumped. And that would be disaster.

At one point, the Universe Three brain trust had been concerned that the United Government would sever the link themselves, leaving them stranded — like U3 was willing to do to UG under that *Icarus* mission. But the economics didn't line up for the UG and the Solar System. The UG, however, had advantages in size, and production capacity that would grow over time. For them, cooler heads prevailed. Why would the UG spend the capital they would need to set a new wormhole gate when they didn't need to?

So, the problem facing Allie and her apprentices was that every engine had a wormhole key with connections that spanned eleven dimensions, each hard-coded into its links. To break that link, and then make an exchange of connections, required separating each level individually, then matching the wormhole physics of the new key on all eleven.

Thomas's random ideas had led Allie to a better understanding of those dimensions, but something was still off.

The solution she was looking for — which it was clear no one fully understood yet — was extremely touchy. The dimensions played with each other. To touch any dimension was to change it, and that change fed into adjacent levels in ways that seemed impossible to predict. That meant that creating the new key required a complex, recursive conversion of tensor tables.

At least the separations weren't as hard as she expected they would be. Mapping hard-coded keys across dimensions was "easy," though it took intense computing and considerable time.

But knitting the whole thing together was a massively powerful piece of theoretical physics. If she got it wrong, the resulting explosion would be like no other.

"At least we wouldn't need to worry about UG finding us," one apprentice had said earlier in the evening as Allie ran through her concerns. She groaned and went on. Being the only person who understood what she was talking about was the story of her life, and the need to constantly explain the unexplainable had rubbed her thin.

She rubbed her temples, getting no further.

The weight was wearing on her.

If she didn't succeed, the Solar System was going to die.

CHAPTER 19

Apogee: 37 Gem System
Local Date: C25/D50
Local Time: 2/10:55

Well past dinner time, which Allie had skipped for the third night in a row, her stomach burned with acid.

Professor Catazara sat at one side of the simple square desk, leaning back, hands over his head. He'd come back to her two nights before, his tail most certainly between his legs and finally admitting that his preferred approach was never going to work.

Simply coming back was the closest thing to an apology she was likely to get.

He was an old man now, the folds of his skin darkening into his wrinkled jaws. Bags lined fleshy lobes under his eyes.

Three apprentices had come with him. They sat in the room's dark corners, sleeves rolled up in rumpled approximations of the professor himself. She'd debated cutting them adrift as simple justice for splitting the first time, but the fact was she needed ideas.

Together, they'd been at it for hours, and the apprentices were as tired as Allie and Catazara were.

Outside the office, a vented window left an opening for the rhythmic grunts of amphibians that rolled through the moist nighttime air. She blew stray hair from her eyes. She was letting it grow again, a decision she was now regretting.

"I still don't understand that leap," she said addressing a logic box in which the algorithm Catazara had proposed was supposed to span dimensions in leaps of five.

"Like I said earlier," Catazara said. "Think about it like you're building a bridge. Or a tent. The idea is to use D-1, D-6, and D-11 as foundations — or like bumpers on slides. Get those three keyed properly, then work inward to build stability."

Allie paused to keep from snapping at him. She wasn't in preschool anymore. Jorge's propensity for analogies as simplifying tools always annoyed her, especially because they were often not right, and even more because — even when they were on course — they obscured the details that made the problem both real and interesting.

In this case, the proposal he was simplifying would result in a spaceship disintegrating under a quantum fusion event more massive than anything less than a supernova.

She shook her head.

"I don't know, Jorge," she finally said. "Even if we cut the dimensional spectrum into segments, the pressure and velocity of the energy flow through the gates are just too much. The model doesn't hold up in virtual at all."

"Virtual can't model interdimensional losses well enough," an apprentice replied for Catazara. "That would lower the flow pressure."

Catazara jumped in again. "That's right. When we add variables to model a loss profile, the three inner dimensions come close to stabilizing."

"*Close to stabilizing* isn't good enough," she said.

"We won't know for sure if we don't try," Catazara said.

She sighed.

If it had been an apprentice who'd brought this to her tonight, Allie would have long ago discounted it and gone off to bed, but even though he'd bailed on her, Jorge deserved more attention. Truth told, she had originally wondered if one of the students had come up with the idea, but after the hours of this conversation she'd bet on Catazara himself. The apprentices were not that smart.

At least that part made her happy.

Nothing was worse than seeing Processor Catazara gasping for breath in places he shouldn't be floundering.

"Resources are too tight, Jorge. I can't take that chance. If we screw up, we destroy the only ship we're going to get."

"All right, then," Catazara said. "What can we do to slow the flow?"

"What's that?" Allie replied.

Catazara's blinking told her the question caught him off guard, too.

"I was just thinking that if we could slow down the flow from the new source as we made the connection, we could give the algorithm time to stabilize. In the meantime, we could create a process that could kill the process if that stabilization didn't finish in time."

"I don't think that would work, Professor," an apprentice said. "At least I don't think it's possible for a virtual process to slow flow in the physical."

The four of them began a new conversation, throwing around deep mathematical constructs and even playing with the model in front of them.

But Allie's brain was somewhere else.

Wormhole throat tensors.

Multiple dimensions.

Hundreds of combinations.

Feedback loops.

And through it all, Professor Catazara's question loomed: What can we do to slow the flow?

Slow wasn't the right word.

Or it was the right word but wasn't right enough.

Slowing it wouldn't be good enough.

She laid her head back against the wall she'd been leaning on.

Thinking.

What would it take, she thought, *to stop the flow of energy through a functioning wormhole gate?*

REFUGEE

All of Esgarat
Local Season: Eldoro Leading, Year of Second *Piela*, Cycle 57

Chapter 20

Esgarat Mountains
North Slope

In a far corner of the rocky chamber the quadars used as their production facility, Torrance Black stood alongside the young engineer and scanned the finished casting. It looked perfect: a rocket fuselage about twice as tall as Torrance was, properly configured with a segment large enough for the engine and another for the payload.

Edart Kel, the youthful but brilliant quadar who had just now showed him that the cooling lines cast in the fuselage were open and operational, stood beside him with an aura of anticipation that colored her expression.

Around them, the assembly area was even busier than normal. They'd had an issue with connecting fuel coils to the main engine. Torrance gave in inward grimace as he considered that problem. He had looked at it before. He would look at it again. He was certain they would solve the issue soon, but something was always going wrong, and the process was wearing. Louratna had insulated him from this kind of thing when she was alive. The thought made him miss her even more.

Edart, though young, had risen to this occasion with passion and skill. Along the way, she'd become a force of her own. Her work drove this collection of Louratna's quadars, inspired them to accomplish things he hadn't thought possible. Despite the constant ache of his planet-worn body, Torrance found his thoughts filled with an admiration that bordered on hope.

Perhaps Edart could take Louratna's place.

Someday, anyway.

These quadars would follow her because — beyond her obvious skills — she'd proven she would be there in the trenches with them.

Now Edart stood before him, clearly holding her tongue.

"This is very good work," Torrance said, running his hand over the casting's surface. It was cooling now, but still held heat.

"Credit to Janti," Edart replied. "He knows what he's doing."

"Indeed."

"Where is Baraq?" Edart Kel asked directly, doing nothing to hide the frustration and anxiety she was clearly feeling. "We need his wave talker now."

Torrance clicked a sense of calmness. Over time he'd grown a better appreciation for the quadarti language. It was now coming so naturally that he sometimes found himself thinking in it.

"He's being pulled too many ways now," he said. "You know that."

"Is there anything more important than this effort?" The young quadar's primaries were wide now, colored an iridescent brown and purple so deep as to be almost black. The folds of skin around them were tight. Her central, too, was slitted open despite the natural light that filtered down to the factory floor — another sign of her dissatisfaction.

"I know you're pressing hard, Edart."

"Pressing hard?" Her jaw clenched. She craned her gaze around the expansive factory. "We are not *pressing hard*, Torranze. We are working as if our lives depend on it. All of us. We're working as if our lives depend on it because we all know that they do."

She wasn't wrong.

Torrance understood that better than anyone else.

Regardless of how fighting among the quadarti Families played out, their planet wouldn't last much longer. The goal now was to get as many rockets as possible outfitted with the Waganat radios — wave talkers in the quadarti vernacular — and then launch an entire fleet toward the Solar System in hopes that a barrage of cohesive messages broadcast in a human language would draw attention.

He envisioned a flotilla of glass bottles floating in the seas of space.

Of those in the compound, only Baraq knew how to make the wave talkers. And Baraq had to do what Baraq had to do. *What is it worth to save the planet if there are no quadars to come with it?* Baraq had told him during one late-night conversation.

He was a complex creature, Baraq Waganat.

He had been through much — been involved in everything.

Torrance had begun to collaborate with him only recently, but it wasn't wrong to say Baraq was the first quadar he had ever truly seen. The quadar was an inventor. An engineer in his own way, a quadar of privileged background, but who had seen devastation at the hand of his Family's power. His public persona carried a blackness now, too. Torrance had heard stories. Tales of Baraq's personal vendetta against his own Family and all Families. Stories that said Baraq Waganat was, himself, the spark that lit the flame of this Family war.

Likely those stories were true.

If so, Baraq Waganat was dealing with pressures Torrance could only begin to relate to.

When Torrance had broached the subject last afterdark, Baraq had pursed his lips into a sharp line and simply said, "I did what I had to do."

Torrance followed Edart's gesture, though, taking in the assembly floor that Edart and her team had now finished retooling to accommodate the production of yet another classification of rocketry.

It had been the second such retooling they'd required — the first coming after the Families had demolished their original facility and altered their plan from building one large vehicle to transport quadars to an approach that would result in smaller rockets. The goal then had been to seed the atmosphere, or even to create a weapon that might change or even avoid the war. Now the plan had changed again, pushing the team to design more moderately sized rockets that would carry that radio equipment built by Baraq Waganat.

Torrance couldn't blame them for their anger.

Edart's group — who was responsible for building the rocket itself — was ready.

Baraq was not.

"I'm sorry, Edart," Torrance said. "I know how hard this is for everyone. But you know why he's splitting his time."

"I know he's wasting that time with the Orange Ring."

"It's not a waste of time."

Edart's primaries blazed, but she didn't say anything.

Anxiety formed in Torrance's gut.

There was every chance she was right, that Baraq's time spent helping the rebels gather refugees had little real value. Politics were hard to analyze, and even his years as a science ambassador hadn't made him any better at it. Still, Torrance had spent enough time with Baraq to know the effort was important to him, so it had to be important to Torrance, too. And who was to say Baraq wasn't right, too. If no quadars remained after the Families had destroyed each other, what value was the rocket?

To be fair, Baraq was making real progress on the production of wave talkers while also spending large chunks of time in expeditions back to Esgarat City. Already the Orange Ring had extracted many quadars, and Baraq expected the first fully functional units in a handful of days. Whatever that meant.

"We're ready to run the trial," Edart said, regaining a calm demeanor. "All I need is his wave talker."

"I'll speak with him."

Edart's expression showed how far she thought that would go.

"In the meantime, I think we could find something to model the wave talker with, which would let your testing continue on plan."

"We could do that, but then we won't know if the wave talker itself can survive the launch."

"I understand," Torrance said. "But let's do the best we can do. At least we'll know if the rocket breaks under expected conditions."

"The rocket won't break."

"Never tempt the fates," he said.

Edart hung her head and clicked annoyance. "Sorry. I know better. Anything that can go wrong, will go wrong. It's just..." She drew a bigger breath and straightened her shoulders.

Torrance put his hand on her shoulder, feeling the weight she'd been carrying in her tense muscles.

"It's all right," he said.

She took a deep breath, then steeled herself.

"I'll make the model," she said.

Chapter 21

Esgarat Mountains
Nectani Gap

Anger burned though Baraq Waganat, starting at his cheeks and swelling through his shoulder plates.

Ezi Waganat sat hunched over as if in contemplation, on a striated rock that jutted from the mountainside. Her throat gave a subtle motion as she swallowed, an action that told Baraq she was holding her thoughts to herself.

Ezi was his dead whelp's *kalla*, and, though the leadership ring was democratic of a sort, she was the most important leader in the Orange Ring as it stood.

It meant she had a lot to hold on to.

A cool breeze flowed from upslope.

A distance below, Baraq saw Crissandr, his own *kalla*, as she worked to triage the last of the quadars they'd retrieved from Esgarat City this past mission. The sight of *hedgie* refugees grew into balls of stone in his stomachs. Watching Crissandr work with them simply made the ache worse.

Baraq finally spoke. "You've seen it yourself, Ezi. The *hedgie* community responds to Lelo. And for better or worse, I am now Lelo to them. I need to go. Every mission I travel with brings home more lives than those I don't."

"The numbers support him," Oast'el said from his perch on another flat rock to Baraq's left. The leader of the Orange Army and Ezi's second-in-command was large for a quadar.

"Only some of them," Ezi snapped.

The three had agreed to meet outside the mouth of the cave that served to host the Orange Ring leadership circle — agreed to discuss specifics of the *next* mission to Esgarat City, specifics that were becoming routine: supplies needed, routes to take, a review of safe havens in case Family scouts caught them entering or leaving the city. They'd also gone over the last damage reports — knowing that recently abandoned buildings were places to treat with care and caution.

Now Ezi had dropped this idea on him.

She did not want him to join the mission.

Wanted him to stay home like a coward.

"Which numbers don't support me?" Baraq asked from his place, seated cross-legged on the ground.

"You know which numbers."

"No, I don't."

"You are getting old, Baraq. The numbers I'm talking about are duration of the missions. When you travel with a team, you slow them down."

"I do not."

Baraq looked to Oast'el for support.

Oast'el, who commanded each mission, put his lips together hard enough that dark wrinkles formed in the looming afterdark. His primaries fell on Baraq with regret. "Ezi is correct on that matter," he said. "Operations that include you are away from the mountain for at least two extra days — sometimes more."

Ezi jumped in. "Every day added to a mission adds to chances renegades can ambush the team. Not to mention that we can run five missions *without* you in the time it takes to run four of them *with* you, so if you add up refugee counts over those spans, any advantage we get from assigning you to those missions goes away."

Oast'el remained silent.

More heat burned in Baraq's face and shoulder plates.

The accusations hurt him mostly because he knew they were true. He did slow the group down. He could feel that in every step he took. And in combat he would be a detriment.

The idea of stepping away hurt, though.

Ezi finally broke the moment. "You know what Brada would say."

Baraq winced with the name. "Brada would say I should go with them."

"No, he would not."

"I know my whelp," Baraq snapped.

"Apparently not as well as you think." Ezi turned to face him. "We need you here, Baraq. That's what Brada would have said, and you know that."

"I can't leave him."

"I'm not asking you to."

"Yes, you are."

Ezi stood up, brushing dust from the legs and back of her *kami*, which were thick and tough leather. She came to Baraq, then stooped to sit before him, crossing her legs over as his were. She narrowed her primaries but opened her central wide in an expression steeped in compassion.

She put her hand on his knee.

Baraq bowed his head.

Brada had been his whelp. His youth. The second whelpling he'd lost. The missions made him feel something deeper than he could describe. When he was in the city, he recalled the image of Brada, of Lelo, body jerking with Family bullets, and he recalled the sensation of stepping forward against the Families in the only way he had left at his disposal — as a lone vigilante.

He was not proud of everything he had done, but it was all he had to give. The only way he had to hold on to his blood.

The idea of leaving Brada now...

"I can't let him go," he whispered, feeling heat from her hand on his knee.

"I know, *Dada*. I can't, either."

Baraq looked at her — Brada's pair-mate — but could not speak.

"You promised me earlier that you would do your role. You said we both knew I was the leader, and that you would do your part."

"And..." Baraq was going to say that this is exactly what he was doing, but looking into Ezi's gaze and feeling Oast'el's strength at the periphery of his vision, he knew better.

Ezi took his hand.

"Stay here," she said. "That's what Brada would have commanded. Stay here and make your wave talkers. Then," Ezi continued, pointing to where Crissandr was now stooping down to examine a *hedgie* whelpling, "when we bring each new gathering of quadars from the city, introduce them to Lelo by joining your *kalla*. That's the message they need from you now. Connection. Togetherness. Each playing their parts."

Baraq nodded, feeling the harshness of loss but knowing Ezi was right.

"She deserves you, too," Ezi said.

After several beats, Baraq nodded again.

"One last time," he said. "I need one more trip to say good-bye."

Ezi laughed then, a soft peal that was bitter enough at first that it brought Baraq anger, but a moment later settled into him.

"I see where Brada got his obstinance," she said.

"So, I can go?"

Ezi glanced at Oast'el, who gave a resigned shrug. "One last mission," he said. "We will leave at Eldoro rise."

"Thank you," Baraq said. "I will be ready."

Ezi stood, then helped Baraq to his feet — aid he accepted easily.

He held on to Ezi for an extra moment.

She paused, glancing at him from an angle that told him he was free to speak.

"You are good in your hearts, Ezi. You are the only quadar in All of Esgarat who could have told me that."

She smiled. "Then I am glad I am here."

"I am, too," Baraq said.

He gave her hand a final warm squeeze, and together they returned to the caves.

Chapter 22

Esgarat City
Foothills

Tierra Waganat gripped the head of his father's walking staff, wincing in pain as he slipped into the lean-to he'd found earlier. It was a tiny thing, just three fiber board slabs fastened into a ramshackle shelter. But its size also served as a deterrent. No one wanted it.

No one with any power, anyway.

No one with any strength.

His heavy stick had fended off two near-dead scavengers last darktime. He expected the need to do it again this darktime. Time was short, though. Soon enough even this splint of shelter would be attractive, and he'd have to leave or die defending it.

He sat back, biting off pain and watching the city before him transition from raids made by Family guards to the darktime dangers brought on as loose gangs of *hedgie* renegades emerged.

Sounds of movement came in the distance.

His throat clenched against the hazy smoke that settled over the landscape.

His ankle hadn't healed well from his fall through the abandoned tenement building rooftop where he and Jee El had cornered Baraq. He wondered if he had cracked a shoulder bone in that fall, too. It had been many heats since that debacle, and the pain was no better. He hadn't eaten in two heats, which meant he was going to have to get out and scavenge, soon.

Leaving the lean-to that long worried him. The only bright spot in the situation was that scavengers out here were working mostly on their own, and the community that remained behind was derelict, filled with mostly the old and sick. The Families would get to this section of the city after the real fighting stopped, but when they came the Families would focus first on rooting out healthy workers who they could conscript to become their guards.

Regardless, he knew of storehouses he might be able to sneak into — maybe.

He wished he had a gun.

All the Tegra weapons he'd had access to in recent heats, and he'd not taken a step to acquire one for himself. Stupid.

He hefted the weighty walking stick. With luck he could find an unsuspecting vandal and take one. Could work. The only challenge would be to find a lone quadar on the hunt, which shouldn't be that hard. It seemed every *hedgie* in the city was out some nights, many looking for safe passage to the commune that rumors said Lelo was forming.

Lelo, he thought. The depth of his anger at that name consumed him.

Lelo.

That name seemed to seep from the dirt every time he came near a *hedgie* now. *Lelo, Lelo, Lelo.* Tierra's body seethed with fire when he thought about his brother — Baraq — donning the façade of Baraq's own whelp, as if he was half the quadar the rebel had been.

Baraq Waganat was weak.

He had always been weak.

There'd been a moment when Tierra had the chance to kill Baraq and had let that opportunity pass. It was a moment he would regret forever.

Tierra truly had lost everything now.

Even Jee El, his most trusted confidant, was now dead, killed by Lelo's Orange Army.

Lelo.

He spat.

Find Lelo, and he would find Baraq. Find Baraq, and if nothing else, he could have his revenge.

As the heats faded and the sky darkened, Tierra used his walking stick to pry himself off the ground. His ankle throbbed, but he hobbled into the darkening terrain and twisted pathways that served as streets here.

He had to eat something.

And he had to get a real weapon.

Chapter 23

That last morning, coming out of the mountains, was so cold that portions of *havra* the group carried had to be broken apart to prepare for their first meal. Cold enough that Baraq's muscles spasmed painfully until the group got moving.

When he woke, he'd found Oast'el staring gape-mouthed up to the peaks, and, when Baraq followed that gaze, he had taken in something he could never have imagined — those same peaks shining with brilliant white shimmer in the golden light of Eldoro rising.

The cycle was in Convergence — the period when Eldoro and Katon raced over the sky together, and when darktimes were the coolest. But this sight was something new. He had to shield his primaries just to take it in. By the time the mission began its last leg, the whiteness had retreated to leave the sharp-edged columns and majestic slopes as barren as they had always been.

But he had seen the brilliance with his own eyes.

The aura of the sight stayed with him as they left camp.

Aware of his deficiencies now, Baraq pushed himself to keep with the group. They were five strong, Oast'el and three lower members of the Orange Army — one, a middle-aged worker named

Kiltian, who had been among the first group of *hedgie* quadars they'd brought to Nectani Gap.

The quadar had worked in a Denari mud field, mixing the soil of Esgarat into the various pasty amalgams the Family sold to other Families — primarily the Festia and Elganjo — for their use in building the city. Cycles of wielding hard tools and operating heavy machinery had gnarled his body. His skin had thickened and grown rough from toiling under the heats. Baraq was older than Kiltian by considerable margin, but Kiltian's body looked like a tangled mess, which made the *hedgie* appear to be the elder. He wore a heat-faded, leathered outfit that made him blend in with the terrain.

Baraq had suffered Kiltian's glances throughout the three heats it had taken to reach the city's outskirts.

He understood the cause of them, too.

Kiltian understood Baraq was not the original Lelo — a topic Baraq still remembered discussing with the *hedgie* as they had first extracted him — but something about Kiltian's glances still made him uncomfortable.

"What are you thinking?" Baraq asked now as they made their way toward Esgarat City.

"I am thinking that life is hard," Kiltian replied as he bit off an end and then chewed on a gnarled piece of *kado*.

"It is."

"I am thinking I have lost three whelplings in my life."

"I am sorry to hear that."

Kiltian grunted. "I'm thinking that most quadars I know have had similar stories over their lives."

Baraq heard an accusation in that commentary.

The losses this quadar had suffered were the norm for his family, whereas Baraq's loss of little Hara to disease and Brada to the Family's murder were unexpected.

"There is much wrong in the world," Baraq finally replied.

Kiltian clicked in low affirmatives, then picked at his teeth with a gnarled forefinger. He pointed to his head.

"I carry their names," he said, then he looked at Baraq. "As you carry your whelpling's name with you." He smiled then. It was a strange smile, part joy and part ache. "Thank you for that."

Baraq understood then.

Kiltian was not holding Baraq accountable for his advantages.

"You would have carried their names even if I did not," Baraq said, feeling something that might have been gratitude or might simply have been the pure rawness of what it meant to be here on the trail.

"I would have held their names, but I would not have done anything else. I would not be here to help others."

Again, Baraq wasn't sure what to do.

"I was not a good father," Kiltian continued.

Baraq grunted this time, thinking about his own path.

He had been a good father. Not always, but sometimes, anyway. He felt closer to Brada then, felt the strength his whelpling had built inside him.

"We do what we can when we can," he said. "And now is always a good time to start."

Kiltian smiled, crunching more *kado* and staring down into the city.

"I will save many quadars tonight," the *hedgie* said.

"Yes," Baraq said. "I believe you will."

CHAPTER 24

Oast'el clicked his soft commands as the extraction team arrived at the designated place. The sky was growing full dark now, the time a hand after Eldoro down. The stars were gaining their full brightness.

Before the problems had come, this area had been open ground, a center of sorts, or a gathering square that hosted festivals and markets. Baraq was embarrassed to admit he did not know exactly what it had been.

This was *hedgie* territory before. Why would he have cared?

The city was quiet now, transitioning from open fighting to nighttime vigilantism — everything so still that even breathing sounded too loud. Though Baraq did not know the area, the destruction here still hit him like hammer blows.

Burned huts.

Cleared streets.

The darktime split by an edge that felt carnivorous.

Esgarat City was eating itself. The Families had nearly completed seizing their conscripts. What came next would be horrifying.

Oast'el motioned Baraq forward, his own central wide. With a final sharp hand signal, he initiated the operation.

This was the most dangerous moment of the night.

Each team member set out on their own, targeting separate dwellings they'd scouted the darktime before.

Inside each *should* be a family — multiple quadars, huddled down low to convey an empty dwelling. Having gathered the family, each team member was to return to the designated rendezvous to make the return trip together, Orange Army soldiers running point and rear guard.

Through Baraq's now wide central, heat patterns lingered on the street and doorways.

His target was the simplest — a sturdy brick building — tiny but solid. The family inside should consist of five quadars who — including the two youngest whelplings — had once worked for the Ombat Family. As he stepped into a twisted alleyway that led to his target, Baraq's body burned with ire at the fact that the *hedgie* family was still here. In a time when every greater Family was either killing or hoarding resources, how could the Ombat Family not know where their workers lived?

He turned the question on himself, though.

He had been high in his Waganat hierarchy. Had he known where the cook called home?

No. He had not.

As Baraq crept through the city, the question festered in his bottom stomach. He came to the alleyway that led to his target and crouched in darkness against a wall.

He'd taken body precautions. Cooling himself through his plates before the exercise commenced, using slow movements to lower his thermal profile. In normal times, if he'd done things properly, he'd be hard to find. But these were not normal times. Quadars were on full alert now.

A glance at his assignment showed patterns on the wall. A crack in the doorway showed the hazy heat shadows of at least two quadars he was here to retrieve.

He took a breath to stabilize himself, then, looking down the ally, stepped forward.

Tierra Waganat could put three fingers together with three more fingers to calculate a full hand. He'd watched the Orange Ring well enough, and he'd kept his ears open as the few independent quadars who remained free whispered to themselves. He could guess their timing. He knew the process they would use, and he knew *Lelo*, meaning Baraq, would be with these raiders.

He may have lost the Waganat Family, but it was time now to finish the task he should have done a long time ago.

He still did not have a gun, but he'd found enough food to keep from starving, and the passing heats had dulled the pain from his wounds. He was strong enough now. Yes, Tierra thought as he gripped his father's walking stick and slipped through the darkness, he was strong enough. The staff was warm in his hands, its weighty head levered with a heavy pleasure as he let it gently wave. It was a good weapon.

Beating Baraq to death with his Family heirloom would provide a value over a simple shooting.

When Baraq arrived in his sights, Tierra's chest tightened.

From a distance, he followed.

When Baraq split from the rest, Tierra approached closer.

When Baraq crouched in the darkness, so certain he'd been heat-blind, Tierra had crept closer still.

And when Baraq left his cover, Tierra pounced.

If it were earlier in the cycle, when the night was warmer, Baraq might have missed it — the smudge of heat, just behind him, just beyond the dark alley. But in the chill, he sensed the swift essence of movement against the darkness, and he turned just in time to get his hand up and deflect the weapon that whipped down to crack across his forearm.

Pain exploded.

The shattering of bone split the darkness.

Baraq gave a yelp as he twisted, then fell to the ground with a solid thump. His chest screamed with a breath that wouldn't come. Above him, darkness filled with a cloaked form, its heavy club falling on him, crashing into his shoulder, then aimed for his head.

Baraq rolled.

The club gave a solid ring as it struck bare ground.

The wheezing of heavy breath came, then the weapon whirled again. It was longer than a club, Baraq realized. A staff. A walking staff. Heavy and firm. He raised his good hand to the attacker's next swing, and caught it in mind arc — the hard, stony surface slapping full against his palm to raise a burning pain.

His lungs cried with a deep, wracking breath. Strength returned, and with that strength came the crystalline moment of this darktime, filling his mind perfectly and pristinely.

"I'm going to kill you now," the attacker spoke.

"Tierra," Baraq said, recognizing the voice and the weapon at the same time.

The markings on the stick glinted in starlight. The smell of hard-packed ground was raw below him. The building nearby seemed suddenly more vivid, and the stars in the sky gave enough light that his brother's features came to him from under the hooded cloak.

Tierra was breathing hard now.

He took a half-moment to raise the cudgel in both hands, lifting it high in preparation of crashing it over Baraq's defenseless head.

The air sizzled as Tierra grunted with the effort it took to whip it downward. Baraq lashed a leg out and hooked Tierra's closest foot. The blow struck Baraq's shoulder, but Tierra stumbled enough that the cane's power faded.

A clatter came, and for a moment, Baraq's hearts soared with the thought that Tierra had lost his weapon. A moment later, however, the cane came down on his leg — a half-blow made from Tierra's knees as his brother regained his footing.

Baraq tried to get to his feet, but Tierra's next blow came to the ribs and instead he fell face-forward to the ground.

Pain flared through his body.

Tierra approached him again, wind blowing the tail of his cloak into a cloud of darkness above him.

Baraq rolled and tried to raise his hand to cover his face, but the arm wouldn't move.

It was over.

Tierra stood above him, then spat a dollop of his life-giving liquid on the ground beside Baraq.

"I hope this was worth it," Tierra said.

Then he raised the stick one more time.

The sound of a door opening came in the distance of darkness.

A footstep fell.

Then a blast ripped through the darkness.

Tierra's body gave an ugly lurch, and a splatter of liquid fell across Baraq's face, warm and metallic.

Blood.

The Waganat above him gave a gurgling sound that might have been an exclamation or might simply have been a last breath escaping as his body fell in a slow topple.

Baraq knew Tierra was dead before his brother hit the ground, which he did with a meaty thud and the hard rattle of his weapon dropping against stone.

Baraq lay his head against the ground and sucked in deep, hard breaths.

His vision swirled with stars both real and imagined.

He gasped air and tasted blood.

His stomachs churned. Pain burned from everywhere at once.

And, as Baraq blinked in a vain attempt to get his bearings, another face hovered over him.

A *hedgie*.

From the building.

Young, but strong, holding an ancient Tegra gun.

"Lelo!" the *hedgie* called, bending to his side. "Lelo!"

It was the last thing Baraq saw.

Chapter 25

Esgarat Mountains
Nectani Gap

Crissandr, who had been preparing clean blankets all morning, called to Pella, then handed the whelpling an armful of them when she arrived.

"Take these to Vareta," Crissandr said.

The fabric was soft now, freshly cleaned and beaten, full of the air that had dried them. Though the whelpling had grown again, that pile was tall enough to come up to her chin.

"I've got it," Pella said. "When I return, can I take the time to plant?"

Crissandr stifled a grimace.

"We need all hands to help," she said, her gaze scanning the masses of quadars, *hedgie* and otherwise, whose numbers were already beginning to grow large enough the community was going to have to consider new housing soon. Esgarat City was still hemorrhaging refugees, too.

She would need to go to the North Slope, too.

As the refugees moved from here to Louratna's old center, they would need to renovate that community, too.

Unable to stop herself, her gaze flickered down mountain to the opening where Baraq's mission should already have returned.

Her mind wandered.

One more mission, he had said.

One more time out into the dangers of the war-torn city.

They were late, of course.

Baraq's trips were always late returning. She folded another blanket, trying not to think about it.

Even if those missions stopped completely, word passed easily, and independent quadars were showing up in steady waves all on their own. Quadars knew where they were. It made her wonder when the Families would return. *When they finished absorbing the city,* she thought, answering herself. The Families would come here when they ran out of labor there.

"We will need food," Pella said, pleading her case while struggling under the load of blankets. "I can learn to plant."

"That is a good thought," Crissandr said. "One that should be considered in the leadership circle."

"They talk forever and then never do anything."

"Sometimes the best ideas take time."

Pella grumbled. She did not like being condescended to.

Crissandr felt the hollow ring of her response even as she was making it. The whelpling wasn't a whelpling anymore — physical growth alone was proving that. But in Pella's case, it went deeper than physicality. The world around her had conspired to make the young quadar grow up before her time, and Pella had met that call. She wasn't wrong, either. Whatever remained of this outpost after the Families finished their convulsions were going to need to eat. If Ezi couldn't broker an agreement with the Banits, she would have to concoct another plan.

Ever since little Pella had returned with Ezi from the Banit exercise, she had been obsessed with planting.

It was to the point that the whelp was doing her normal work, then staying out in the darkness to dig patches of root fiber and sweet grasses. Crissandr had followed Pella two evenings prior. She had a small crop of *katja* going, too. The memory of their fresh scents coming from deep in Pella's chasm made her smile.

Whatever the Banit whelp had imparted on her had taken solid root.

"Tuber," she said gently aloud, smiling at a memory of Torranze in the wild.

"Tuber?"

She waved a hand.

"It's nothing, young one," Crissandr replied, shooing Pella away. "Yes, when you return, you can work on your planting. For two hands only, though. Then you will need to return to help prepare the broth."

"Thank you, Crissandr!"

Then Pella sped away to deliver the blankets, moving fast, Crissandr assumed, to ensure she did not change her mind. She laughed then, watching Pella scurry off — her thin body lithe and strong. Crissandr remembered when she could move like that, remembered being so firm in her convictions even if her understanding of those convictions were so unbaked as to be raw.

Pella was different in that way.

Pella's mind seemed always in the right place.

Crissandr let her gaze fall to the cracked, barren desert lands that spread into the distance before her. She gave an involuntary glance at the peaks that had blazed white when she'd first emerged from the caves.

What would Pella's life be like?

Crissandr didn't want to think about it.

When she and Baraq had such moments for reflection, he seemed so sullen that she was afraid to bring the subject up. Still, she could see the truth inside the cracks of his mountain. Baraq was worried. He wore himself thin traveling, then drew himself even thinner, forgoing sleep to teach himself again how to make his Family's wave talkers.

He was a good quadar, though.

Always stronger than he gave himself credit for.

Like little Pella, Baraq always knew the right thing to do, even if at times he'd let the need for today's survival override that knowledge.

She wished she could help him.

But, mostly, in her hearts Crissandr wished she could keep him here. Baraq's body was broken now. His back was beginning to stoop from age and with the weight of his efforts. His arm was still bruised from where the fall had nearly ripped it from its socket.

One last expedition, he had promised her. *One last set of quadars under Lelo's name.*

It was what he wanted, but she was afraid.

The mission had left six heats prior.

Her gaze flickered down mountain again.

"The little one is rambunctious," one of Crissandr's co-workers said as he placed another blanket on the line to air out.

"What's that?" she said, starting.

"Rambunctious," the co-worker said, giving a head-nod toward Pella as the young quadar disappeared behind the patch of bramble growing around the cliff face.

"Yes," Crissandr said, forcing herself to click delight to cover her malaise.

She wished things were going to be better for Pella.

All she could do to make that happen, though, all she could contribute in any way, was to keep working. Keep making food and keep working to turn fabrics into garments and blankets. Keep helping nurses welcome new quadars. Keep moving forward, even when she was so tired she couldn't take another step.

Now, at least, there was one more thing she could do.

It was time to give the whelp room to grow.

Time to talk to Ezi.

Pella wasn't wrong in her assessment of the circle, but Crissandr had seen Ezi grow more adept at managing those talks. Ezi was learning how to force decisions quickly if need demanded. So, yes. Later tonight Crissandr would have that conversation.

Pella wanted to plant and grow.

It was time for her to do that.

Crissandr returned to the blankets.

Chapter 26

Esgarat Mountains
Nectani Gap

In the distance, the extraction team returned.

Crissandr Waganat stood taller to watch them, bending her back in a useless attempt to ease pain.

Two new members strode forward, carrying a stretcher between them, another quadar lying motionlessly on it.

Her hearts dropped.

Her knees turned to mash.

"No," she cried softly. "Please. No."

She dropped the knife she'd been using to tan a *rela* skin, then, moving forward, grabbed dirt and dust to dry her hands with before wiping them on an already dirtied towel of rough fiber cloth.

She ran then.

Down the mountainside, lifting her *haldi* so her feet could carry her faster.

"No!" she called in a wild voice that drew attention. "Baraq!"

Chapter 27

Esgarat Mountains
Nectani Gap

Baraq woke in a dark mountain alcove. He opened his central to find Crissandr, primaries and central closed, seated in quiet meditation, back against the stone mountain, head, too, against the wall.

It was late now.

He could sense that much.

The operation would have been reported out. The day's work finished. Eldoro and Katon had long before fallen.

His head hurt. He was tired and sore everywhere.

He tried to roll over, but pain from his arm shredded him so sharply he hissed as he tried to breathe. Memory flowed back. A system of three rods strapped together held his broken arm in place.

"You are awake," Crissandr said.

"You say that like I should be happy for it." He lay back, panting while the sizzling pain subsided.

"Drink," Crissandr said, lifting a bowl to his lips. "It will dull the pain." She dribbled a bitter elixir into his mouth. He swallowed without complaint.

"You should heal," she said calmly, "but it could be a long time."

He grunted acknowledgement. "I'm old."

She laughed at him then, in that way she had, and he knew things would be all right. She put the bowl down and leaned back against the cold mountain wall. Her breathing was a soft sigh.

He put his good hand on her thigh, and she opened her central farther as she drew a blanket up over them both.

"I thought you had returned to the mountain," she said, craning her neck.

Her body warmed his hand. "I did, too."

"I don't think I can do this anymore," she replied.

"We are all going to return to the mountain sometime."

"I know," Crissandr said. "I know we are."

Her expression carried the question clearly. She wasn't going to hold him to his word, but she wanted to know.

"I won't leave you again, Crissandr."

"I don't want to make you do anything—"

"I have better purposes here."

Baraq hesitated to find additional words that wouldn't come.

He wanted to say that Lelo would live on now, even if he — like his whelp before him — didn't. But he couldn't make his lips form them. Something about the young whelp who had saved him felt important. Something in the way Kiltian's voice had come to him so strong as he marched toward the city dressed in his field leathers. But what that *something* was, Baraq couldn't distill into words. Instead, he clicked resolution and left it at that.

Despite his ineptitude, his words caused a wave of relief to roll off Crissandr. She took his good hand. Pressed her palm onto the back of his and intertwined their fingers.

"There's work to do here, too," she said.

"Yes," Baraq replied, almost laughing. "I am sure Torranze would agree with you at that. I'll need us to go to the North Slope."

Crissandr nodded.

"We will worry about that next heat," she said, sitting against the wall again, contentment covering her face. "This darktime we sit."

Baraq tightened his grip over her fingers.

"Yes. Worry later."

Right now, he was happy, or, if not happy at least content. At one point, not so long ago, life had broken him. But he was here, in the place he should be, with his *kalla*.

Life was hard, but no matter what happened, Crissandr's hand in his would always be enough.

Chapter 28

Esgarat Mountains
Nectani Gap

Several heats later, sharp panic surged through Ezi as she raced to the triage station. Reports said a sniper had hit Oast'el, but no one knew how bad his wounds were.

As usual, Oast'el had led the last extraction team, a team that had just now arrived back at the Gap.

They couldn't afford to lose him.

She couldn't.

Not now. Not ever.

The Orange Ring had just started to meld as a useful leadership council — had just begun to hit their stride after she had pieced them together from the remains that survived Brada's killing. Beyond all that, Oast'el was also her connection to Brada. She needed him as much as the community did.

Hearts beating, Ezi came to the open chasm lined with the harsh brambles and stubborn sawgrasses that grew from cracks in the walls — to find him seated on one of the benches Crissandr had assigned to those needing medical attention. She marched to him, both relieved to see he was mobile, but angry at the way he held his arm against his wound. Dried blood matted his shirt's coarse fabric, but his coloring looked good.

Seeing him sitting up and complaining broke her hearts into

strange little pieces. She wanted to cry but couldn't manage it.

There was so much to do. So much at stake.

"Are you well?" she said.

"I'd be better if these nurses would leave me alone." He moved his arm and winced.

"Eat your pride."

"It's not pride."

She clicked neutral, then in a slow movement, sat down across from him.

"What happened?"

"They were ready for us."

"Ambush," she said, worried. "That's not good."

"It's also not surprising. The Families are poor learners, but they didn't gain control by being dull."

"So, what next?"

"We'll have to change our approach," Oast'el replied, his voice deadened.

Ezi put her hand on his shoulder, then pulled it back. "We're coming to the end, aren't we?"

He clicked a wistful affirmative. "The real fighting is ending. Tegra and Festia are still in conflict, but they have dealt with the others. As the Families turn their attention to us…" He shrugged. "Let's just say our next missions will be harder to hide."

"The numbers we retrieve are smaller each mission as it is," Ezi said. "It's not going to be enough, is it?"

Oast'el shrugged again. "It will have to be."

"Spoken like a true soldier."

He laughed and grimaced as he reached a water cup beside him.

She watched him take a greedy drink and understood how much he was hurting.

"Truth is truth," he finally said, wiping his lips. "It won't be long now before every independent quadar in the city will be conscripted to a Family — and when that happens, any quadar we bring here will be seen as stealing Family property outright."

Ezi felt what Oast'el wasn't saying. "The ambush says that the Families know we are here."

"Yes."

Ezi glanced at Oast'el, then let her gaze focus on the dry desert horizons, feeling walls close in on her despite the open plain.

The Families knew about Nectani Gap.

And they knew where Louratna's caves were.

If they were now laying ambushes for their raids, it meant those Families understood what the Orange Ring was doing.

The Families' next step was obvious.

Once the Families had settled their war, the free quadars of Louratna's North Slope would be next. The idea turned her stomachs sour. She would have to talk to Torranze about it soon. They may need to turn his rockets to different ends.

One problem at a time.

She sighed and patted Oast'el's knee, then she stood.

"I need to tend to assigning living spaces to our new additions, and then arranging their trips to the compound. I'll check back when I can."

He nodded.

"Heal up," she said to him.

"Don't worry about me."

She gave a crooked smile. "Yes," she said. "Like a true soldier."

As she left the triage station, a sense of omnipresent dread came over her. The war the Families fought would be over soon, but the one every other quadar was waging may never end.

CHAPTER 29

Crissandr sat her aching body down at a table carved from the rock.

She had followed Baraq to the North Slope, had come to Louratna's compound to discuss modifications the area needed so it could house more quadars. She was in the large, oblong chasm that served as a kitchen. All around her, quadars hustled and scurried from station to station, calling out to each other with voices that echoed amid the overheated aromas of brothy stews and racks of cooling *banka* bread.

Even if they had enough food, preparing it would be complicated.

This time of the heat, lighting was mostly soft, coming from a naturally cut shaft that allowed Eldoro's rays to splay vividly against the far wall. Reflected radiance overpowered the luminous moss that would take over in the darktime. That lighting, combined with the chamber's size and functionality, had made it the natural choice for use as a community kitchen.

Crissandr was bone weary now.

She'd come here because she wanted to be alone for a moment, too. Her tasks were broad and varied, and she'd decided she needed to let the world fade, if just for a moment.

She took a calming breath and closed her primaries, leaning her elbows against the table and propping her chin against her fists.

"Are you well?"

Edart Kel, the engineer Baraq spoke so highly of, stood before her.

Now that he had focused on building wave talkers, Baraq had been spending considerable time with Edart. She was the one who, along with Torranze, was going to make everything they were working on happen.

The engineer had a plate with her, filled with a *havra* dish Crissandr had worked with the staff to prepare earlier.

"Yes," Crissandr said, stifling a sigh. "I am well enough."

"I'm sorry to make you jump. May I sit?" Edart motioned a place across from Crissandr. Other places were available, so Crissandr understood Edart's question had more to it.

"Yes, please," Crissandr said.

"Are you sure?"

"Yes, yes," she said, now motioning Edart Kel with vigor. "Please tell me what you are thinking."

The plate clattered against stone as Edart sat.

"Seeing you here," Edart said with an awkward pause. "I wanted to tell you something."

"All right."

"Baraq," Edart said, taking a bite and chewing quickly. "He's quite proud of you, I think. He's always talking about you. *Crissandr is working on garment factories*, he'll say. Or *Crissandr is arranging the kitchen staples. Crissandr is assigning quadars to medical needs.* Crissandr is this, and Crissandr is that."

"That is nice to hear."

"I know how hard things are, so I thought you might like to hear that."

"He says such things about you, too, Edart."

The young quadar clicked a humble tone. "I'm just trying to make things better."

"As are we all." Crissandr was suddenly hungry but didn't feel right leaving the table. "That's not really why you asked to sit here, is it?"

Edart pushed her plate gently aside. Her lips slid left, then right as if contemplating her next words.

"Is it going to matter?" she finally said.

"I see," Crissandr said, feeling the real question in Edart's posture.

With All of Esgarat falling into shambles, and with the deeper chills coming to darktime portending desperate projections about their homeland's future, this youthful quadar with such passionate drive was asking if anything would be left to save even if the Families' war came to an end.

"You have seen so much," Edart added. "And you are not like Torranze or Baraq. I believe you will tell me the full truth — not just what I need to hear." She paused for a breath. "I want to know what you think."

"I understand that, too," Crissandr said with an amused grin.

Torranze and Baraq were engineers. Inventors at heart. Their optimism was their strength. They could not accept that ultimate failure might exist because to consider such a thing would be to die themselves. Edart was like Baraq and Torranze, but she was also like Crissandr: They were both doers. They understood cause and effect in a more pragmatic way than either Baraq or Torranze did.

Crissandr's realism made for a different kind of strength.

Edart sat quietly, fidgeting her fingertips together.

Crissandr put both hands on the tabletop and let the stone's strength bring her closer to this entire chasm of chattering quadars.

"There was a time," she said, "not so long ago, when this chamber hummed with a purpose. I remember working in this very kitchen. Standing with three lines of quadars. There was a feeling of hope in those days. An essence of..." She paused, looking for the right word. "Camaraderie."

Edart's nod let her know she'd picked the right word.

"While Louratna was alive we felt like we were doing a service. She was saving Esgarat, you know. Everyone understood that even if she did not. That idea gave us purpose, and it was that purpose — the idea that we could make All of Esgarat better for all quadars — that attracted free-thinking quadars to the mountain."

Edart stopped fidgeting and instead wrapped her fingers into a ball. She clicked a soft affirmative. "That feeling is what brought me here."

Crissandr nodded, watching the cooks work. "The place feels different now, doesn't it?" she said.

"It feels desperate."

"Fearful."

"That's right."

"Before Louratna was murdered any fear we had was easy to ignore."

"Now it's real," Edart said.

"And fear is powerful."

"More powerful than hope," Edart said.

Crissandr gave a smile she knew was too wry. She reached across the table with her knobby hands and put them over Edart's supple young ones.

"That's the problem with engineers."

"What do you mean?"

"Always so focused."

"I don't understand."

"Look at the quadars here." She waved her hand to encompass the whole chamber. "Take a moment. Watch them as they struggle to stretch stores designed to feed only as many quadars as Louratna once housed but are now feeding hundreds more. See them toil. Watch them work the root stores with their bare hands. Admire how they chop the meats to spread them among us all."

Edart gazed around the cavern.

While Crissandr waited, her hunger rose.

"I see them," Edart said.

"These quadars are afraid now, Edart Kel," Crissandr said. "They are worried about the Families. Most of us understand the true dangers to all of us now — those of Esgarat itself. Those dangers that make your work on the rockets so important. There is much to despair, but still they come to the kitchen each heat and they work hard until afterdark."

She hesitated, then drew Edart's gaze to hers.

"Why do you think that is?"

Edart spent another moment watching the kitchen workers.

"I don't know," she said.

Crissandr gave a gentle chuff.

"You are a leader, Edart. I know you feel that, though you are too young and, more important, too focused to see what that means." She raised a gnarled hand to cut off Edart's protestations. "That's all right. You are who you are. But I see what Baraq sees in you, too. You are every bit the leader that Ezi is, or that Louratna was. So, in response to your feelings of fear, let me tell you this: Fear *is* stronger than hope. And sometimes those who fear are right to do so. Maybe this *is* the end for us.

"But as powerful as that fear is, it cannot sustain."

Crissandr smiled, feeling the lines crease around her lips.

Plates clattered and the hum of voices echoed in the open cavern.

"Hope, though. Hope is eternal and if you watch these workers in just the right way as they go about doing their parts, you can see that hope seeps through. And if you see it that way, you'll know that this hope is because quadars like you exist.

"Your work is important, Edart Kel.

"Every worker here believes in you."

Edart's chest rose once, then fell. An expression hard to decipher came over her face.

"Thank you," she eventually said. "I needed to hear that."

Crissandr clicked her own thanks to Edart. "You are welcome. I needed to say it."

Crissandr took a slow breath, dwelling on the warm aromas around her, and realized that was right.

She felt better now.

Stronger.

Her body ached less, and she felt refreshed.

She had things to do — hunters to assign, and the textile weavers to address. She wanted to spend time with Baraq, to hear how he was progressing and to chastise him for doing stupid things while his arm was still healing.

First, though, she had to eat.

Chapter 30

Esgarat Mountains
Nectani Gap

Pella leaned over the seeds she had just planted, squatting in the way only youth can, bony knees jutting skyward like angled posts, arms wide and bent at the elbow, rounded head craned downward to stare so intently at her work that she could be living in a different universe. Lovingly, she touched fingertips to the dusty soil, and — as she had taken to doing for some time now — whispered to the seed.

"Grow strong, little kado *root. I'll see you tomorrow with water and some more of your family."*

That was something she'd learned while she was visiting the Banits and when Anko, the young Banit, had taken her to the growing pits. Plant the seeds, he'd said. Make sure they received enough water (*but not too much!*) and then till ground root shells into the soil around it. All the while, talk to the plants to make them feel more welcome.

There was more to it than this. Of that she was certain.

The holes in her knowledge were obvious, even as she was working with what she had. The secrets of growing a garden were more complicated than a quadar could impart during a single conversation. But it had been enough to get her thinking, and now she had decided that with enough work she could learn the rest herself.

Anko's facial expressions came to Pella as she whispered to the seeds. She thought of him every time she spoke to her plantings, and other times, too. More often than she wanted to admit. He'd been laughable enough, covered in mud from the pits, but sincere in his conversations, and only a little annoying with the sideways glances that told her he knew how little she understood.

Just being with someone her own age had made her comfortable, but he'd also been equal parts shy and excited as he'd given her his lessons.

Without that day, she'd never have thought to create this little garden on the flat floor of a mountain shaft — a sink-space large enough to pace around in and deep enough to protect young plants from the heat and elements. Without Anko's first lessons she would never have known enough to make it work.

Was he even alive now?

She hoped so.

Pushing that thought aside, Pella looked up the sheer walls to where the sky was darkening.

It was time to go back.

With a grimace she wrapped her shawl over her shoulders. The air was already sharp. The woven fabric was coarse, which she found she liked better than softer, but heavier skins that others were coveting.

Her work this time had resulted in another row — the fifth such line.

The first and third appeared to be failures, but the second had sprouted and were already budding with flowers that smelled sweet in the shaft's enclosed space. The fourth row was nearly as successful. This time she would reduce the water by a quarter and see what happened. Next heat she would begin planting a larger patch using the approach she'd tried in the third column, but with more ground shells. If it worked like she thought it would, she'd have a *kado* patch before the next Katon Following.

One last time, she breathed in the aroma.

It made her happy. Almost refreshed after a day spent on the never-ending chores Ezi and Crissandr piled onto her.

Then Pella scaled the shaft wall hand over hand.

She did not begrudge the work Ezi and Crissandr asked her to do. New quadars arrived daily, carrying expressions of shock and fatigue over their bodies.

These refugees rarely had anything.

The effort to feed, clothe, and attend to them took everything Ezi and Crissandr had, and all around her other quadars were working equally as hard: foraging, hunting, cooking, and addressing wounds and suffering.

That was another reason she came here, though.

Tending the seeds made her feel better. Working the soil made her feel less alone. These seeds were hers. They were the only things she could give herself to.

Pella climbed out of the shaft and stood at its edge. "Thank you, little garden," she said. "I'll see you next time."

The walk to the caves was not long.

Pella used the time to think about her tasks for tomorrow.

She had to darn garments, and peel the clean rootstock that went into the community soups Crissandr had created. Her hands hurt from that work earlier today, and they would hurt from it again tomorrow. Flexing her fingers in reaction to the idea, she came to the primary cave opening and saw Ezi standing backlit by light from the craggy mouth. The older quadar wore a loose *haldi* of faded yellow that seemed etched with the light behind her. Her body language said she'd been waiting for some time.

Pella's backbone grew firmer as she walked, preparing.

I am no longer a whelpling, Pella thought. *I can handle myself.*

While she understood the work, Pella did not like the curfew Ezi and Crissandr had agreed was a good thing for her. After having received blessings from her garden, she was in no mood for a dressing down now.

From behind Ezi came another quadar, though, smaller and slight, stepping back close to stand beside Ezi.

Something about Ezi's smile — which was a bit too gleeful for the moment — made Pella look more closely. Even in the approaching darktime she could see the new quadar's *kami* were sturdy but worn at each knee. His shirts — two layers — were plain but in good repair, too.

Another moment passed before the truth registered.

"Anko!" she called.

The young quadar broke into a large grin.

Chapter 31

Esgarat Mountains
North Slope

Torrance stood on a wide slab of mountain rock, desert wind blowing its oven-hot blast to burn against his face and whip his robes against his forearms and calves. He squinted against the light of two suns, and tried to stand firm in the heat.

This planet was killing him.

Below him, three units had just finished being prepared for launch. Their alignment was picture-perfect, something he found both powerful and worrisome. He did not know what to expect.

He wished he had a camera, though.

Baraq Waganat and Edart Kel stood beside him, one to each side, a pairing of age and youth that felt almost poetic to his mind. Behind them stood more quadars, each having worked for many heats to see this day.

Now was the time. Testing was over. Launch day was here.

Memories flashed — *Everguard* crewmates on edge as they watched clocks count down on the series of wormhole pods the United Government would launch into Alpha Centauri A. In a hard juxtaposition, hindsight made him acutely aware of the difference between anticipation and desperation.

That comparison came with a bitter taste he would never be able to describe.

He had created this problem.

Now here he was, trying to deal with it. All he could say for sure was that whatever he did would never be enough.

A chill breeze from upslope whipped his loose robes with a whomping noise that made him picture flags in a stiff wind.

He shaded his eyes.

The cycle had progressed over the heats, and smaller Katon now preceded Eldoro as they plodded across the sky, casting closely spaced double shadows that sprung from the base of each rocket. It had been a long time since he'd thought about the one-dimensional shadows he'd grown up with as a boy in Wisconsin.

The idea made him smile.

The shadows here seemed so natural to him now.

"Are the wave talkers operational?" Torrance asked with the same formality he would have carried on *Everguard*.

"Operational?" Baraq asked. His arm was still in a loose sling that Crissandr had first made, then required him to wear.

"Are they ready," Torrance said, in their shared qualish. "Are the wave talkers working?"

Baraq clicked affirmative even before looking at the small receiver he'd placed in a corner nook where two rocks had fallen together to create a natural table. The quadar looked up from the receiver. "Wave talkers are working."

Torrance saw a sense of strength on Baraq's face that he'd only recently come to understand. Now focused on his wave talkers, the elder quadar had shown a deep dedication to making his part of the project work. It was about Lelo, he understood. About Baraq's son.

Torrance clicked a supportive tone.

If nothing else, Torrance understood loss.

"Engines?" he said to Edart.

"They've all passed Expectation Testing."

It was a coy answer. Expectation Testing was a euphemism for inspection, and inspection only went so far. The only way to fully test a rocket was to do what they were preparing to do now. He understood what she meant, and appreciated the smug pride that covered Edart's expression. He wasn't going to begrudge her the moment.

He scanned the rockets one more time.

The three stood at pristine attention as dust devils rose, and twirled, and fell behind them. The rockets were not massive by human measurements — only twice his height, and as big around as his thigh — except at the nose-end where the wave talker's dimensions required Edart to make design adjustments that left the rockets looking like stiff snakes that had just swallowed a whole mouse. The lower sections of each rocket appeared wider, but that was an optical illusion created by the triangular fins Edart had affixed to the engine segment.

If these three made it, the team would launch three more tomorrow, and three more the day after, and three more each day until they depleted either rockets or wave talkers.

Production was ongoing.

"Well, then," he said, looking to Edart. "I'd say it's about time to light these babies up."

She didn't understand every word, but her bright expression said she got the gist.

Edart Kel engaged the ignition command, and smoke appeared below the first rocket, a wisp at first, then a coiling cloud. The third fired next, then the second. Sound levels rose like thunder over the horizon, and in clouds of exhaust, the three spikes made their way off the ground to rise into the sky.

Torrance found he was holding his breath.

A tear clouded his vision as the three streaks rose.

Then the second rocket wobbled.

Just a small blip at first, but a moment later it became obvious something was wrong. The rocket twisted away from its expected path, leaving a jagged, smoky contrail in the sky. Another moment later a flame burned its way down the fuselage, and then the engine died, leaving the rocket to loop in an agonizing arc, upward for a moment, then bending downward to tumble with gravity toward the planet's surface.

The downrange impact was a loud crash, but when Torrance raised his gaze, he found the other two rockets still streaking upward.

Excitement seemed to grip the collective.

Chattering erupted, then came the sharp whistles that were quadarti cheers.

A long minute later, nothing could be seen of the two but floating contrails dissipating in the sky.

Torrance turned toward Baraq, his question on his gaze.

"Wave talkers operational," Baraq replied, smiling.

Torrance bent at the waist then, hands on his knees in the heat, but feeling only pressure falling from his shoulders.

"You did it!" Edart pounded those shoulders hard enough that the blows hurt. "You did it!"

Torrance stood up as tall as his bent frame could manage, and pressed his lips together, thinking about Louratna and thinking about life in the Solar System.

Those rockets had a long trip ahead of them — decades at the speeds they could achieve. He would certainly be dead before they neared their target. And given his rudimentary understanding of navigation and ballistics, most of the launches would miss their targets. The idea made him think about a summer vacation sitting on a beach and listening to a historian talk about endangered baby turtles as they waddled to the shallows, some dying before they made it there and some becoming grist for the food chain. Even among those that made it to the ocean waters, most would die, the guide had said.

Some made it through, though.

Some lived.

That was life, really.

In this case, it might take only one: one rocket, blasting a message, to find the right target.

Above them the contrails had disappeared now. The sky was unbroken and clear.

"Those two are for you," he whispered into the desert wind, imagining Louratna sitting beside him and cheering. He smiled then, knowing he'd done at least what he could do.

His best.

As meager as it was.

THE MESSAGE

MESSAGE

Local Date: November 8, 2256
Local Time: 1442 (Earth Standard)

The message arrived — undeniable and clear — in two blasts, the first long and rambling in the way Ambassador Torrance Black had when he wasn't thinking too hard, the second, sharp and concise, both broadcast on standard radio frequencies.

The message was received not only by official channels but also by thousands of independent operators across the Solar System.

The waves were a touch past four standard years old by the time they crossed into the Solar System, frayed gently by time but still cohesive enough to be clearly heard as they fell upon receivers and were processed back into audio.

Four years the waves had traveled, traversing the distance between Alpha Centauri A and the Solar System.

Just as it had been four years since the events of Oscar Pentabill's death and Torrance Black's departure.

Four years since Black had found himself on *Icarus.*

"This is Ambassador Torrance Black, Captain, Interstellar Command," the first blast started. *"Icarus is dead."*

Black then outlined the technology behind Universe Three's — hopefully failed — plan to set a black hole into Alpha Centauri A, and hence cut the United Governments' Star Drive ships off from their source of fuel. He stopped short of directly saying a United

Government Intelligence official had sent him to kill Pentabill, but the insinuation was there. Then, hoping someone might come to retrieve his remains, Torrance finished the first part of his message by giving his coordinates — a set that defined Alpha Centauri A.

"Look out for my girls." Torrance finished that first blast with a resigned sadness to his voice. *"Whoever finds this, let Mercy and Ana know I love them. And do the same for Oscar Pentabill,"* he finished. *"Tell his wife ... tell Glory ... that he loved her."*

The second burst came just over a minute later, this time spoken in the direct and clipped tone of voice that said Black was suddenly dialed in.

"Strike those coordinates," Ambassador Black had said.

"I'm going to Eden. I'm going to see for myself what's down there.

"If it's still possible, come and get me."

RESPONSE

Chapter 32

Arlington, Virginia
Local Date: November 8, 2256
Local Time: 1515

Zina Nichols connected to the virtual node and settled into her seat. As security protocols flashed, her lioness, the dynamic tattoo she had chosen when she was so much younger, spread itself across her hip. The lily on her shoulder remained closed.

The node's strong security left the room feeling ephemerally barren — the walls cloudlike and shifting with slow-moving points of gray against a navy background. That the lighting was oddly good at the table made her happier.

She did not care for virtual, but Willim Pinot was traveling, and this was the only way to chat now.

So, Zina waited.

She liked being the first one to meetings. Taking her position early was like staking out the high ground. Watching other attendees as they took their seats made her feel like she was seeing them at their least guarded moment. It gave her a moment to peer underneath their game faces.

This session with Pinot was going to be a hard one.

News of the message was barely a half hour old, and the airwaves were already buzzing with Torrance Black's name.

The message could not be squashed now, which meant her boss was going to be on dicey ground.

The story that Black had been a Universe Three agent was unraveling before their eyes, and everyone who mattered knew the operation had been Pinot's baby. So, personal triage was on the agenda.

His agenda, anyway.

Hers was a little more complex, and now she was ahead of the game.

Her agent on Triton Station 12 had been the first to receive Torrance Black's message, and she had pinged Zina before the news cycles had caught up to it. Sitting here, waiting for Pinot, the confidence that came from knowing more than the other player gave her, if not comfort, an air of anticipation she found tantalizing.

She shifted in her chair, then crossed her legs.

She was nervous, but it was a good nervousness.

She calmed herself with a deeper breath.

Zina Nichols was still officially the youngest person in UG history to have filled a deputy director's role, but a delicate tingle came over her when she considered how it might feel to be the youngest person to occupy the full *director*'s seat.

Pinot snapped into focus.

He stepped through the virtual hallway and into the null node. As he took his place, Zina noted Pinot's left hand gave a small, but perceptible tremor. The old man was losing it. He should have gone to life extensions a year ago, but vanity had kept him from doing that. Now he was paying the price.

"Good evening, Director," Zina said. "I hope your dinner was lovely."

Pinot grumbled. "Gave me heartburn."

She smiled as warmly as she could. "I'm sorry to hear that. Eating while on travel is always such a gamble."

Pinot had been on Ceres Station to attend a gathering of agents from across the asteroid belt when the message dropped. It was a trip he would usually have sent Zina to deal with but had taken upon himself this time — justifying it by saying he wanted to meet with Ambassador Newzarik to discuss her relations with, and understandings of, the wildcat miners who were causing such a stink these days. Zina didn't buy it. Pinot could have accomplished that conversation through the same node they were using now, or even via agents in the field. If she had attended the session, she could have distilled the situation into the concise blocks he preferred. This made her wonder if Pinot's trip meant he'd become concerned about her — that he was on to the networks she had been creating inside the agency, and that he wanted to test those waters himself.

Of course, rumors were also swirling that three companies were going to merge to form a conglomeration that would attempt to mine the Oort cloud. That meant money.

Pinot was likely working that angle, too.

Time would tell.

Maybe she was just being overly paranoid, but the government paid her to be overly paranoid so that idea didn't bother her any.

When Torrance Black's message hit the news cycles a few minutes ago, Pinot had fended off questions and called her directly.

Hence this emergency session.

"So," Pinot said, having settled himself. "Torrance Black has returned to us."

"It would appear so," Zina replied. "What are you thinking?"

"We give the bastards an alternative story," he replied too sharply. His lips compressed into a hard line.

Yes, Zina saw, her boss was truly feeling stress. "And that story would be?"

Pinot sat forward. "It's a decoy. We've got Universe Three on the run now, so it makes sense that Francis would run a counter op."

Zina gave a small, silent nod. "A ruse from Universe Three." She considered the angles. "I suppose that would play for a while. Long enough to get something else going, anyway. Everyone knows Deidra Francis is as cunning as she is savage. She's simply trying to divert attention from our primary mission. The message from Black is a U3 ploy they devised years ago to seed distrust in us."

A smile touched Pinot's eyes. "Yes."

"I can arrange that."

"We'll need to address the push for any mission to Alpha Centauri A, though. It's important that never happens."

Pinot was right about the push. Pressure was already mounting for a trip to Alpha Centauri A, and it would get more intense over the next few days.

Launching such a mission sounded reasonable on its face, but Pinot would not win if a mission were to jump to Alpha Centauri A.

Proponents argued that even a one-day jaunt would be enough to determine what had happened, but no one believed politicians would ever limit such a mission to a simple spot-check. Pulling off a full search-and-salvage operation would be a detailed and meticulous process. Still, in just the past few minutes those proponents were already making proposals to use *Orion* or *Voyager* to perform a surveillance mission — both of which were in upfit stations now. If *Icarus* was derelict in orbit around the star, it would be found, and if Black's quest to make it to the planet had failed, his shuttle could be retrieved.

Pinot's concern — and to a degree, hers too — was that finding *Icarus* could serve to authenticate Black's latest message, something that would support the idea the ambassador had *not* been an agent for Universe Three as Pinot and the UGIO had claimed.

And if *Icarus* was *not* recovered, certain factions would simply twist Torrance Black's message to suggest U3 was so desperate that it had sacrificed a ship to the star — which is what Black's message insinuated.

That kind of story could twist in the wind forever, and lead to problems inside problems.

If nothing else, every intelligence officer worth their salt understands that uncontained problems multiply to cause even more problems.

Better to cut that dragon off at the head.

Zina cleared her throat. "I agree. I don't see any upsides to letting that kind of mission run. I've already begun pushing counterarguments into our information channels. How the logistics required to change a Star Drive's mission will be both huge and complex," she recited. "Stocking supplies — even for one day — takes time to enact, and, once everything gets delayed, adjusting the repair and maintenance efforts for ships already at dock for upfit will cause immense ripples in the system."

"Yes," Pinot said, pleased she'd already acted. "Don't forget to focus on people, too. Our workers have lives to live."

"Of course." Zina smiled. "Station leaves would need to be revoked. Families with plans would get disrupted. I'll add those to the mix."

Pinot gave a nod as she talked.

"And then there are the ramifications of delays to other missions these ships were intended to complete," Zina said, sitting back as she finished. She spoke in exaggerated news-voice, then. *"Do you want to derail scientific advancement and push the entire agenda of the United Government back simply to run a boondoggle operation based on a single message that most likely is a Universe Three plant?"*

Pinot's expression softened, letting Zina know she was hitting her mark.

He scratched his chin in the way he did when he was calculating options.

"We need to get experts to flood the news wires," Pinot added.

"I'll handle it."

"I want to put pressure on all the key players. Everything you've discussed are the right steps for public consumption, but we'll want to squeeze a few lemons inside our walls before they start pissing lemonade."

She knew what Pinot meant the moment he said it.

"Marisa Harthing," she said.

"Among others."

Captain Harthing was a big name in Interstellar Command. Zina had dealt with her years back, during that first action against Black's reputation. The captain was driven in the way most career officers were, but she was also a mother, and — unlike Thomas Kitchell — she had been able to read the room properly. Zina had already planned to check up on Captain Harthing's daughters before the call. It was time to squeeze her again.

She liked it when her own agenda overlapped with Pinot's, because it gave her cover to run unimpeded.

"We'll want to start our own investigation of Torrance Black, too," Pinot said.

"Of Black?"

The idea bothered her because it caught her off guard. When she first took this job, she promised herself she would always be thinking ahead of her boss. That she wasn't sure where he was going with this thread worried her.

"Yes. I want to know everything we can about what happened to him. I want to know about his claims that U3 might have been trying to set a black hole into Alpha Centauri A even back then. I want to know how that idea plays with issues we see with the sun today. Whatever there is to find, I want to find it."

"That's good," Zina said with relief. She'd already started that task, too. Pinot's planted story to the counter, they both knew Universe Three had taken Black, and, since nothing in the ambassador's original service dossier suggested he had turned to U3, she assumed he was now dead — tortured and left to rot in some dank prison cell out in deep space. She'd wanted to know for sure. It made sense that Pinot would, too. "I'll get a recent scan on Centauri's spectrum, too. It might give us an idea if there's extra metal profiles there."

"It might," Pinot said. "But I'm guessing metalicity resolution isn't going to be good enough."

"Probably not," Zina said. "I'll get somebody moving on everything, but it's going to take some time."

"I understand," her boss replied. "Three days?"

"Four. Maybe five."

Pinot wasn't happy with the answer but having been in the pits early in his career, he *did* understand it. If he assumed she had just started, then four days wasn't a bad estimate.

Of course, she had started earlier.

She expected answers in two.

"All right, then let's get to it."

She disconnected, then stood up and straightened wrinkles down her pant legs before leaving the room.

Four days.

The Torrance Black story would pin Pinot down for longer than that, but questions about the black hole were where the real power lay. If it was true that U3 had advanced their wormhole technology that far four years ago, that meant they had better scientists than she expected.

She needed to know where they could be now, and she assumed that the answer had a *lot* to do with the problems they'd found in the sun.

She had four days to get ahead of that game.
It was time to make her move.

Chapter 33

Navigation Command Office
UGIS *Explorer*
Local Date: November 9, 2256
Local Time: 0215

Marisa Harthing froze when she first heard the message.

It *was* Torrance. There was no question about that. Even after years apart she would know that voice anywhere. There wasn't a nay-saying government hack alive who could convince her otherwise.

She sat stoically in her office — which today was a comfortable chamber on *Explorer*, UG's newest Excelsior class Star Drive spacecraft. Just off the production line, the ship had finished its safety shakedowns and now Marisa was overseeing the process of upfitting her with the latest, most advanced navigation profiles UG engineers could manage. She'd stayed up all night to finish reviewing the test logs, and now she was tired.

But every news outlet in the system had Torrance's message on loop. It was proof that the stories about him were false. He was no U3 spy.

Was it real? That was the news agencies' first question. If not, who concocted it, and why? Infinite experts produced an infinite stream of patter about everything from what it would take to create such a forgery to what it could mean for Supreme President Jihansen's next confirmation election. Jihansen hadn't been in the seat at the time of the cover-up, but someone would have to pay, and if nothing else he had remained quiet after being briefed.

You might find the people want another president so much they are willing to suffer through a real campaign again, said one expert.

Marisa's personal system was filling up again — journalists asking for comment.

She wasn't stupid enough to answer them yet.

This would be her second time through this mill, and she understood the danger of responding too quickly. She needed time to sort through it all. She wasn't going to go spouting nonsense into this already rancid stream of speculation. On top of everything else, as a moderately high-ranking member in Interstellar Command, Marisa Harthing also understood exactly how bad this message was for certain officials — the groups that had devised and released the stories that said Torrance Black was a Universe Three spy and, specifically, the UG Intelligence Office.

Her mind flashed to that night with Zina Nichols.

Her stomach burned as she realized that Torrance *was* a spy, just not for Universe Three. The message made it clear now that the UG had coerced him to kill Pentabill, but Deidra Francis had beaten him to the punch — then kidnapped Torrance, taken him aboard the soon-to-be scuttled *Icarus*, and threatened his daughters in response to a bluff he'd given them.

That last sounded so familiar.

Ice ran through her veins.

The details made sense now — Nichols was covering for her bosses. Bosses who had used Torrance, then tried to keep it quiet.

And four years ago, Marisa had done her part with no little duress. She had deflected questions when journalists had come calling — had simply said, *I never saw anything untoward from Torrance. But people are hard to know, so I can't say what he did on his own. And it's been years since we were together for any real lengths of time.*

All those were true statements, but they were also lies — lies that had saved their daughters' lives as well as her own career — but lies, nonetheless.

Her answers had satisfied the journalists well enough that after a few weeks they'd moved on to chase other shiny objects.

She still remembered the bitter taste of those answers though, remembered how they made her feel like a traitor to Torrance.

She didn't know how to feel right now.

Angry, certainly. Lost. Self-righteous.

She would pay a month's salary to see Zina Nichols's face as she heard that message.

Marisa realized then that she would receive another call from the deputy director.

She was going to enjoy that session.

So, she sat in *Explorer*'s office, stewing and thinking and listening to Torrance's voice over and over, low and gravelly, calling out through the distance of time.

If it's still possible, come and get me.

That's when Marisa Harthing, Captain, Interstellar Command, Navigation, attached her dataclip and adjusted the security protocols.

"ABKE," she said. "Get me in touch with Ragnath Gavarian."

Chapter 34

Pallas: Asteroid Belt
Local Date: November 11, 2256
Local Time: 1145

Hoping to blend into the bustling lunchtime crowd, Marisa Harthing ditched her uniform in favor of informal slacks — plain blue heading toward purple — and an unassuming shirt of faded gold. A thin band restrained her hair, which had once been dark but was now shot through with gray. After having worn her IC uniform for years, she felt at odd in the informal clothes.

She was, however, still overdressed.

Ragnath Gavarian sat across from her, looking more like the local he was, in a dark, collarless shirt that clung to his thin frame. The journalist had retained his dashing cut, his dark hair had grown out to curl around his ears, and his skin was still smooth over his sharp cheekbones. His fingers were long and graceful as he twirled a spoon around his soup bowl.

They sat in a highly public and crowded pavilion that had been carved out inside Pallas, which, due to its orbital inclination, was a difficult station for standard spacecraft to access — a fact that made it optimal for certain factions who mostly just wanted to be left alone. The table was small enough for just them, barely large enough to hold their lunch — eggs on rice for her, spiced noodle soup for him.

If she hadn't been so anxious, she would have considered the public chamber to be interesting. The place smelled as wild as its reputation — filled with warm aromas and a wall of never-ending sound that echoed from a rounded, but well-lit ceiling. Its architecture felt expansive inside the otherwise tiny asteroid, and its people were full of movement.

Despite Marisa being overdressed, the foot traffic here seemed less than interested in her, something that made her happy.

Pallas was a place where people came to be alone together.

Usually, anyway. That was its reputation.

Growing impatient, Marisa leaned in.

"Thomas Kitchell was your contact," she said.

"I can't answer that question, Captain," Ragnath Gavarian replied.

"I'm not a captain for this conversation," she responded.

"Begging your pardon, Captain, but the mere fact that you were able to contact me so quickly speaks to your captainship — for this conversation, or any other."

"Fair enough," she said. "You're not easy to find."

"That trait makes for a good journalist. Or—" He gazed around the chamber. "—at least one who remains alive."

"I'm sure that's true enough."

After his news piece on Kitchell, the heat had gotten intense for Gavarian. He'd dropped off the grid for a considerable time, popping up only here and there before fading away again. She knew his background. He was smart, well educated, and from a family of equally smart people. Her research said he had levers to pull when he needed to get things done but tried to stay independent. Ragnath Gavarian's whole brand was that of a lone wolf, but Marisa understood he couldn't pull this kind of life off if he were truly on his own.

It made her wonder about his contacts.

Her own situation wasn't much less cloak and dagger.

By her duty log, Marisa Harthing was still on *Explorer*, scheduled to depart in a few standard hours. But after Gavarian agreed to meet, she'd managed to convince one of her subordinates she needed a day to clear her head. After all the work it had taken to complete the upfit, she wanted a bit of time to herself, off the books.

A few journal entries later, she hopped a one-seat jumper to come here.

Gavarian was going to cover Torrance's message, of course. The story was too juicy to ignore. So, he was looking for angles, and hers was too tempting to ignore.

She checked her dataclip.

Three hours remained until she had to be back on *Explorer.*

"Let's not waste our time pretending what this is about," she said.

"What do you know?" Gavarian said.

"I know you wrote an article about Thomas Kitchell, and that Kitchell was killed shortly thereafter."

"I thought this was about the message from Torrance Black."

"It all ties together, doesn't it? Please. I mean, don't even try to tell me that Ragnath Gavarian, the system-renowned journalist, can't feel that."

"All right," he said. "I feel it."

"So, when you spoke with Kitchell, what did he say?"

"I told you I won't reveal my sources, but I'm sure anything he said that was worth repeating went into the article."

"Seriously, Ragnath. I may not be able to find you all by myself, but — *as a captain* — I am big enough that I can make things uncomfortable for anyone who publishes you. So don't play that game with me now. Your story quotes someone close to Torrance Black, and Thomas Kitchell disappears the same day. I don't need your confirmation to add the math. Hell, I *know* Torrance better than anyone else in the system. There aren't that many people close to him. It's either Kitchell or me, and I didn't talk to you."

Gavarian laughed but didn't say anything.

Marisa twirled her fork between her fingers and thumb. "You want a story about Torrance Black," she said. "I want the truth. Either we're going to work together, or we aren't."

Gavarian's eyes blazed with artificial sharpness.

Theoretically, the UG restricted such augmentations now, but it was public knowledge that the journalist had been modified. Marisa assumed he could see into various spectrums — particularly infrared, which she assumed would be a benefit to a journalist attempting to read a subject. If he was reading her now, she hoped he saw *she's pissed off enough to make his life hell.*

"What do you want?" he said.

Marisa left her fork inside her bowl.

"I want to take down the United Government Intelligence Office."

Gavarian raised an eyebrow and indicated respect. "That's a big order."

"They killed Torrance, and they killed Thomas."

"Well, Torrance just dropped us a note, so I'd question that."

"We both know he can't have survived four years on a shuttle in deep space."

He shrugged.

"It won't matter," Gavarian said. "Torrance Black's story isn't going to bump the world at all. Universe Three spy or not, he did agree to go kill Pentabill, so no one will care much about that. It's a fine line between traitor and assassin, but, in the end, people *want* their side to be doing the dirty work. No intelligence officer in the system is going down for ordering the killing of a Universe Three spy — which Oscar Pentabill most certainly was."

"They killed Thomas, too."

He shrugged. "Water under the bridge."

"They did the same thing with me as they did with Thomas."

"What do you mean?"

Marisa hesitated for only a moment. "The UGIO threatened my daughters to keep me quiet."

Gavarian's eyes narrowed, and his gaze grew more intense. Marisa felt exposed. Hair on her arms raised.

"That makes sense," he finally said.

"What do you mean?"

"Your statements. Back then. I was watching. Everything you said was so milquetoast. I should have caught on then, but they make sense now."

"So how do we do this?"

Gavarian stared at her for a long time, obviously thinking through steps and trying to decide how to fit puzzle pieces together. Marisa gave him space. "We don't," he finally said.

"What do you mean, we don't? This is the story. It's what you do."

"No. I don't go half-assed out into a nebula cloud. This is *part* of the story. But there's another part of this thing we'll need in order to bring it around full circle before I go any further."

"Another part?"

His eyes darted over the chamber, then he leaned toward her.

"One you don't know anything about."

"All right, then," she said. "Tell me about it."

"Thomas Kitchell."

"What about Thomas Kitchell?"

"He's alive."

"What?"

She sat still, confused, then realized Gavarian was still looking at her with something she'd call expectation on his expression. She felt like the entire universe was pressing in on them as they sat in this tiny little place in space.

"Thomas Kitchell is alive," Gavarian said.

"I don't understand. I saw his office."

"I can connect you. That is, I can connect you if you are not actually a captain."

She let his comment settle again.

"You're with Universe Three?"

"God, no," he said. "But I can hum a few bars."

He remained silent, then.

Marisa stewed over the comment.

Voices echoed around them.

Smells came sharply to her.

The sound of rumbling movement, footsteps against flooring, voices distant and echoing.

Thomas was still alive.

Fully involved or not, Gavarian had contacts in Universe Three. Now Gavarian was trusting her — a United Government Interstellar Command officer — with information that could get his cohorts killed.

Around them, the milling crowd went about their business as if Gavarian hadn't just taken a humongous chance.

"Why are you doing this?" Marisa said.

"I see the same thing in you that I saw in Kitchell."

"Which is?"

"You both have a good relationship with the truth."

She scoffed. "Hmm."

"Cynical much?"

She raised an eyebrow.

"The real question you should be asking," Gavarian continued, "is what I want you to do in return."

"And that would be?"

"There's something ugly happening in the upper echelons of UG," he said. "I want to find out what it is."

"There's always something ugly happening in the upper echelons of the UG," Marisa replied.

"I'm not stupid, Not-Captain Harthing. And neither are the people who live in this system. They're tired. Or distracted with the work it takes to make a life here. But they aren't stupid. And you know what I mean. There's something going on with the sun, and when I fit events into a timeline, it's clear to me that Torrance Black and maybe Thomas Kitchell have something to say about it. We both knew the *ambassador is a traitor* scheme was bullshit from the get-go. So, that means there's a whole crap-ton of cover-up being covered up." He twirled a glass between his fingers. "I think you're as cagey as you are desperate. You've got position and you've got contacts. I want you to find out exactly what that cover-up is."

Marisa's eyes narrowed.

He was asking her for much more than her story.

"You don't want me to stop being a captain, then?"

He gave a dry laugh. "Probably not."

Could she do it? Could she play whistleblower from within the command structure? Did she want to get caught up in the political machinations it would take to bring down the UGIO, or did she just want to sit back while someone else took the risks?

She thought about the Intelligence Office, about people she knew in positions of power, and the compromises those people needed to make to stay there — compromises including her own. Where was the line?

A memory of Torrance flashed in her mind.

The people needed to know.

She stared the journalist down.

"Thomas is with Universe Three now," she said.

"Yes."

"Can you take me to him?"

"Eventually."

"That's not going to be good enough. Either you get me to him or him to me, or you don't get what you want."

"And if I can make that happen?"

Marisa smiled like a cat as righteousness settled within her.

"Then I suppose I'm a captain-not-captain."

Chapter 35

Apogee: 37 Gem System
Local Date: C27/D35
Local Time: 2/1015

Early in the night shift Deidra Francis waited in Martin Scalese's office.

She knew two things after receiving his missive late in the afternoon, a missive that contained a request from Ragnath Gavarian — or rather, a request that came *through* Ragnath Gavarian — that said Marisa Harthing, a captain in Interstellar Command and a friend of Thomas Kitchell, wanted to come here.

First, she knew she had to talk about this offline.

Too much was happening right now and adding a UG officer into the mix was tempting fates.

Second, Scalese's group would be responsible for any extraction they made — and, if she understood the request properly, Scalese would also be responsible for getting the captain *back* into the Solar System.

Now she sat on one of Scalese's guest chairs, waiting for him, thinking, slumped to one side, one leg crossed over the other, her jaw propped up on one hand.

She didn't know what to make of Gavarian.

The journalist was more flamboyant than she liked. A bit of an enigma. A dashing figure who was independent in ways that both appealed and put her on edge. He'd been that way since the first days he'd begun to work with Universe Three, and to be fair that flamboyance was as much of an asset as a detriment. Gavarian was like a dog on meat when it came to his work, too. Something inside kept him focused on what he considered to be the truth, and the one truth that mattered was that he'd done real damage to United Government officials in his time.

Deidra had been around long enough, however, to know that dogged pursuit of truth could be a sword that cut both ways.

Still, Gavarian had been trustworthy and adroit. If he'd done nothing but get them the services of Thomas Kitchell, Universe Three would be ahead no matter what she did now.

Almost no matter, anyway.

If this was a ruse or not, either way she would be betting her entire community.

The door opened.

"Martin," Deidra said, standing.

"Deidra," he replied as he went to his desk and toggled the display. U3's dossier on Harthing, which was substantial, came into view. He smiled as he took his chair. "I assume you'd like to get straight to it."

She nodded, sitting also.

Scalese wore his usual nondescript dark slacks and a gray pullover that bumped over a gently rounded belly. He wore his brown hair trimmed short.

"Tell me what you're thinking," she said. "Bringing someone like Marisa Harthing into the fold has major upside, but if it blows up…" She blew a breath through her lips.

"Yep," Scalese said, scratching at his neck. "Harthing wants a meeting, and she's willing to let us control all the arrangements. That makes it's hard to pass up."

"Convince me."

"If we control the process, we can double-blind the jumps, and we can scan her in process until we're certain she's clean. We'll need to burn another good mole to make sure we don't screw up and give them something to trace, but what can I say?"

"If it's real, it's worth it," Deidra said.

"Exactly. Having a captain at Interstellar in the fold would be twenty-seven on the Richter scale. So, looking at it that way it's an easy yes." He took a tug on a bottle of water he kept on his desktop before continuing. "Gavarian has been golden for us, too. If this came from someone else, I'd drop it out of hand. But..." He shook his head. "He's been exceptional. And he's got his eye on a big prize."

"You think you can do it without leaving a trail?"

"Nothing is ever perfectly foolproof, but we've done it before."

"The window is tight."

"To be honest, the tighter the better. Constraining the mission lets us focus."

Deidra contemplated the situation while they sat in silence filled with the gentle hum of the computer banks and cooling systems running outside the office.

"Are you going to bring this to the staff?" he asked.

"No. I'll need to tell them, eventually. But this is the kind of thing that gets ugly if too many people are in on it."

"I understand that. And it's an easier lift if fewer people are in it."

"Do you have eyes on him?"

"The journalist?"

"Yes. What do you know about Gavarian right now?"

"You're asking if I think he could have been compromised?"

"Yes, that's what I'm asking."

Scalese shrugged. "I don't think so. Nothing in our tracking data shows it. He's slinky. Hard to pin down. From a family in high places but burned those bridges a long time ago. I know he's got accounts all over the place and a soft place for body modification. Recently did an upfit to allow him to dial down his skin sensitivity — which isn't to my taste, but what the hell, right?

"But comprised?

"I don't see it in any recent tracking. And he's always seen himself as a Freelance Doer of Good who pops up to write definitive exposé, then disappears."

"A vigilante with a datapad," Deidra said, and chuckled.

"Right. Robin Hood in a spacesuit. Then there's also my guess is that if UG captured him, they'd kill him before they'd try to turn him."

She breathed deeply.

Time pushed onward.

"All right," she said. "I understand. Contact him and set up a trip for Captain Harthing. Double and triple blind. No tails."

Scalese smiled.

"That's what I hoped you'd say."

Chapter 36

Aldrin Station, Lunar Orbit
Local Date: November 16, 2256
Local Time: 2015

Marisa had been on Aldrin Station for a week now, which, though the military kept her flying, she considered her home base. It was a short enough time that she was still feeling out of sorts as she returned to her quarters. At least she'd now finished debriefing the Joint Staff for the *Explorer* upfit, which meant she had three days to rest now.

Three days before she was to take a shuttle to the historic abandoned mine operation that had once been Mars Colony Natim.

Sightseeing, she was to say.

An actual vacation. The vice admiral had already approved her leave. Once there, however, U3 would handle the rest.

As the door closed behind her, Marisa found her message signal flashing. It would be Ana, her daughter, calling to tell her about her trip to the falls on Io. She and her partner had been there for a month, researching a crustacean life form explorers had recently found in the superheated streams of that moon's underground oceans. Wanting to take her time catching up, Marisa unbuttoned her jacket, and, feeling less formal, poured a glass of tea before checking it.

It wasn't until she finally sat down that she saw the message's security toggle was set, which brought her hackles up.

She flicked it on.

Zina Nichols. The woman from the Intelligence Office.

The name made muscles around Marisa's face tighten.

Ragnath Gavarian's directions came back to her, too. Their vague nature made her unhappy, but that had been the deal. No questions. No information. U3 wasn't taking more risk than they absolutely had to. *Do as you're told,* Gavarian had said, *and you'll see Kitchell.*

Otherwise, we're done.

Now Zina Nichols was flagging her down.

Of course.

Torrance's message made it certain someone in the UGIO would reach out to her, and since Nichols had been the contact previously — and successfully — she was the likeliest to take it on this time, too.

Still, Marisa wondered how much the Intelligence officer knew.

It didn't really matter.

Marisa had her own agenda now. She wanted to see Kitchell, but she'd already decided that even if she chose not to work with Gavarian, she was going to take matters into her own hands.

She'd known this conversation had been coming, and she'd let it play through the recesses of her mind more than a few times. She wished she'd been more focused at those times. Seeing the flash made her feel unprepared.

You answer the bell when it rings, though. The time was now.

She let out a breath and toggled the message.

All right. Let's do this.

The deputy director was immediately available.

The system created a virtual conference node, and a moment later Marisa found herself in a pleasantly bright office area set in a high-rise building, glass on all sides. A haze of clouded blue sky was visible in every direction. The lighting was mostly natural, but also came from soft coils in the ceiling — a ceiling whose presence kept the conference center from feeling too exposed. The table was a blond wood, bleached toward white. The flooring was deep blue.

The whole thing felt unnaturally crisp, probably because it was.

Marisa took a seat across from Nichols, who was wearing a beige top, which Marisa assumed was as "true" as her own UGIS jacket, which she'd buttoned up again prior to arriving. This was a working session. No reason for enhanced avatars.

"Thank you for meeting on such short notice, Captain," Nichols said.

Though she hid it well enough, Nichols looked tired.

"Think nothing of it, Deputy Director. Meeting with the Intelligence Office is always a pleasant way to spend an evening."

That the response registered on Nichols's face confirmed a certain fatigue. "I expect you can guess the topic."

"Torrance's message. You want to make sure I'm still in the corral. Thank you for getting straight to the point."

Nichols gave a nod to acknowledge the last sentence. She sat back an almost imperceptible distance and placed one arm on the tabletop, fingertips absently rubbing together. Marisa wasn't far off the mark. Zina Nichols's workload must have intensified over the past few days. Things were certain to be hot, and likely to get hotter before long.

"And?" Nichols said.

"I don't have anything new to say to anyone," Marisa said.

"Tell me more."

She shrugged. This wasn't a hard game to play. "The answers I gave the press four years ago were noncommittal enough that they stand today. I didn't know Torrance that well over the last years, but he'd seemed like a stand-up man back in the day. The messages sound like him, but there are vocal records available for a motivated hacker. I could put a fake together myself that was nearly as good. So, I can't say either way."

Nichols put her hands together before her.

"That's the answer, right?" Marisa finished.

"Yes. That will do well."

"How long do you think it will serve?"

Nichols cocked her head and widened her eyes to indicate she wanted more.

"I've already proven I'm willing to play games, Deputy Director. I understand how these things go. But I do know it's a game, and I don't want to pretend. We both know the message is genuine. So how long do you think you have before the heat gets to be too much?"

"That's a question for other ears."

Marisa felt the rebuff, but at the same time sensed an opening.

"I want to be a pair of those ears."

"I don't think that's wise, Captain."

"I don't think you understand, Director Nichols."

The Intelligence officer waited.

"I want in on the game."

"Captains in Interstellar Command do not get access—"

"To make this more than clear, Deputy Director. I'm considering a career change. Navigation is fine, but I plan to live a long and productive life. The steady stream of system upgrades I've been assigned have grown ... mundane now." The deputy director seemed suddenly more interested. "I've served the UG since I was a teenager. I want something more."

The expression on the deputy director's face finished its transformation from combative to intrigued to enlightened.

"You think this is your opening?" Nichols said, now fully focused. "You keep to the story, I give you a job?"

"One takes what comes," Marisa noted, knowing her audience.

"What did you have in mind," Nichols replied.

"You're connected. And you *need* me to be happy right now. Do you have any ideas?"

Nichols gave a terse smile. "This *is* a shakedown."

"I've been washing your back for a while now," Marisa replied. "And I'm telling you I'm still in the tub, so maybe it's time you wash mine. I like Intelligence. I think I could help."

Nichols's lip curled upward in a feral smile. "I see," she said.

Marisa felt calculations happening inside Zina Nichols's mind.

"I have a few tasks I need to finish. But give me a few days. Let me see what I can do."

CHAPTER 37

Buenos Aires, Argentina
Local Date: November 18, 2256
Local Time: 0800

When she arrived at the supreme president's estate, Zina Nichols was tired, but ready.

Too many balls were spinning in the air right now, and between Pinot's assignments and her own machinations, her travel schedule — both on and off the books — had been brutal lately. The air tram had gotten into Buenos Aires late enough that she hadn't had time to sleep, and even if she had it wouldn't have mattered. Given the rocky trip, and the nature of the session with the supreme president, she knew this was going to be tricky. So, as was becoming too common, she spent the night pacing her hotel room and going over her case.

It was okay, though.

She'd have time to sleep tomorrow, and the extra effort was worth it. As security showed her to a claustrophobic little holding room, she was as prepared as she could have been.

She stood still as a series of machines scanned her. As promised, the system logged her in as a tier three, meaning her appearance wouldn't show on Ils Jihansen's public calendar, and not even on calendars observable to those with normal high-security clearance. Tier three was deep-cut, eyes-only. She hadn't been certain she'd get it, but her position, her reputation, and her request for ultra-high security had done the trick.

That she was smart enough to know she couldn't get away with abusing it had to have helped, too.

The supreme president wouldn't accept this kind of audacity if he wasn't certain she had the chops to make it stick.

After she'd passed clearance, two staff members and a sensor bot escorted her through several gates and into an elevator that led eventually to the supreme president's personal office.

Jihansen was waiting for her, seated behind a desk flanked by three staff members in padded chairs — two women and a man, each dressed in professional outfits that stopped just short of military uniforms. They made her own chosen attire — a business suit this time, navy blue with a thin belt and a tight neckline — feel almost casual. She recognized all three and had conducted past conversations with two.

Cups of coffee sat on the supreme president's desk and on side tables beside each chair. The aroma was strong enough she could get a caffeine rush from simply smelling the hazelnut.

Zina wondered what they had been discussing before she made her entrance. Crime sprees? The recent civilian unrest after the UG had pulled resources from Mars to focus on the zero-g production plants on Ceres Station and other facilities scattered around the belt?

A few big companies had their eyes on the Oort cloud, too, something she most definitely had on her agenda once certain prerequisites were settled. Could that have been the topic?

"Good morning, Deputy Director," Jihansen said, standing. "Can I get you anything? Coffee? Espresso? Tea?"

He was as tall as the holoprojection she'd practiced with two nights ago.

"Maybe just some water," she replied as she came to the remaining seat in front of and to one side of the desk. "If I have any more caffeine I might just crawl out of my skin."

Jihansen laughed, then motioned for water.

They made small talk as the server returned.

The chair was at an angle to allow her to feel like she was speaking with all of them at once — which was something she'd practiced also. She'd only anticipated two additional guests, but that wouldn't matter.

Each attendee made sense when she looked at it rationally.

Finally prepared, the supreme president got to business.

"All right, Deputy Director Nichols. What brings you here?"

Zina scanned all three faces to gather up their attention.

"I know you've seen briefs, so I'll cut to the essence of the situation. It is now clear that despite my office having made such accusations, Torrance Black was not an agent for Universe Three."

"Yes," Jihansen said. "That seems to be the case now, doesn't it?"

"That's a big mistake."

"And you are here to take the heat for it."

"No sir. That is not why I'm here."

The supreme president's expression made her think he'd been expecting a call from Pinot on the subject — or maybe he'd already received one. Zina had been watching contact records and hadn't seen anything, but Pinot had ways to operate outside her view — just as she had ways to move outside his.

"That was a big mistake," she continued. "But we all know it's not public enough to get my boss bounced."

"Yes," Jihansen said. His voice was neutral. "Willim Pinot has a good reputation. He's been critical in fending off U3 aggression."

"And yet," Zina said, beginning to play her cards. "They still managed to frustrate us at every point."

"Losing *Vengeance* has reduced their operations," Jihansen said.

"Indeed, it has. They've only run a few operations here and there since that time. But even then, I think it's interesting to note both when and where they run those few operations."

"How so?"

"Each mission has been like lightning strikes pointed directly at places that inflict intense damage to us — that caused more harm than one might guess from the public reports. Scientific delays, or supply line crashes, other breaks in our advances. Two operations killed several key players involved in improving our scanning capabilities. And then there's the whole Mercury operation and the black hole connection in the sun."

As she spoke, Zina felt the temperature around the room drop.

The supreme president's advisers had each put their coffees down.

"Their intelligence organization is well known to be extensive," one of the advisers said.

"But is it, really?"

The supreme president leaned forward. "What are you saying, Deputy Director?"

Zina paused to sip water, feeling its chill flow into her mouth and down her throat.

"Let me ask you a question."

The four waited.

"How did Universe Three know Black would be with Oscar Pentabill?"

"What do you mean?"

"They had to know, right? How else would they have been prepared to abduct him? Which, they clearly did. Or do you believe in random luck? Do you believe that it was just an amazing coincidence that Universe Three happened to be eliminating Oscar Pentabill at the exact same moment that our own agent was in the process of doing the same thing?"

"I see," Jihansen answered.

"Then there's the fact that Universe Three kidnapped the UG science ambassador, then took him onto a Universe Three ship and eventually destroyed him. Message or not, Black is certainly dead now. But what if all of that was a ruse?" Zina sat back. "What if Pinot wasn't sending the ambassador to kill Pentabill? What if he was sending him into an ambush?"

"An ambush?"

"What if I tell you that I can prove Torrance Black was not the weapon, but was, in fact, the target?"

Jihansen's eyes slitted.

"Per the ambassador's message — which no one has been able to disprove — Universe Three was trying to put a black hole gate into Alpha Centauri A over four years ago. What if, Supreme President, Torrance Black had discovered that act, and when he did, Willim Pinot handed him to Universe Three."

"Are you suggesting your boss is a double agent?"

"I'm more than suggesting it, sir. I have records to prove it."

The gasp around the room was soft, but audible.

"And it gets worse."

"The sun," Jihansen said.

"It's a real problem, sir. The Mercury skirmish was a bigger operation than anyone is telling us."

"It *is* a black hole?"

Zina Nichols nodded. "Universe Three used that operation to drop a black hole gate into our sun. The UGIO director knows about it and isn't talking. If you look deeper, I think you'll find enough there to say he's also been inconspicuously deterring and delaying scientists who were trying to determine what is actually happening."

The supreme president locked gazes with his subordinates.

Heads nodded. He turned to her.

"I'll need to see your receipts."

"I'll have the encryption keys developed," she said. "You can expect them before the day is out."

Underneath the controlled expression on her face, Zina Nichols gave a contented breath. It was over now. Everything but the *coup de grâce*, anyway. She had the goods on Pinot — almost all those goods were obviously true and not hard to certify as authentic. The few pieces she'd had to make up to twist the knife were easy to piece together. She'd won. It was only a matter of time now.

Willim Pinot was going down.

The supreme president closed their session quickly thereafter, and ten minutes later security escorted Zina Nichols to a pod that took her back to her hotel.

The building was sleek and glassy in the midmorning sun.

Her mind ran loops as she strode into the expansive lobby.

She had work to do, and she needed to sleep.

If she could manage things right, she could spend an actual evening celebrating around the pool.

Tomorrow, though, she had another tram to catch.

Zina Nichols had one additional loose end to deal with.

Chapter 38

Mars Colony Natim Historical Relic Park
Local Date: November 21, 2256
Local Time: 1015

Marisa Harthing waved her glove over the scanner that logged her presence into the museum tour. Maybe it was just her nerves, but the museum felt antiseptic to her, so regulated.

Which she assumed was at least part of the point.

Touring the historic mining caves at Mars Colony Natim meant signing waivers and wearing the facility's branded environmental protection suits as you trudged down through the tube that would carry you to various sightseeing areas — each suit coded to a particular attendee in a particular group. Officially, the suits were used to allow the tour to take in areas where the air seal had broken in the raid, but they also ensured every photo taken carried the Parkridge brand.

Parkridge Mining Company owned hundreds of these historically charged sites across the system, sites where they wanted people to feel disjointed and out of sorts.

So the suits themselves served both to add distance from reality and provide a sense of disquiet about the place.

But the tourists also needed to feel safe. Which was why guards wearing UG colors lined the entryway to the park — and then the tube to the tram itself. The display of force was particularly relevant here, though. Mars Colony Natim was the site of the earliest and most surgically brutal of Universe Three's attacks on United Government home ground. To feel safe walking its remains put distance between then and now. The guards added to the aura, which was solemn and reverential.

That this was where U3 was going to slip Marisa away was its own form of irony, but those were Gavarian's instructions to her.

Timing would be critical.

Arrive at Natim, take the tour, and be ready to move.

If everything went properly, Universe Three would extract her and then inject her back into the group before the tour was over.

She had not been informed of the contingency plan for if things did *not* go well.

Enclosed in her suit, Marisa's breathing apparatus clicked with each inhale.

Yes, she was nervous.

Her gaze flitted from face to face as she tried to keep herself calm, waiting for whatever was going to happen to her.

She wondered what was happening with her data chain right now. The system would log her presence in Parkridge databases. She wondered how Universe Three was going to deal with her disappearance from the tour. If they could futz with the data center, it meant they had people in interesting places. One does not just hire into that kind of a role by coming in off the street.

All she knew for sure was that she was supposed to get on the underground tram to join a five-hour tour through the mining and research facility, a tour that concluded on the surface amid rubble that consisted of torn-up greenhouses and control systems that remained from when the U3 raid had destroyed Natim forty-one standard years ago.

As she made her way into the transporter, the pumped-in sound of historical news reel material filled her ears. Feelings from her *Everguard* days flashed back to her. Anger. Sadness. The desire for revenge. She'd nearly died in the attack. Her recovery had been intense, long, and painful. Memories from those days still made her unsettled. Which was why now, walking in line to the tram, she felt like a cog in the wheel of the world.

She realized that designers had molded even the tram's dim lighting to make the experience feel even more grungy and claustrophobic than it might have been otherwise.

But she didn't care that her emotions were being manipulated. Recreating the horrific nature of war across the system was the entire point of the display.

Against it all, she felt the presence of Torrance Black and Thomas Kitchell so fully that they might have well been beside her.

She took her seat along the tram's left side. The compartment fit her suit perfectly.

She scanned faces around her.

No sign of anything unusual. Time was ticking. It had to happen fast, didn't it?

The tram lurched forward.

Welcome to Parkridge Mining Company's Mars Colony Natim experience, a voice came over the intercom. *Now that we are in the safety of the tram, you can lower your faceplates and turn off your rebreathers.*

Tourists around her adjusted their helmets, and faceplates slapped into position with a clatter of snaps. The air here was fresh and sweet, but as the tram crawled down its track, that aroma grew dark and oily.

The action began when the tram deposited them into the bomb shelter.

Imagine if you will..., the narrator began as the gathering crowd finished ambling into a wide chasm that early inhabitants had gouged from the planet's stone crust. The lighting was brighter here — bright enough to see easily from wall to wall around the chamber.

Everyone knew the story.

Search crews had rescued seventy-two survivors here — the last seventy-two people so retrieved. They survived here for over a week, starving and out of water, watching as others died around them.

Imagine huddling here in safety as, above, Universe Three bombers, without mercy, strafe the colony.

The sound of bombs exploding came from above.

The floor shook, and fine debris fell from the domed ceiling.

Imagine the fear. The anxiety. Imagine being concerned for your family, scattered around the colony, fighting for their lives.

Marisa knew it was coming before it came.

Imagine as your safe space turns to total darkness.

A thunderous clap shook the floors, and the lights snapped off.

At that moment, amid pitch darkness and involuntary screams, Marisa felt a hand close on her arm above her elbow.

"Now!" a voice said into her ear as the agent pulled her aside.

Of course.

The room behind would remain in darkness for an extended time — that had been a warning Parkridge had made each tour member sign. If they got her out cleanly, they could have hours before Parkridge or the UG would be able to confirm she was gone.

Marisa lurched away, barely maintaining her footing as she followed.

Her eyes had not adjusted, and the pitch blackness around her was disorienting.

The hand grew stronger under her armpit, yanking her hard to the side. They moved together, walking, almost stumbling but for the pressure under her armpit.

Voices grew muffled and more distant as a door closed them off.

Their footsteps reverberated around her.

Her guide snapped a light on, and Marisa saw they were in a service tunnel that seemed to run forever. She glanced at her guide — a man whose face held dark contours. He had been in the tour group.

"We've only got a couple minutes to get to the jumper," he said.

"All right," she said. "Let's go."

Together, they made fast tracks down the tunnel.

THE MEETING

Chapter 39

Apogee: 37 Gem System
Local Date: C27/D42
Local Time: 2/05:55

Allie Feder watched Thomas Kitchell as he stood in the middle of the holoprojection and flipped through her model's representations of each dimensional space.

She had mixed feelings.

On one hand, she was happy to see his mind had settled again after his success with the blind, and it was ... cute ... that he was working hard to learn the theory he needed to understand her own work. On the other hand, he was still not fully useful when it came to helping with problems that were pure theory, and unless he were to spend years at the work, that lack of understanding was always going to be a problem. They were alike in so many ways, and one of them was that their egos were both more fragile than they wanted to admit. She liked being close to him, but she had come to realize she would never be able to share herself the way he wanted her to, simply because he couldn't grasp the idea that she worked on things he couldn't understand.

Their relationship was already complicated, and since she felt him getting ready to suggest they get even more serious, it threatened to get even more complicated soon.

His presence still helped make her feel less alone right now, and that was a good thing. But the eggshells she was beginning to tiptoe around were more than offsetting that advantage today.

As Thomas paged through the dimensions, the model's colors shifted — ruby red, sapphire blue, emerald green, and on. They cast his face in multicolor shadows. While each dimensional representation was simple enough on its own, and each matched with every adjacent pair in the eleven-dimensional grid — which, in theory made for a finite, albeit large chunk of work — the collection was defying her efforts to piece them together across the board.

She knew she could disconnect the jump engines now, but if she couldn't get the matching to work, she'd never be able to re-link them.

"It's the time dimension that screws everything up," Kitchell said as he turned to her, now seated on a padded chair, bent over, elbows on knees.

"Yes. That's right," she replied, trying to keep from sounding patronizing. "The time dimension is always the problem in wormhole physics. Or you can call it a gravity problem if you want."

"How so?"

"Take any triple bond — any three spatial dimensions, that is — and then you add in the time dimension, but every one of those bonds also has its own gravity field, which means gravity and time get intertwined there, too."

"I see. Spaghetti gravity."

He did not see, but Allie wasn't going to spend time trying to impart education he wasn't ready for. Instead, she blew out a hard breath and then adjusted the topic. "Reverse engineering is hard in four dimensions, but almost impossible in eleven."

"What if you tried something full duplex?"

This time she couldn't contain herself. "Seriously? Full duplex? You're honestly looking at this piece-of-crap model and you're coming up with *why not try full duplex?*"

"I'm sorry," he said. "I'm just trying to help."

She lay back in her soft seat and rested her neck against the padding. Closing her eyes, she let the moment ride.

"I'm going to kill an entire system," she said.

"You're doing no such thing."

"If I can't reattach the engine grid, the Solar System is going to die."

"It's not your fault."

"Please stop that."

"I'm not stopping anything. You're a physicist. Nothing more. You don't owe the world any more than it gives."

"Goddamn it, Thomas. Please stop it. I know what I'm working on." She kept her eyes shut and raised her arms over her head, welcoming the feeling as her muscles stretched.

"I'm sorry."

She blew another breath.

"It's all right. I know you'd rather me fail anyway."

"I never said that."

"You don't have to."

Thomas had gotten better at faking it, but he had never fully let go of the idea that Eden might host intelligent life. He had hoped his jamming shields would be enough to sway Universe Three's staff away from going doomsday on the Solar System. In the end, he didn't have any real say in the matter, and Allie didn't believe any middle ground could be found in which he would get his way. Either Alpha Centauri A was going away, or the sun was, and the answer to those equations rested on her ability to solve the problem of multidimensional engine keys.

She didn't have time to babysit him through that situation.

He was going to have to deal with that on his own.

She watched Thomas toggle the models again, simply to watch them fail.

A door to the room opened and one of Allie's student apprentices entered.

"Thomas?"

"Yes?"

"Director Francis would like to see you."

Chapter 40

Apogee: 37 Gem System
Local Date: C27/D42
Local Time: 2/06:05

Thomas Kitchell stepped into Director Francis's office.

She had recessed the walls just enough to give access to a breeze that was at least refreshing despite the uncertainty on his mind. The director looked at him from her position, standing near the edge of the office floor, looking out over the city. Her expression was almost wistful, which seemed odd to him. Deidra Francis was not someone he considered wistful.

"Is everything okay?" he said.

"Have a seat, Thomas," Francis said, motioning to two small couches set at perpendicular angles to each other. A pitcher sat on a small table, cups of tea full and ready for them. A third cup sat empty on the same platter as the pitcher. "I have someone you will want to see."

He took a seat.

"Someone I'll want to see?"

"Yes." She stepped toward the sofas, then sat down to sip from her cup.

He followed that action. The tea was one he knew the director favored, cool but with a bite of cinnamon.

Director Francis put her cup down.

"I'm sorry this is so uncomfortable, Thomas. But I admit I'm not sure how to approach it."

"I hope it's not bad."

"Me, too," she said with a smile that was equally sardonic and wistful.

"Well," he said. "Who is it?"

Francis toggled her communicator. "Show her in," she said.

The door opened a moment later, and a woman walked in.

Thomas's jaw nearly hit the floor.

"Marisa?" he said, suddenly standing.

She was older now, her dark hair shot through with gray, but her eyes still blazed with the same intensity. Her lips were still thin, her cheekbones still prominent. Rather than her UG uniform, her clothing was informal, loose pants, loose shirt rolled down at the collar with sleeves to mid forearm.

Uniform or not, it was most definitely Marisa Harthing.

"My God." He went to her.

"Surprised?" Marisa said, as he engulfed her in a huge hug that she returned with just as much vigor.

"Just a little." He held her back from him. "I can't believe it. I mean ... I can't believe it."

The moment collapsed around him.

Marisa was here. In Director Francis's office.

It was suddenly too much for his brain to process.

"What's happening?" he said. "How are you here?"

He turned to look at Francis, who was standing now, too.

"How is she here?"

"Captain Harthing has some news," Deidra replied.

"I'm not sure how much more news I can take."

"There's been a message from Torrance," Marisa said. "He sent it from a shuttle while in the Alpha Centauri A system."

Thomas took a step back, furrowing his brow, taking a breath, and putting both his hands on his head. He wanted to laugh or scream but his brain was caught in an endless loop, and nothing seemed to register.

"Torrance is alive?"

"Probably not," Marisa said. "The message is four years old. He sent it from a shuttle he stole from *Icarus.*"

Thomas nodded. That made sense.

Four light years from Alpha Centauri A to the Solar System. Still the idea that Torrance had been alive to send a message pounded in his heart.

"Alpha Centauri A," he muttered.

Marisa's expression urged him on.

"He headed to Eden, didn't he?" Thomas said. He didn't need her answer to know he was right. "Tell me everything," he said.

There, in Deidra Francis's office, Marisa imparted the content of Torrance's message — his assignment, kidnapping, transfer to *Icarus*, and eventual escape on the shuttle.

Director Francis confirmed Universe Three's portion of the operation — something Kitchell already basically knew.

The whole thing felt surreal.

"Could he still be alive?" he asked.

"I doubt it." Marisa shrugged. "It's a very long shot."

"Torrance has always found a way to survive, you know. That's who he is. We need to jump *Defender* there now." He turned to Francis. "We need to know."

"No," Francis replied, her gaze flickering to Marisa. "At least not now."

"Why not?"

Marisa replied. "Because Universe Three has survived by being wise."

Between the rock of Allie's work and the hard place of this conversation, Thomas wanted to pull his hair out with his bare hands. His entire body felt like it was melting. He dropped back onto the couch.

"What Captain Harthing is saying," Director Francis replied, "is that we still can't take that risk."

Marisa nodded. "I am a wild card, Thomas. Director Francis can't tell if I'm here on the terms I've stated, or if I'm part of a more complex game. She needs to know I'm not setting her up for an ambush that would cripple her community."

"All right," Kitchell said, shaking his head absently. "Don't take this the wrong way, then, but if you're not here to try to get to Torrance, why *are* you here?"

She smiled. "That's a fair question."

"So?"

She explained the pact between herself and Gavarian.

"But I came here because I needed to see you again. I'd gone to your office and seen the bombing. I was certain you were dead. But Gavarian told me you were alive, and I needed to know if that was true."

"And now that you know I'm here?"

"I know I can trust him."

"I see," he replied. "And you're going to work with him now?"

"I think I am."

Kitchell sat back in his seat, feeling the soft cushions give around him. He felt deflated.

"Are you okay?"

"I don't know."

For a moment the only sound came from the city outside the open walls of the director's office.

"What is this all for?" he finally said.

"What do you mean?"

"I don't know. I ... I just don't know anymore. The UG. This place. It all seems so ... senseless. We're just going around in circles."

"You've been with us for a time now, Thomas," Director Francis said. "You've seen there's a difference between us and the United Government, right?"

"I don't think there's as much of a gap as you'd like to think."

"Maybe not. But whatever gap is there is real. And the universe is a big place. If the UG would simply leave us alone, things would be better. You know that is true."

"Tell that to Captain Keyes."

Francis pressed her lips together.

"None of that matters to me," Marisa said. "Maybe your Universe Three structure is the right way and maybe it's not. I don't care about that at all, though. All I can say for certain is that I've seen the UG up close too often. I've spent my life trying to do the right things, and I'm proud of what I've accomplished. Torrance was, too. He and I raised two great people in that process. But—" She paused, looking for words. "Something has to change, though. I'm tired of being a foil. Tired of fearing for my girls' lives and tired of watching people higher up the chain shove good people like Torrance into corners simply because they hope to climb higher.

"I know you can't go to Alpha Centauri A now, but you need to go sometime. And that sometime has to be soon."

"If you could get us the UG jump schedule, that might change the dynamics around that decision," Francis replied. "It would mean we could be certain there's not a trap waiting at the end," she added.

"That's a big ask," Marisa replied.

"Big asks make big differences," Francis said.

Marisa stared off into space, then shook her head.

"Maybe the time will come when I can do that. But today it's too much too early. I'm going to give Ragnath Gavarian the truth about corruption inside the UG's walls," Marisa replied. "That's all I can really do. It's as far as I can go right now."

"That's fair enough."

The interchange gave Thomas a moment to assess things, and as the truth fell, anger rose. "Neither of you actually cares about Torrance."

"I care about him," Marisa pushed back.

"If you did, you'd find a way to go get him."

"It's not that simple."

Kitchell stood up, angry red coming to his cheeks.

"Then you're no better than the rest."

"That's not fair."

"Fair or not, it's true." Anger burned through his body now, heat rising to his face. "A trip to Alpha Centauri A might help us. It might tell us what happened to Torrance and *Icarus*, or it might not. But those aren't the reasons we should go. We should go because Torrance was a good person — and because good people deserve better. We should go because, small chance or not, there's an actual chance that Torrance is alive!"

He left then.

Steamed out of the office. Steamed down the stairs, and steamed out of the building to disappear into the streets.

His sight blurred as he nearly ran away from the leadership center. Now that he knew Torrance had been alive, he knew one true thing, and one true thing only.

They had to go to Alpha Centauri A.

The only question was how.

Unhappy with how their reunion ended, but short on time, Marisa Harthing left shortly after Kitchell stormed out.

189

Chapter 41

Apogee: 37 Gem System
Local Date: C27/D42
Local Time: 2/09:10

After sitting alone in silence for long enough to gather her thoughts, Deidra Francis went to her door, paused, and then — despite the early hour — left the building, too.

She walked alone through the streets, watching the effect she had on people as they worked. Recently laid pavement was hard against her feet. The heat of the day was warm against her back.

She walked until she came to the peak of a grassy mound that rose before dropping down to a riverbed.

The aromas of reeds and water mixed to form an earthy smell that played into the heat that beat on her shoulders. 37 Gem was a star like the sun. The water in the river was the same, two parts hydrogen, one part oxygen. She sat at the tangled root system of a thick tree, remembering a night so many standard years before when she sat with Katriana Martinez — her mentor, and her friend.

This would be Deidra's call.

She knew it would be.

The staff would hold a heated conversation. Sides would be taken. But a decision would need to be made, and she was intimately aware that to not decide was a decision in itself.

Her staff would look to her for final mediation.

For better or for worse, that was leadership.

She didn't trust Marisa Harthing yet, but something inside told her she should.

Kitchell was right when he said Deidra didn't care about Torrance Black. How could she? She'd never known him. She'd known Katriana Martinez, though, and try as she could to shake her image, Deidra couldn't get Thomas Kitchell's words out from her head.

Katriana Martinez was a good person.

And good people deserved to have their stories told well.

She sat there for a long time, feeling the breeze in her hair, and smelling the earthy aroma of the river around her, its currents flowing slowly and steadily onward.

Chapter 42

Mars Colony Natim Historical Relic Park
Local Date: November 21, 2256
Local Time: 1400

The U3 agent was pushing her so hard that Marisa nearly had to jog through the service tunnel to keep up. The lower Martian gravity helped.

"There's not much time," he said.

Her breathing quickened, and their rapid-fire footsteps reverberated off the tunnel's raw concrete walls.

On his direction she'd opened her faceplate again so she'd match the others at the tour stop they were going to inject her back into. Still, the helmet muffled the space around her, giving the moment a ragged desperation that accentuated the worries she already had.

The jump from Universe Three's home base back to Mars orbit had been as rapid as the initial jaunt there had been, and then they'd slipped her onto a standard charter transport carrying goods from the asteroid belt. The brief shuttle back to the historical park's service bays went as planned.

Once back on Natim's grounds, she'd shimmied into her assigned Parkridge suit — which she'd left on station to ensure tracking algorithms didn't toggle. Now, another agent, dressed as a service tech, rushed her down a service corridor.

The idea was to take her through the service tunnels to install her into a lavatory station near the group's final stop, then have her rejoin the group as if she had just returned with them. Getting to the room alone wouldn't be hard, but that lavatory was for workers, not visitors — and, in fact, the visitors' suits themselves included operational recycling and reuse systems for just such occasions. To cover that track, the U3 agent had manually disabled the waste management cycle on Marisa's system to give her an excuse if necessary.

It should work.

She checked her suit's internal clock.

Not that it mattered.

Timing was the critical element, not time itself.

They needed to sync up properly.

Without direct access to the group's status, that timing could be a mess. If security noticed her while exiting, she was to indicate the broken system, and, if that wasn't enough, she would claim ignorance about the rules that said she was supposed to stay with the group.

A closed doorway loomed ahead.

She caught her breath while the tech's proximity key synched. A light flashed red, then blue, then green. The door opened, then without a word the tech motioned her to wait as he slipped into the short hallways that led to the lavatory.

Marisa flashed on everything that had happened in the past few hours. Thomas Kitchell was angry with her, but he was alive. Not that she could blame him. She could still feel that first hug. It made her miss Torrance that much more.

The tech reappeared, and motioned her in.

A moment later, she was alone in the lavatory, the door closing behind the tech with a hollow latching that reverberated sharply in the little room.

She felt anxious, but oddly in control.

Everything was on her now, and the anticipation she felt was not unlike those she felt while waiting in green rooms for someone to introduce her. She took breaths to calm herself, then went to a UV cleansing station, leaned on the counter, and stared at herself in the mirror. A headache was beginning to build. She was tired, and her eyes were dry and red. Too much travel in too little time.

She laughed. How many light years had she jumped today?

Add in a double helping of stress.

Noise came from outside. Her heart rate spiked. The tour, arriving? She wasn't sure. Footsteps came close. The door slid open. The suit was bulky enough Marisa had to crane her back and neck to see it was an attendant who stepped through. A woman. Young. Security of a sort. An all-purpose communicator flashed from her wrist.

"What are you doing here?" the woman said.

"The group sent me ahead," she said too quickly.

"Sent you ahead."

"I had a suit malfunction."

"No one is supposed to be alone. Are you okay?"

"Yes, I'm fine now. Thank you. Just had to use the facilities."

From behind the security attendant, the initial arrivals from her group entered the pavilion outside. If she could just get out there, she could scan herself out with everyone else and no one would be wiser.

The attendant glanced to her communicator.

"I hope I haven't gotten anyone in trouble," Marisa said hurriedly. "I'd hate to see anyone get dinged just because they let me take care of myself."

The woman pressed her lips together.

"All right," she said. "I don't suppose it's a problem."

"Thank you," Marisa said.

The woman stepped aside, and as the tour gathered in the pavilion, Marisa joined in.

THE JUMP

Chapter 43

Apogee: 37 Gem System
Local Date: C27/D42
Local Time: 2/12:00

Thomas Kitchell didn't know what he was doing anymore. Sitting alone on the chaise in the darkness outside his quarters, he felt small. Useless and weak. At least when he was working on the blind, he had something to focus on. Now he had nothing to do but see how little he mattered.

Above him was a field of stars.

Around him city clamor had given way to insects and the lizard-frogs Allie liked so well.

He drank the lemonade he'd decided on over harder stuff. Not that he would have minded getting drunk, but he wanted to be able to think now and he didn't trust himself to stop drinking once he got going.

He was still angry. Deidra Francis, he understood. The woman was born hard. But Marisa? How could Marisa Harthing be so cold?

He would never stop being angry about that.

Looking into the darkness, Thomas felt the loss of Torrance as strongly as he'd ever felt it. He wasn't a physical person, but every time he thought about LC his brain spun out of control and he found himself needing to get up and pace. Even now, sitting on the balcony, restless energy made his skin crawl. He wanted to punch something.

Hard.

Gazing into the starfield, he swore he saw one point moving in the sky and imagined Torrance in a derelict shuttle. A sense of desperation overwhelmed him. He pictured LC in a shuttle, lost in the Centauri system. No. Not lost. Stranded. Some unknown chain of events had stranded LC in the Alpha Centauri A system, and then moved him to find out for himself the answer to the question that had fueled both of their entire lives. The idea made Thomas want to scream.

He closed his eyes and laid his head back, trying to calm himself by recalling the hazy sizzle of the data files from his now long-lost Eden set. He'd listened to them sometimes after learning that Torrance did. The sound had always felt so intimate.

What had LC seen? What had happened to him?

Could he have found Eden?

If so ... Thomas was suddenly jealous.

Why wasn't there more to Torrance's message, or even more messages? He couldn't stop his brain from churning over this question.

What did it mean that the message stream stopped when it did?

Had the shuttle broken?

Had Torrance simply been conserving energy?

The number of possibilities were infinite, and that infinity made his brain freeze.

He drank his lemonade, feeling so deeply alone now.

The lemonade had grown too warm.

Maybe he should go to the harder stuff.

He sighed. Even Allie was pushing him away more than not. She had been so distant the past few days — which he knew meant her mind was working on something, but something he still couldn't get a real grasp on. Darkness felt claustrophobic. He imagined her in her lab, still working, still testing options on the skimmer the U3 staff had assigned her. At this rate he would be an old man before they got to Eden.

How it would feel? To get there after the fact? How would it feel to arrive too late, to find out there *had been* life on Eden, but they'd left it to falter? The image of dead aliens spread out over a barren landscape flooded his mind. What if they got there to find nothing but that? What if Torrance had made it to Eden? What if he was still alive, and what if...?

Suddenly, his heart nearly froze, and his entire body went numb.

The skimmer the U3 staff had assigned her.

Allie Feder was testing her models on a Star Drive jump-capable skimmer. And that skimmer was in the flatlands outside her laboratories.

Resolve fell over him like the darkness itself.

"I'm not going to be a pawn," he said, flashing on the events that had gotten him away from the Solar System in the first place. Deidra Francis herself had suggested as much. The memory burned in his heart.

"I'm not going to be a pawn," he said once again. "I'm not going to be a pawn."

This time as he said those words, he stood up and moved off into the darkness, toward the city outskirts and toward Allie's lab.

Chapter 44

Apogee: 37 Gem System
Local Date: C17/D42
Local Time: 2/12:00

In retrospect Allie would say the answer was obvious.

This time it didn't come from any sudden flash of insight, nor was it accompanied by a sense of universal joy. Instead, Allie asked herself a simple question and struck on a relatively simple idea: If she set recursively interdimensional flow gates that, themselves, were built across the dimensions — gates whose latches called on each of the other latches, essentially — and then iterated through the algorithm until she found the right settings for each, she could build a multidimensional dam that was strong enough to stop material from flowing through the wormhole's throat tensors for long enough for the rest of her algorithms to run to completion.

Looking back on it, the whole thing was a special case that fell out of Kransky-Watt if you dug down deep enough into the quantum structures of the universe.

She came upon the core of the thought just as her student apprentice had called Thomas Kitchell away from her office, which was fortuitous timing because that meant she had time to stew over the idea.

An hour turned to two. Two to three.

Outside turned from daylight to dusk, and then dark, but by that time Allie didn't care.

She was on to something.

The world is fractal in nature. Dimensions on dimensions on dimensions. Turtles all the way down. She sat in her office for a few more hours, playing with the model, setting the latch code across every software dimension the model mimicked. Starting flow, then stopping it.

Opening her mind, she pondered real-world implications, particularly thinking about dark matter, and about black holes and what might be inside them. A black hole stopped time. Or it condensed it, and therefore it had to change space, too. If she could stop matter transfer through a gate, could she reverse it? Kitchell and Black had been concerned about stealing a planet's sun, and for good reason. But was what she was doing any better by playing with black holes?

The math here said it wasn't impossible to pull material from a black hole. That idea set her back a notch. If she did that, what would she find?

What could she change?

Could intelligent life exist across the dimensions?

Her brain ran free.

Scientists still didn't understand black matter. Not fully. Her idea described how energy and, therefore, matter could be held in interdimensional pockets for what could conceivably be infinite time periods. Could this be the math behind the enigma? Could another species have "stolen" material from this universe? Could dark matter be the result of interdimensional mining?

The whole thing was unsettling.

That was the thing about science that had always attracted her — the more you knew, the more questions you had. And something else, too. To understand science was to understand that everything you touch, you change. Transferring energy through portals that rode the dimensions would alter those dimensions, though she could not say *how*, or by how much, but if she were guessing, it would look like mass conversion in cross-dimensional universes. Energy here became mass there, and vice versa.

She clicked the model again.

When she finally emerged from her mind-funk it was late.

She was suddenly ravenous and tired, but it was a good hungry, and a great tired.

Despite the multitude of questions she had, Allie Feder knew one important thing: She could make it all work. She could plant a black hole connection into Alpha Centauri A and save the Solar System. She could staunch flow from a gate, strip a spaceship of its original gate, and then connect that spaceship to another source.

More work was needed to set parameters for the new throat tensors that were strong enough and flexible enough to take extra stress of a full wormhole flow. But creating the systems to do it was now officially an engineering problem rather than one of theory.

She understood, also, that the application was broader than she'd first thought.

Much, much broader.

That would come tomorrow, though.

Now was time for dinner.

Chapter 45

Apogee: 37 Gem System
Local Date: C27/D43
Local Time: 2/12:20

The dark of night, the cover of insect song, and the fact that the security systems knew his profile had been his friends. Ten minutes and a brisk walk after leaving his quarters, Thomas Kitchell climbed through the rounded entrance way and into the Star Drive skimmer.

Even though the skimmer was small for a spacecraft, its body still spanned fifteen meters — most of that associated with the squat, oblong engine compartment. The cockpit was a cylindrical tube that seemed pasted onto those engines. A small passenger bay sat behind the controls. Gunmetal seats, gray painted walls, and a flooring lined with thick rubber compound made the whole thing feel more functional than aesthetically pleasing.

The door irised closed as he engaged the straps.

He toggled on the navigation and guidance display, revealing bright control lights that made him blink against the darkness.

He engaged a preflight checklist.

Throttle. Aileron control. Orbital configuration. Deep space navigation.

The fuel gauge showed enough.

It wasn't like he was going far under conventional drive, anyway. The Star Drive engine status light remained on standby.

Kitchell had been studying the Eden files — records of the first radio emissions from the planet — for so long, he could code their coordinates in his sleep, which meant the challenge for his skills would be simply getting the skimmer off the ground. He'd played simulations in his younger years, and he'd flown a few rudimentary craft, too. He thought he could pull off the basics, but deep down, he wasn't sure.

"Only one way to find out," he muttered.

He kicked on the primary engines, and once the rumble settled, pulled up on the yoke.

The craft levitated, banked left, then too far right.

He wobbled upward as around him the ship kicked up a dust cloud that pelted the fuselage in the darkness. The wobble made his stomach lurch. He gritted his teeth and pulled further up while also pushing a thruster throttle to get velocity. The craft shot forward heading directly toward Allie's laboratory. He pulled hard on the yoke, and the skimmer stood on its tail, rocketing upward so hard Kitchell's head cracked back against the seat and his dinner fought to reappear.

He'd missed the lab building at least.

The skimmer climbed harder. Gravity pressed him down and the thick atmosphere buffeted the spacecraft's body with white noise. Ahead the star pattern showed. He pressed harder on the throttle, and the craft roared forward.

A radio burst nearly made him yelp.

Skimmer C, what is your flight plan?

Kitchell concentrated on the controls, listening to the skimmer's ascent.

Skimmer C, please return to the surface. Your flight is not authorized.

Then everything got suddenly quiet. He was in near Apogee orbit.

Toggling the jump drive, he entered a location code for Alpha Centauri A. He didn't have much time. If he didn't leave now, they'd get *Defender* or its fighters on him soon.

Repeat Skimmer C, please return to the surface.

Kitchell engaged.

CHAPTER 46

Apogee: 37 Gem System
Local Date: C27/D43
Local Time: 1/00:15

Allie Feder already knew she wasn't going to be getting any sleep tonight, anyway. She'd eaten, and that was good, but ideas about the model kept streaming through her thoughts, and she could do nothing but toss and turn in her bed.

Still, that the call came so late both startled and annoyed her.

"Come to the lab," Martin Scalese had said. *"Thomas Kitchell is gone."*

Her first thought was that this meant Thomas had died. Heart attack or a stroke. Her heart froze.

"What happened? Where is he?"

"The Star Drive skimmer," Scalese said. "He took it."

"I'll be right there."

She rang off and turned the light on.

"Oh, Thomas," she said under her breath as she stood up and got herself ready. A moment later she was striding purposefully through the damp nighttime.

"Maybe we shouldn't have trusted him," one of the techs was saying as Allie stepped into the room. Director Francis was there with Deego Larsi and Communications Director Scalese. "The skimmer will have its navigation coordinates registered. I'd bet anything that the UG will have our location the minute he hits the Solar System."

"He's not going back to the Solar System," Allie snapped.

"One step at a time," Scalese said. "Let's check the logs."

Larsi was out of his league, so simply scratched his collar bone and remained silent.

The fact that the tech jumped to such conclusions annoyed her.

She was fighting a sense of betrayal from Kitchell, but she had come to know him, and that knowledge gave his act of desperation the Quixotic essence of tilting at deep space that made it possible to defend him.

Still, what he'd done was stupid.

And it made her look bad.

She was going to give him all kinds of shit for this once he got back.

"Then where is he going?" the tech asked.

Deidra Francis responded. "Alpha Centauri A," she said.

"That's right," Allie replied. "Go on and check the logs, but there's no doubt in my mind that's where he is right now."

"Assuming he made it," Larsi said, pulling his hand from his neck.

"Yes," Allie sighed, her body posture concurring. "Assuming he made it."

"We can't have him doing this, you know?" Director Francis said to her.

Allie looked at Scalese. "Can we at least confirm I'm right?"

"Yeah, it's already coming in." Scalese checked a projection display from his datapad. "You're right. The jump log coordinates say he went to Alpha Centauri A."

Francis closed her eyes and ran both hands through her hair.

"Nothing ever comes easy."

NEWS

SOURCE: INFOWAVE — NEWS for the 23rd century
TRANSMITTED: November 22, 2256, Earth Standard
HEADLINE: UG Intelligence Official Steps Down

Buenos Aires – In a surprise announcement, Supreme President Ils Jihansen said today that Willim Pinot, the United Government's top Intelligence official, was leaving office effective immediately.

"Director Pinot's service has been excellent for an extensive period and played a formative and substantial role in efforts to keep the population of the Solar System both safe and prosperous," the statement said.

The announcement provides no specific details, and Pinot has not made public comment, but the statement itself strongly suggests that Pinot made the decision unilaterally, and with the desire to step away from the stresses of holding such a position.

Jihansen has not named Pinot's replacement, but people close to him say he has a front-runner.

ZINA RESPONDS

Chapter 47

Alexandria, Virginia
Local Date: November 25, 2256
Local Time: 0115

Zina had received the call three hours earlier.

Sitting now in cold darkness, on a bench in a park outside her apartment building, Zina Nichols tightened her fists again, then released them. Even with several hours under her belt, the movement did nothing to quell her anger. She lit a third hit and drew smoke deeply into her lungs before letting it seep slowly out her nostrils.

She'd been in college the last time she'd indulged in grunge, but she was far too good of an intelligence officer to not know where to get it.

The taste was coarse, but oddly sweet.

Tonight, she needed it as badly as she'd ever needed anything.

She'd run her play, run her game.

And the dice had bounced an unexpected direction. She felt dumb now, which isn't something she would ever get comfortable with. This was her fault. She should have considered Jihansen having a flunky or two at hand, and she should have placed barriers in their paths.

It would not have been particularly difficult.

Her body felt like it was water, rippling in a cold stream, her fingertips numb in the cold. It hadn't snowed yet this year, but it had been cold. The bench's planks pressed hard against her back. Movement from her body art was as aggravating as it was comforting. They, too, seemed changed by the grunge.

She ran the message through her mind again.

"I wanted to let you know you have a new boss," Supreme President Jihansen had said as he told her who he had chosen in Willim Pinot's place — a name that most certainly was not hers.

Five years of work.

Kaput.

At least the asshole had the guts to call her directly.

She lit a final hit, then tossed the remnants to the side.

Releasing the last of the smoke, Zina Nichols stood in the darkness.

Her head swam with the heady combination of resignation and intoxication, and fatigue nearly overwhelmed her. She drew frigid air into her lungs and breathed it out in a long, stress-relieving stream of white frost.

She stretched and straightened.

This wasn't the end.

The game wasn't over. She felt that now more than ever.

She wasn't giving up that easily.

She had work to do. Lots of work.

Tonight, she would sleep.

Tomorrow, she would get back to work — not the least would be completing the process of bringing Marisa Harthing on board.

That had taken weeks of solid work.

Every evening. Off the clock, technically, as if off the clock meant anything for a deputy director in the Intelligence Office.

But Zina Nichols had done it.

She should have assessed the situation when she first ran into it — or, rather, should have taken it more seriously. She'd seen Marisa Harthing's expression as she put forward her thinly veiled request to join the organization. Only a complete idiot would miss that this was more a self-aggrandizing ploy than any need for a midcareer change. Marisa Harthing wanted *something*, and the fact that her request came just after Torrance Black's message arrived meant that *something* was going to be a problem.

Zina had seen that much.

She'd failed to take it in as deeply as she should have, though.

Only after she'd started processing Marisa Harthing's transfer requests had warning bells started going off.

So, Zina had spent the time since that request working backward and forward on the timeline of Marisa Harthing's whereabouts. Where had she been, and why had she been there? What steps had she taken? What transportation? Who had she seen, and for how long?

Which is how Zina found the gaps.

And how, when she laid routine reports of locations over jump-craft movements, she came to her conclusion regarding what had happened.

Everything is tracked, she thought as she searched through the tangled network of systems and data, *so everything can be found.* The challenge, as always, was in separating the unimportant from the important.

In the end she got a little bit lucky finding the answer as quickly as she did. Data did not come from the darker corner of the system cleanly — or cheaply, for that matter. But a series of indirect sources matched a jump-craft signature with a departure, and then a series of bank deposits and another set of convoluted searches got her the rest.

When she had her answer, her next step was clear.

Chapter 48

Aldrin Station, Lunar Orbit
Local Date: November 28, 2256
Local Time: 0117 (Earth Standard)

Aldrin Station's night shift had progressed far enough that Marisa's soft bootsteps against the composite floor was the only sound in the corridor. As she approached her quarters, the door clicked to unlock itself, meaning it had sensed she was alone.

The sense of solitude felt good.

Travel was normal for her, but it wore her down — not just the physical demand, but also that any work she did while on the road always felt so much denser. Constantly being on travel also meant constantly being hosted. This most recent travel — her "vacation" to Mars Colony Natim and her jaunt to wherever the hell Apogee was — was different, but still more of the same. It all added up to say she was grateful for the few days of downtime she'd had here.

The door slid open as she reached it.

Her time should be drawing short, though. With luck, Marisa would be in Intelligence before the new year. Then it would be time to contact Gavarian and get to work.

The game she was playing was dangerous, but she was tired of pretending she didn't care, and she owed Torrance that much. She was going to find the truth. And, for Kitchell's sake, that could even include a trip to the Alpha Centauri A system.

Before stepping through her quarter's doorway, she paused.

The light was on, as it should be. But what registered suddenly was that it hadn't clicked on after the door opened, as it usually did. Instead, it had already been on. The dissonance slid a cold slice of anxiety down her spine.

"Hello?" she said, putting a hand to one wall.

The front chamber looked untouched — lounge and table in their normal corners, the far wall displaying the slowly undulating representation of the icy sludge found in the depths of the Europa Seas that she used because it reminded her of her daughter Mercy's work.

Its prismatic, deep blue churn flowed to purple.

Her data wall was a dark, cold square to her left. The aroma was neutral, colored only by the faint remains of potpourri that had now gone stale.

Nothing else moved. Nothing felt out of place.

Just the lights, which were now on further into the chambers — down into the kitchen and over toward the bunk and then out to the observation porch that, as a longstanding captain, she'd earned the privilege of having.

The sound of a knife slicing down to a cutting board came from the kitchen.

Marisa clutched her fists tight.

"Come in, Captain," a voice said, clear and firm, female, but neutral enough to be deceiving. "You must be starving."

She stepped into the room, and the door slid shut behind her.

"Who is it?" she called, still waiting at the entrance.

"Now is not the time to be shy, Captain. We're going to be working together, after all."

The knife fell once again.

"Deputy Director," Marisa said, remembering the timber of that voice. A feeling of discomfort came from physical tension draining at the same time as her emotional shields went up.

She stepped into the kitchen.

The lithe form of Zina Nichols stood at the island, dressed in simple athletic wear — dark leggings and a loose-fitting sweatshirt with a line drawing of a panther's head made in whites and grays.

She had chopped a pair of apples into slices. The aroma, tangy and sharp, made Marisa suddenly hungry.

"I think we should begin this relationship by you getting used to calling me Zina," Nichols said, sliding the blade into a cleansing slot in the wall, then returning it to a decorative holder at the end of the island. "I'm your boss now, but I don't see any need to be formal."

She handed Marisa one plate and took the other for herself.

"How did you get in?"

Nichols gave a low breath that was at least partially derisive.

"I wouldn't be much of an intelligence officer if I couldn't manage to slip into and out of places at least mostly unseen."

"Mostly unseen?"

"I'm glad to find you can listen."

"Is that supposed to mean something?"

"Suppose you tell me?"

Nichols gave her a dark-eyed glance that Marisa felt might be more of a challenge than an acknowledgement. The intelligence officer gave no hint of which direction might be right, simply left the question hanging there while she crunched an apple slice, then took her plate to stand at the observation port.

The lunar surface loomed outside; its silvery white arc carved like a brilliant slice against a backside lobe of the brown-black dark side that lay exposed to the station.

Marisa examined the plate of apple, feeling tension. What was Nichols doing here? What did she know? What were the chances she had poisoned the fruit? The tone of the deputy director's voice said something had to be going on.

She picked up a slice, still deciding.

"Thank you for the snack," she said, glancing at Nichols. "I didn't realize how hungry I was." She ate the slice, swallowing quickly.

"Vacations will do that to you, I've found."

There it was again. The tone.

Nichols ate the second half of a slice. The apple crunched softly in her closed mouth. "I'm here to bring you the good news," Nichols said after she swallowed.

"My application was approved."

"Exactly."

"That was fast."

Nichols shrugged. "Could have been faster, but it is what it is. You report to me starting now. Officially, your first assignment is a two-week transition of duties to your replacement in Nav Command."

"An unofficially?"

"You *are* quick," Nichols said, and nodded. "We'll make a crack analyst of you yet."

"I'm quick enough to note that's not an answer."

Marisa took a half step backward to lean against the kitchen island, then waited. Nichols also centered herself by leaning against the portal view, then leveled her dark-eyed gaze directly onto Marisa's.

"Your first real assignment is to explain to me why I shouldn't expose you as the Universe Three agent you are."

"I see," Marisa replied, reflexively using the phrase to give her mind that split second to process the situation. "Less than an hour on the job and I'm already up to my neck in cloak and dagger. I suppose I should be flattered."

"Is that your answer?"

"I can't imagine I need to answer that. My record is—"

"Do I really need to walk you through this step-by-step, Marisa, or are you going to give me the respect I'm due and simply acknowledge the fact that you met Ragnath Gavarian off-line a short while back, and then a few days later disappeared from the Solar System for four hours while on a tour of the lost colony on Natim?"

Marisa's stomach dropped. It was all she could do to hold the plate steady. As it was, she had to prop it against her belly to keep from showing her vulnerability.

She'd been careful. They'd all been careful. But Nichols was too good. What had she gotten herself into?

"I was lying earlier when I said we'd make you into a crack analyst," Nichols continued. "You need to know right now that it's too late to ever make you into a real intelligence officer. I knew that the minute you said you wanted the job."

"I'm quick enough."

Nichols gave a chuff. "Being an analyst isn't about being quick. It's not even about being smart. Not really, anyway. Those are just entry-level traits. Becoming a real analyst is about reading data and asking the right questions. It's about understanding people and seeing where they're going even before they do. A real analyst is always ahead of the game. You've made a fine Interstellar officer. But Intelligence?"

Nichols gave a sound that might have been a laugh.

She picked up a slice and waved it haphazardly.

"No one will ever take you seriously."

"Then why—"

"Your inability to be a top player is your value."

Marisa frowned.

"Once you see it, you'll understand. You'll be like Torrance Black was as a science ambassador, which I suppose makes this situation all that much more endearing. Everyone knew the science ambassador was a simple engineer. Not a real scientist. And that meant he was not a threat. In the end, all those theoretical physicists and mathematicians could let their guards down around him without fear."

"I see."

She did, too. Torrance was a great engineer, but his skills had always been limited when he'd gotten into the more philosophical nature of navigation science.

"And you have connections," Nichols continued. "At first, I discounted those, mostly because nobody here really thinks about Interstellar Command with anything more than a passing interest. But it turns out I hit the jackpot, didn't I? Not only do you have connections, but you have connections with a capital C."

Marisa ate the next slice, letting the tang play in her mouth as Nichols's words settled. The intelligence officer knew Marisa had been with Universe Three, and if what Nichols said was true about her transfer, she held Marisa's fate in the palm of her hand. The combination soured her gut.

"What do you want," Marisa said.

"I want to know what you talked about with Gavarian. I want to know where he sent you. And I want to meet him."

Marisa pursed her lips.

She'd been wrong. Nichols *didn't* know about her meeting with Deidra Francis.

"I don't know how to do that."

It was a lie, of course. Gavarian had given her a contact under strict directions on how to execute that contact without burning them. The idea of giving it to Nichols now made her skin crawl.

"I think you'll find a way," Nichols said.

"How...?" Marisa stopped herself before she could complete the thought.

She took Nichols in, then. Looked at the entire idea that was Zina Nichols. Nichols knew a lot, but not everything. She knew about her vacation, and her contact with Gavarian. She knew Marisa had jumped from Mars Colony Natim, but not where she had gone. If she knew Marisa had contacted Deidra Francis and Thomas Kitchell, Marisa was sure this conversation would have jumped those rails a long time back. Regardless, Marisa had read about Zina Nichols in the time since their first meeting. Rumors said she was precise with her mental gymnastics. Now Marisa saw how true those rumors were.

"Let's leave it at this, Marisa," Nichols said, answering her question anyway. "I make my living by asking myself questions that I think are important, and then putting information together from otherwise disparate places to answer them. This is no longer a game. You're the one who put your foot into this ring. You're past the time you can take it out."

She picked another of her apple slices, and examined it closely, turning it from side to side.

"So," Nichols said, her voice sounding dangerous. "Let's take another shot at getting off on the right footing, shall we? I say I want to speak to Ragnath Gavarian, and you say..."

The air in the room seemed to settle.

"And I say, all right. But I'm going to need some time."

Nichols's lip curled into a smile that carried something close to satisfaction. She lifted herself from the observation panel and crossed to the kitchen to leave her plate on the island counter, half the slices still uneaten.

"Come to my suite at zero seven thirty," she said. "I'll get you started. Rules and procedures, you know, take you Earthside to your station and introduce you to the team. All the usual stuff."

Marisa nodded. "I'll be there."

"That's good," Deputy Director Nichols said with a nod. She left, then. The door opened, then clicked behind her.

Marisa sighed and took another bite of an apple slice.

Chapter 49

Aldrin Station, Lunar Orbit
Local Date: November 28, 2256
Local Time: 0135

Zina returned to her quarters, satisfied.

Bringing an agent into the office from another service wasn't unheard of. The background checks, for example, were routine — a case agent was assigned, a full background tracking would be enacted, and a verdict rendered. Marisa Harthing's service record — though a tad mundane after the *Everguard* incident — was about as sterling as one gets, and the way she handled the whole Torrance Black affair gave her additional points from those in the know on the political side.

Harthing's case was as much of a lock as any résumé Zina Nichols had ever seen.

On the surface, anyway.

Zina wasn't stupid, though. People like Marisa Harthing don't just wake up one morning and decide they want to be in Intelligence. Something bothered Zina about the whole thing. She'd never had a subject of an operation ask for a job, especially not a subject of such interest.

It was going to take work, but that was the game.

And if this session had proved anything to Zina it was that Captain Harthing *did* have value.

Depending on that motivation, maybe Marisa Harthing could be useful. Otherwise, Zina could dispose of the captain as easily as she had acquired her.

REUNION

Chapter 50

Undefined
Local Date: Undefined
Local Time: Undefined

The light show inside the Star Drive skimmer was, if anything, more intense than what Thomas Kitchell had seen on Excelsior class spaceships.

The flow was closer.

More intimate.

Watching the multidimensions break down over a cruiser's form was awe-inspiring in the same way that looking at crashing mountain streams or billowing nebula clouds was awe-inspiring. Seeing it up close in a skimmer was like what he imagined diving into the ocean might be.

He came out a few ticks off from where his informal calculations would have put him.

He chuckled. Marisa would be proud.

Then he looked through the view screen and saw Eden's rounded sphere lying before him, reflecting light from Alpha Centauri A and B and Proxima, and for several moments he was stunned to the point that nothing at all went through his mind.

He'd seen planets, of course. His work alone had taken him to every planet in the Solar System except Mercury. Still, looking at

Eden — seeing her brown crust marked by dark lines and broad, featureless plains, and then seeing the large, circular pattern of the mountain range he and Torrance had discussed so often he felt he could map it by hand — well, it felt like meeting a distant pen pal for the first time. He knew this planet. He felt its proximity in his bones.

Coming back to full awareness, Thomas determined he was now in an orbital position around the planet.

A moment later a truth struck him.

"Where are the clouds?" he said to himself.

Eden was supposed to be blanketed in hazy clouds that were somewhat acidic in nature, but — as Torrance had decided — were "helpful" because they would shield the surface from Alpha Centauri A's more intense emissions. Yet here the planet was, starkly barren. Thomas ran environmental scans.

"Crap."

The cloud cover's disappearance meant the acid had dissipated into the ground — which would change everything. He'd trusted Torrance's assessment of the situation.

So much had changed.

The clouds gone.

The surface baked to a dun tan.

He'd have bet his apartment back home on the fact that there was life here. What he saw made him fearful. Had this been their fault? Projections had suggested the drain would be slower. Could the draining of the star have created this much havoc already?

And, despite his rational mind telling him otherwise, Thomas let another question in, too.

Could Torrance have survived?

A scanner pealed with a sudden bleep.

He frowned, looking at the scanner.

It registered an energy release on the planet. No. It had been multiple releases. Three.

Thomas trimmed the skimmer and put eyes on the distant ring of mountains, able to find it easily even from this distance, and, with even less effort, able to put his sight on a brightness flaring upward, streaking away from the surface. A moment later, that brightness dimmed, and Thomas could not believe what he was seeing.

Missiles.

Rockets.

Piercing Eden's thin atmosphere then looping their way into deep space.

The radio pinged then. Messages available.

"They know I'm here," he said, flipping his radio receivers on and letting the frequency scan find a source.

"This is Ambassador Torrance Black," the receiver crackled. *"I live on the planet Eden, along with a whole collection of new life forms. We are peaceful, mostly. We need help. Alpha Centauri A is going away. Without you, everyone here will die."*

The message looped.

Thomas Kitchell's brain spun.

Torrance Black was alive. And he was broadcasting from those rockets.

CHAPTER 51

Esgarat Mountains
Harshish Point

As she often did from her home here at Harshish Point, Karshi Fael watched the lights stream up into the sky. It was happening daily now. Always at this moment of the heat.

The display would start with a flash, and then the lights would raise up slowly in the distance before the wind would eventually carry a low rumbling to her perch.

She was alone here — alone with the old *neantha* beast she'd picked up along the way during the trek to this distant place, Harshish Point, where free-range quadars had once called home. It was a dead place now, holding only enough succor that she'd been able to scratch out her own existence, but not enough to support a community. The beast could still hunt some. She augmented that. And the few *katja* plants that flourished on shaded hillsides captured enough water to keep her alive.

For a while, anyway.

She'd long since stopped wondering how long that would be — for her or for the *neantha*. She'd grown to appreciate the beast's presence, but it seemed clear now that the animal would return to the desert before Karshi did. Still, she didn't know. The desert takes when the desert takes. There was nothing to be done other than to breathe, to eat, and to be one with All of Esgarat.

Today, though, after the lights had risen, and as Karshi was about to retreat into the caverns, something different happened. Another light. Arcing over the sky. Falling this time rather than rising, falling like another light she had seen so long ago.

She shielded her eyes from Eldoro's heat to see it loop down through the sky, glittering in the light as it drew nearer the surface. Nearer to the fields that had first birthed the lights that rose from Esgarat's surface.

She watched it until it disappeared over the horizon and the world went silent once again.

Chapter 52

Esgarat Mountains
North Slope

"I'm receiving something unusual," Baraq Waganat said.

Torrance turned to see Baraq bent over the receiver, fiddling with the three knobs that adjusted frequencies and cleaned up noise. The sight made him feel grounded somehow. They'd been working together for some time, and Torrance found a certain kinship with him. They were about the same age, or rather, the same stage of life. And they had a certain kindred spirit when it came to invention and development. With full training, Baraq would have made a good engineer.

They shared a certain sense of what power meant, too.

Over time, Torrance had learned more of Baraq's story.

He understood the quadar.

Now Baraq was confused by his equipment, and the sight of the quadar's long fingers twisting dials and muttering to himself made Torrance remember times in his Systems Command aboard *Everguard* doing the same thing.

The heat was still early, but it was already too hot for Torrance. A burning hot morning after a bitter cold darktime. Torrance pulled his hood to keep his face shaded, but he couldn't ignore the fact that his entire body ached now, and that he was old enough and human enough that no amount of rest would ever completely remove that pain that came from living on Esgarat. It was the same for everyone here now. But Torrance's body had not evolved to survive on Esgarat, even if the entire planet were not undergoing convulsions.

He breathed oven-hot air, then blew it out.

He wished they could use a different launch time, but his ability to deal with ballistics wasn't good enough to take gambles if he wanted a reasonable chance that these darts in space might make their way to the Solar System. The program was going well now. Almost too well. The joy of launching new rockets had faded to a basic drudgery. Most production workers didn't even come to the launch pad anymore.

More than anything, he wanted to go back into the cooler regions of the mountain community.

"What is it?" Torrance finally said.

Baraq gritted his teeth rather than reply, but Torrance could hear the answer regardless: *If I knew what it was, I would have told you.*

Instead, Baraq looked up to the sky.

Torrance put his hands on the small of his back and arched his gaze upward, too, to the place where the last three rockets had left Eden orbit, seeing their contrails still drifting.

He blinked then.

Hand shading eyes. Peering.

It was a white dot at first. Then turned into the arcing trace of a white contrail.

"Did we lose one?" he said, but that didn't make sense. A rocket that made escape velocity would not return to the planet.

The dot moved slowly across the sky, and suddenly he remembered being a kid in Wisconsin and watching airplanes with his father. His heart pounded, then.

"It's a spaceship," he said despite finding that idea hard to believe.

But he watched it.

Ignoring the heat now, Torrance kept his eyes glued to the white streak as it moved.

Falling.

Flying.

Turning on a gentle path to head toward their position.

He felt Baraq's presence beside him, silent, mouth gaping.

"It *is* a spaceship," Torrance said, suddenly hit with such intense emotions he couldn't manage them. "It's a spaceship," he said again as he put his hand on Baraq's shoulder, and felt his friend's arm around his own waist, holding him upright.

It was, indeed, a spaceship.

Chapter 53

Eden
Local Date: Unknown
Local Time: Unknown

The landing was rugged enough that at first Thomas thought he was going to plow the skimmer into the jagged edge of the mountain. He got it down, though, and as he switched off the various systems, the brown dust clouds his arrival had kicked up began to dissipate.

He unclipped and, as he prepared to exit, took a quick scan at the safety meters that indicated the atmosphere was breathable. With the external temperature reading fifty-four degrees Centigrade, he would be uncomfortable, but at least he would survive.

The air lock disengaged, the side pod irised open, and a furnace blast of stifling air confirmed that temp reading. The smell came next, a strong and bitter mix of rock dust tinged in sulfur.

He peered out, and his heart gave a clench.

Several figures stood along the mountain slopes, mostly robed against the heat and the wind.

The sight drove fear first.

They were startling, those figures. Tall and upright, standing perfectly still and wearing robes of unknown fabric that whipped in the stiff desert wind.

A stab of survival instinct made him think he should slam the door shut again and get out of the place.

Then one of the figures broke ranks and headed his way.

Its bent posture and ambling limp made its pace slow, yet still the motion felt familiar enough that Thomas swiveled his seat to watch more closely, then stepped down onto the small platform that had extended as the door opened.

In direct sun, the heat burned against his cheekbones. His boot hit the ground, and he stood taller.

"Thomas?" The voice from the shamble of a figure was thin in the closing distance, but he'd know it anywhere.

Torrance Black.

Kitchell stood, waiting because that felt like the right thing to do.

Torrance arrived to stand before him. His body was frail now. A patchwork of wrinkles covered his face, and growths of blackness dotted his cheek — growths Thomas knew were bad news. But Torrance's eyes were piercing, and the skin that wrapped around his suddenly smiling lips reminded Thomas of late hours in the Systems Command room trying out new ideas.

"Hey, LC," Thomas said, a loopy grin crossing his lips.

Torrance broke then.

His eyes suddenly glistened, and he stepped closer, wrapping Thomas in a hug that might never end.

"My boy," Torrance finally said, his head leaning hard against Kitchell's shoulder. "My boy."

When the hug had, indeed, finished, Torrance peered up at Kitchell.

The kid was older now. He'd put on weight and, perhaps because Torrance's time on the planet had been filled with gaunt creatures with equally gaunt faces, Kitchell's cheeks seemed fleshy to the point of being bloated.

"Am I dreaming?" Torrance said.

The hood of his robe flopped over his eyes, and, leaving one hand clamped around Kitchell's biceps, he lifted the hood with the other.

"Not at all, LC. I'm right here."

"How?" he said.

"It's a very long story, LC," Kitchell replied.

"Tell me everything."

"Of course. That's why I'm here. Part of it, anyway."

Torrance patted the kid on the bicep. His strength faded in the heat. The muscles of his legs and back ached.

"I'm too old to stand out here much longer. Let's get inside, and you can tell me everything. There are some quadars I want you to meet."

<h1 style="text-align:center">CHAPTER 54</h1>

Esgarat Mountains
North Slope

"This is incredible," Kitchell said as Torrance walked him up the mountain and toward the flat plateau where the quadars were standing — equally astounded to see Kitchell as Kitchell was to see them. "I can't believe what I'm seeing, and I have no idea what to say."

"Well, whatever it is, I'll have to translate," Torrance replied.

"Oh, really?" Kitchell joked.

Torrance laughed.

When they arrived back at the platform, Torrance clicked a greeting, then made introductions.

"This is Baraq Waganat," he said, putting his hand on Baraq's shoulder, "and this is Edart Kel," motioning with the same hand.

Kitchell bowed his head, then nodded and smiled as he offered his hand. Tentatively, Baraq took Kitchell's five-fingered hand into his own of six. As Edart followed, Torrance turned to the quadars. "This is my friend Thomas Kitchell."

They clicked.

"Toe-miss," Baraq replied, pronouncing the last syllable in a strong hiss.

"How has he come so quickly?" Edart added.

Torrance couldn't help but give a wide smile.

"Always the pragmatist," he said. "Let's discuss when we get inside."

Baraq clicked affirmative.

Torrance introduced others in the team as they walked, but he could tell they became a blur to Kitchell.

"It's all right, Thomas. It was all a blur to me at first, too."

"I'll bet."

The quadars were excited, though. Confused and worried, too, but as they progressed to Louratna's compound, news of Thomas Kitchell's arrival made its way through the community, and Torrance could feel their attention grow to a buzz.

They went to the group's production facility to talk, and Torrance felt the presence of the whole quadar community slipping into the corridors outside simply to get sight of this second human being. Kitchell's arrival carried the dashing aura of bravado that came from having fallen out of the sky, like Torrance had. If they didn't know how to take Kitchell at first, Torrance could almost hear them working through their reasoning: *Torranze had welcomed Toe-miss, and Torranze was on their side.* That settled the deal. For now, anyway.

When they first arrived at the production facility, Torrance gave Kitchell a tour of the floor, explaining each station and letting the workers display their processes.

"Leave it to you to create a rocket facility on Eden," Kitchell said as they finally took places around a carved table in a quiet nook of the facility.

"All the credit goes to Edart," Torrance replied, motioning the quadar as she and Baraq joined them. It was good to get off his feet, and the cool air of the mountain chasm combined with the chill of the carved rock he sat on to make him breathe easier.

"How did you get here?" Torrance finally said.

"Well, LC. It's complicated."

"I imagine so."

Kitchell filled him in on his story, Torrance translating as best he could — which he quickly found was impossible. How do you describe a black hole to beings that hadn't even seen stars until a few cycles ago? And the political mechanics of jump systems and intergalactic skirmishes was beyond his ability, too. The quadars understood Families and their own form of apartheid, feudalistic capitalism, but the concept of oligarchy posing as a faux corporate democracy, and a strong band of rebels making their own dash toward a separate Utopia wasn't going to land, either.

He tried, though. Despite the difficulties, Torrance didn't want to leave the quadars behind.

When Kitchell finished telling his story, Torrance didn't know whether to chuckle or cry. "You weren't kidding when you said it was complicated."

"No, I wasn't."

"Universe Three?"

"Strange, I know."

"That's going to take some getting used to."

Kitchell shrugged. "That's okay," he said. "It was all a blur to me, too."

"Touché," Torrance said. "And you stole the skimmer?"

"Sometimes you just gotta take a chance." Kitchell grinned and he suddenly looked ten years younger.

Torrance sat back, absorbing it all and feeling something that was a disquieting mix of contentment, happiness, and deep, deep anxiety.

"We need to get you back to humanity," Kitchell said, leaning in conspiratorially. "Both of us know that. If I can take you back, I know the U3 command will do the right thing."

"Humpf," Torrance replied. "Do the right thing. Good luck there."

"To their credit, I've seen their discussions. No one in U3 really wants to kill a hundred billion humans — which is a reason I can stay with them I guess — but it's the same old story. They'll do it if they have to."

"But they won't have an issue killing a separate species, right?"

"I don't know. All I can say for sure is that the problem is the same — no one in the Universe Three hierarchy knows there's life here, either. I mean, it's all hypothetical until it isn't. The only difference is that U3 seems to have the ability to make it happen in real time."

"I see," Torrance said.

Both glanced across the table from where Baraq and Edart were sitting patiently, still waiting for his translation. Torrance paused, feeling tension rise to his chest. Just how does one go about telling a person that another civilization is going to exterminate their entire world?

He glanced back to Kitchell, then again to the quadars, this time feeling a connection in the depth to Baraq's gaze. It was the same depth that had been there the first time they'd locked eyes — back in the small room in Esgarat City where the quadars had first taken Torrance to recover from his crash.

Despite himself, Torrance smiled.

How much had Baraq sacrificed for his people? How much had he sacrificed simply for Torrance?

He turned back Kitchell.

"Are you thinking what I'm thinking?"

"That depends on what you're thinking."

"How many of us will that skimmer of yours hold?"

This time, Kitchell returned the grin.

CHAPTER 55

Esgarat Mountains
North Slope

Strapped into the skimmer, Torrance took in his co-passengers.

A sense of amazement washed over him.

After all this time, he shouldn't be surprised at what the quadars could do. In fact, Louratna would be either embarrassed for him or offended by his lack of expectation by now. They'd had almost no time to put the party together — *the U3 leaders will be making decisions any time*, Kitchell had said, *and I doubt the fact that I swiped their skimmer will delay them much* — and yet they'd gotten the gist of the problem almost immediately, and then chosen the perfect set to send with him.

To Torrance's right, Baraq had been an obvious choice. Across the cabin, Ezi — the rebel leader had also been a natural candidate. She held the hand of little Pela, who sat beside her, barely constrained by the straps.

Torrance had been against Pella's inclusion at first — hoping for Crissandr, instead. Or Oast'el or Vareta. But the whelp had argued her case to be here and seemed as ready to meet these humans as either Baraq or Ezi were. Ezi was the one who convinced him. Pella was the future, she had argued. Pella represented everything that needed to be saved. Who better to be here?

The skimmer seemed so ... human ... as they sat in it, their primaries, dark pupils surrounded by purple and golden hues, their central shut now, but even so Torrance could feel the iridescent natures of them burning inside him.

The angles of the skimmer's equipment felt out of place to him now. The clean lines of its design felt almost pristine when placed against the rudimentary technologies that the quadarti had developed. He opened his eyes and let the oddity of the quadarti forms sitting in the passenger bay settle over him — the way the straps were too wide for their thin shoulders, and how obviously uncomfortable the seats were against their "alien" backplates.

Torrance closed his eyes, trying to get a grip on the fact that all this was truly happening.

Brave. All three of them.

He tried to imagine how he would have felt if an alien species had swept down to Earth when he was Pella's age. All he could do was shake his head and hope.

Kitchell had landed less than six standard hours ago, and now here he was clambering into the pilot's chair as the door irised shut.

"Everyone ready?" Kitchell asked, as he toggled the control system on.

"Mata?" Torrance asked the quadars.

"Mata," Pella said, raising her fists.

The others smiled and clicked affirmative.

Torrance stifled a chuckle. Everything was happening so fast he could hardly take it in.

"We're green for go here," he said to Kitchell.

Ten seconds later, the engines kicked in.

Despite Torranze warning her that liftoff would be loud, Ezi was still unprepared for the high-pitched roar of the engines, and the way the skimmer shuddered as Toe-miss played with the instruments.

She recoiled, covering the wide flaps of her ears.

Her uncomfortable seat gave her an angle to watch from as Toe-miss's fingers depressed keys and toggled buttons. Eventually, he pulled on a lever, and the shuttle rose off the ground, shifting first right, then left in abrupt bumps that scared her even more. The shuttle lifted farther, and things became smooth enough that she ventured a breath.

"It's all right, Ezi," Pella said from beside her, putting her fine-boned hand on Ezi's knees.

The sincerity of the whelpling's gaze made her laugh at herself.

"Thank you," Ezi clicked.

Outside, the ship's altitude and rotation gave her a panoramic view of the mountains she'd called home, then, slowly, she looked out over the foothills before finally taking in the vast desert plains.

In the far distance, columns of sand twisters rose into the heated winds as they ran toward the wastelands.

The desert takes, she thought.

She'd heard that phrase since she was a whelpling herself. She wondered if it was true now.

Or perhaps a portent.

Torranze had explained that if they did nothing, other humans would do something that would destroy All of Esgarat. He had spoken like that before, but never with such flare, and never with such urgency that made her recall Brada's speech. Torranze needed members of the community to go with him. Quadars to prove that they existed.

At first the idea annoyed her.

Of course, they existed.

How could they not?

The quadarti had been here since time before their ancestors crawled from the mountain depths. No human could say otherwise.

And yet, Torranze persisted.

She wished her pair-mate was here now, if nothing else, simply to see this. Brada would know what to think about the moment. He would know what to do. But all Ezi had this heat was her own instinct, and an undying hope that she was doing the right thing.

Vareta did not like her leaving. Not now. And Ezi understood why. The trip was dangerous. What if she did not return? Whether it took or not, the desert *was* harsh and the mountains no better. Life was hard, and it was going to get worse before it got better. If it ever got better.

She had finally gotten the free quadars working together.

Now she was taking this risk.

Her decision to join the trio had been hard until she accepted Torranze's word that such a task had to be done. If that were the case, then assigning anyone else would be an abdication of her position. *Don't ask others to do what you will not.* That was something Brada had said to her one night as they lay together, tangled in blankets. She had asked how he stayed so committed. He had run his soft fingertips over her shoulder and said those words.

When she recalled them, she knew what she had to do.

But, as the spaceship climbed into the air above All of Esgarat, as the nose tilted upward to climb into the sky and the land below grew smaller and smaller, drawing her view of everything — including even their great ring of mountains — down to a size so small she could cover them with her thumb, Ezi wondered for the first time just how true it was that the desert took.

Perhaps her quadarti lore had been wrong.

If what Torranze said was true, the world was so much bigger than she had understood. As still the skimmer rose toward the darkness above and the grounds below shrank, Ezi let herself dwell on her life and on Brada's as well, and on the lives of all quadarti.

Who were they?

Where did they fit?

What was the desert, after all?

Where did it end?

When he was younger, Baraq Waganat dreamed about what lay beyond the hazy clouds that had once covered his homeland.

He remembered that now.

Sitting in the compartment, watching Toe-miss point the spacecraft upward into the clearness of what was there now, he remembered how his hearts raced the first time he saw the Light That Fell from the Sky. He pressed his palm against his seat's armrest, and wrapped his long, but now knobby and gnarled fingers around the holds there.

Low vibrations from the skimmer entered his body.

Those vibrations made everything real.

They ran from the hard seat, through his arms, and over his shoulders. White noise. The physical manifestation of the sound of random output of the wave talkers. Without the physical nature of that noise, he could have convinced himself that this was just another dream. Without it, he might have been able to convince himself that he was simply dying, and the things he was seeing were nothing but fictions his own breath-starved brain was concocting.

That's what they said happened when you returned to the mountain. Or at least what some said. His own father believed that passing gave you visions of what was to happen, anyway.

Of course, he would say that.

Rayna Waganat was not one to dwell on the past.

For Baraq, though, the vibrations reminded him of when he was a whelpling, listening to wave talkers in the nighttime. Feeling the noise in their signals as the perfect impurities they were. The rest of the family used the devices simply as they were designed to be used, as basic machines to speak to one another. But Baraq had always loved taking one into his sleeping chambers and letting the noise filter over him. Hearing the occasional pop or a glitch that seemed to him like someone was talking to him from places far away.

He imagined they were messages from the future — something he'd never told anyone until he told Crissandr one late evening as he was listening to them with her. That had been before they were pair-mates. Before everything, really.

Her reaction was to put her hand over his and simply listen with him.

That was when he knew who she was.

The memory made him feel close to her again.

He recalled those glitches as Toe-miss steered the craft up into zones where the air was first thin, and then where the atmosphere barely caught the light, and then further to where there was no atmosphere, and where the outside turned the darkest black he'd ever seen.

The cabin grew silent then.

His body lifted from the seat and caught on the looping belts Torranze had strapped over his shoulders.

He felt odd.

"It is as if weight has left," he said.

Torranze laughed then. "I should have told you about gravity," he said. "Enjoy it." Torranze lifted his leg then and pulled off his sandal, leaving it to hang in the air, rotating with slow motion. "It's fun," he said, giving it a whirl with one finger to set it spinning.

Baraq clamped his gaze on the sandal, stunned.

He looked out the porthole and saw a star field that blazed as bright as any light he'd ever seen, and he became frozen with such a sweet, lacing exhilaration that he thought he might die right here and right now.

His eyes clouded, then. His throat grew gauzy and tight.

He'd always wondered.

He'd always hoped.

Then the light show started.

After Toe-miss guided the spacecraft out of its jump and into the place Torranze called Apogee, gravity returned.

Pella edged up on her seat to see out the window.

Land flowed past below. It was so different from All of Esgarat. So green. Green so dark and so vivid it took her breaths away.

She wondered what Anko would think of this land of green.

What would he think about these plantings? Most were free-growing, random like patches of *katja* or *havra*, but then as the skimmer drew near the encampment Torranze called Universe Three, the growing became more like the controlled lines the Banits had perfected and that she had stolen for her own planting — only much longer and much broader.

The plantings here were green, too, and lush.

More vivid than anything she'd seen before.

Everything was so ... different.

Buildings like those in Esgarat City, but also bigger and made of materials she couldn't determine.

Odd machines.

People. More humans like Torranze.

Then, in the distance, a shimmering surface that reflected light from Eldoro — or from the heat Torranze called "37 Gem," which was a name her tongue could not quite say properly — or just "the sun," which seemed an odd name to her.

"What is that?" she said, pointing to the reflecting brightness.

"A lake," Torrance replied, clicking interest. "It is a pool full of water."

A lake, she thought. *A pool full of water?*

Was that even possible?

No wonder their plantings were so large.

As the skimmer flew on, she stared at the *lake*.

The roar from the craft's engines drowned out all other senses, and as the skimmer flew further, the angle of the sun changed so that the whole thing, the *lake*, became a dark blue that reminded her of certain cave passages in the early hours of Eldoro rising.

When the craft passed the *lake*, she laid her head against a rest, feeling the word on her tongue.

What would it be like to live where water simply pooled in places, rather than in Esgarat City, or in the mountains that had been her home for the past forever?

She closed her eyes and imagined.

Torrance enjoyed watching his quadarti friends as they experienced the rumbling takeoff, the wild lights of the jump, and reentry to Apogee amid a fiery shower of sound.

A certain muscle memory helped Torrance place things together as they came back to him, but for Baraq, Ezi, and Pella, it was all so much. He wished he could be inside their heads now.

They looked alternately stunned and invigorated, constantly pointing out new things and clicking to each other.

He enjoyed that.

Calm before the storm, he thought. Calm before the storm.

"Is this your homeland?" Baraq asked.

Torrance clicked three soft times in the negative. "The people here are like me, though," he replied.

Apparently satisfied, Baraq sat back.

But Torrance knew he'd just lied. Yes, these were human beings. These people were Universe Three. Kitchell's commentary aside, he seriously doubted they were like him.

APOGEE

CHAPTER 56

Apogee: 37 Gem System
Local Date: C27/D43
Local Time: 2/04:30

Deidra Francis called the emergency session late that afternoon.

There was no reason to wait, Deidra decided. With Kitchell jumping, Allie's new revelation that she could manage the process of changing over a Star Drive connection, and Keyes turning up the heat, things had gone to shit.

And that didn't take into account that she'd decided to receive Marisa Harthing on her own, which was news she wanted to present before it slipped out and gave Keyes even that much more ammunition.

Better to address it all now.

Deego Larsi, Martin Scalese, Timmon Keyes, and Kazima Yamada — the whole crew had filtered in by the time Deidra arrived.

The room felt warm to the point of stagnation, and the closed roof gave the whole environment a claustrophobic sensation. Even the lighting felt harsh. Allie Feder sat catatonically in her seat, her body posture creating that cone of preoccupied silence around her that she got when she was focused. Deidra understood Kitchell hadn't talked to her before stealing the jumper. That had to bother her.

Among all the bluster that was getting ready to fall out, it was Allie's work that might well change everything. Deidra hoped Allie understood exactly how important that was.

Deidra took it all in as she strode intently into the room.

She wore dark pants and a white collared shirt under a green jacket that carried a U3 patch on one shoulder.

"Good afternoon," she said as she came to her place at the table and stood resting both hands on the back of her chair.

Staff members grew silent.

"I have several things I want to discuss tonight," she said. "The first is that I want everyone to know that early yesterday morning, I hosted a secret meeting with Marisa Harthing, a captain in United Government Interstellar Command. We held that meeting in my office here on Apogee. The captain has since returned to her home in the Solar System."

"Are you serious?" Kazima Yamada said.

"That's unacceptable," Timmon Keyes added, pounding the table. His cheeks suddenly flooded with a blood rush.

The rest of the staff sat in various states of stunned silence. They'd heard news of Kitchell's thievery and expected that was the primary topic of the session. They would need a moment to gear up to something like this.

"Our intelligence operations indicated she had expressed interest in working with us," Deidra said. "She has a connection to Thomas Kitchell, and as a condition she wanted to confirm Kitchell was alive and well. When Martin confirmed he could manage that transportation without risk, I decided it was the right thing to do. So, I invited her here."

"You can't bring an active member of the United Government into our home system and expect anyone to be happy with it," Keyes said.

"It's like painting a big WE ARE HERE sign on ourselves," Yamada said. "I can't believe you didn't tell us."

"I designed the operation," Martin Scalese said, interrupting to support the director. "I can vouch for our security processes. The operation was flawless. We've moved people like that before. There was no trail left behind, and given the window of opportunity, I can also confirm there wasn't time to inform the staff."

"Thank you, Martin, but that isn't necessary," Deidra said, looking directly at him before turning back to the staff. "Opportunities to work with such a high-end asset don't happen often, and I thought this was a risk I needed to take. The only real question left was whether I would let her return to the Solar System."

Keyes crossed his arms over his chest and leaned back. "Which, of course, you did."

"I did."

"Surely even you see that was a mistake, right? The addition of a high-level operative is not tempting enough to risk full exposure of our home."

"Marisa Harthing has intimate knowledge of UG's Star Drive navigation practices and is also in the process of transitioning into the UG intelligence structure. If she sticks to her word, she'll give us valuable information. But she is more than a high-level operative."

The statement hung in the room.

Allie Feder was the one who finally responded. "She was Torrance Black's partner, wasn't she? She was on *Everguard*? That's why she needed to see Thomas."

"Yes," Deidra replied. "The captain has connections to both Kitchell and Black. It also turns out that recent events surrounding Ambassador Black have also given Marisa Harthing cause to be disenchanted with her employer."

Keyes's gaze was carnivorous now. His passion was rising.

"Of course, now the fact that Thomas Kitchell has jumped into Allie's little skimmer and run off back to the Solar System changes things, doesn't it?"

This was his opening. Or at least he thought it was his opening. He wasn't aware of where Kitchell really was, and he was going all in. This was Deidra's chance to at least defang Keyes a bit.

"I've seen the enemy working up close, you know?" Keyes continued. "I understand things about the United Government that you apparently don't."

"When you are a hammer, everything looks like a nail," Deidra said, stepping around the room in the direction opposite of Keyes's seat. She moved slowly, using the time to feel out the room, lightly touching the back of each chair as she went.

"What is that supposed to mean?"

She stopped in a location directly across the room from her usual seat.

"It means that not everything is how you see it, Timmon. I know you're unhappy with things today. I know you've floated the idea of taking a vote of confidence on my behavior — which I'm guessing you're preparing to present tonight. But this case is not a nail, and you are not the hammer to deal with it. Nothing here is as you see it."

The idiot laughed. "Since you bring it up," he said, turning to the room and winding up for his proposal.

Deidra cut him off. "Thomas Kitchell is not ratting anyone out, Timmon. He did not run to the Solar System. He went to Alpha Centauri A."

His expression morphed to confusion. "Alpha Centauri A?"

"You don't know anything about him, do you?" Allie Feder said.

"I know enough."

"Apparently not."

Deidra broke in. "There are other things you don't know yet, Timmon." She waited the right amount of time for the staff to recognize Keyes was on the defensive. "Among those things are that Captain Harthing brought us news that hadn't filtered through our networks yet."

"I don't know if we can handle much more *news*," Keyes said.

Deidra ignored him. She hoped he'd back down when painted into that corner, but his stubbornness in the face of defeat meant it was unlikely he could stay on the council.

She proceeded. "Captain Harthing relayed information that the Solar System has received a message from Torrance Black."

"A message?" Yamada said.

"Yes," Deidra said. "From the man who was on *Icarus* when it was lost."

Even Keyes seemed taken aback.

"As Allie said, Marisa Harthing was his partner for much of their lives. The two have daughters. So, you can see why a message from Torrance Black might change the game."

"You're going to use her?" Yamada said.

"I have ideas," Deidra responded, her gaze directly on Keyes. "But after speaking with her, I expect the relationship could go two ways."

"What does she want from us?" Yamada asked.

"Help," Deidra said.

The room rustled for a moment.

"How real is this?" Keyes said. "Can we hear the message?"

The director smiled. "I thought you would never ask."

She nodded to Scalese, and he toggled the system.

The gravelly sound of Torrance Black's voice filled the air.

"This is Ambassador Torrance Black, Captain, Interstellar Command. Icarus *is dead..."*

A moment later, the group sat in silence as they absorbed it.

The captain's expression twisted, then settled. "Have we confirmed the message was really from *Icarus*?"

"Martin?" Deidra deflected.

Scalese, elbows on the table, spoke in controlled tones. "We ran a copy of the message through analyzers. Subdimensional signatures match profiles of shuttles on *Icarus*, and the date stamps on the meta footers are convincing. The forms were more than four years old, but four years of vacuum don't dissociate the signal too far. The profiles were still strong."

"And all that gibberish means?"

"The chances of it not being from an *Icarus* shuttle are exceedingly small."

Yamada spoke up. "Could it have been spoofed?"

Scalese responded. "Nothing is impossible, but a scan over the spectrum shows everything is cohesive, and the fractal structure shows no signs of splicing or raw editing. Not even traces of sound engineering. If it's a forgery, it's better than about anything I've ever come across."

"I suppose Harthing is also convinced the message is real?" Keyes said.

"She said she would know the voice," Deidra said. She had completed looping around the room as the others were speaking, and she took her seat. "Captain Harthing reported that UG officials are already spreading stories that we created the message. Obviously, we didn't do that. We've confirmed her information, though, so I'd say the fact that the Uglies are fishing with fake bait says they think the message is authentic."

"Yeah," Yamada added. "Someone is trying to cover their asses." The engineer fidgeted, then glanced toward Keyes. Couple or not, she was coming around. "The timing is odd, too," Yamada continued. "Why would UG create a fake message now?"

Deidra cleared her throat. "That's something I keep asking myself. What advantage would anyone in the United Government have to create that message?"

"I suppose it could be a fringe group trying to cause problems," Yamada replied, clearly thinking through things now.

"Or an individual in the UG structure trying to create an incident," Deego Larsi added.

Yamada responded. "If it were independent rebels, why would they pick Torrance Black? And how would they even know Black had been on *Icarus*?"

"All right," Keyes said, unable to hold back any longer. "Torrance Black sent a message. So what? What do you want us to do, Deidra? Why do we care? The important thing here is that you let a UG agent into our city, and now her close friend has skipped out with one of our most important assets. What are we going to do about that?"

"That's the best question you've asked all day, Timmon," Deidra replied, bringing the room to a halt. "It's another question I've been thinking about ever since Captain Harthing left Apogee. What do we want to do?"

She leaned forward and clasped her hands together before her.

"This becomes especially important because there's one more piece of information I need to put before you."

"What now?" Keyes said. "Are we planning to host the new supreme president?"

"That's enough, Timmon."

"I'm not sure it is."

"I've given you leeway so far, and your voice is an important one. You can have your vote soon," Deidra said. "But as of right now, I am the director of Universe Three. If you cannot comport yourself appropriately, I *will* have you removed."

The captain sat frozen in place. He finally seemed to understand that his position had eroded during this conversation. His gaze flitted around the room, and his chest rose with a big breath that he released slowly.

"That won't be necessary, Director. You are right. I apologize."

He sat back, waiting.

"Thank you," Deidra said, not certain what it meant that Yamada remained silent. "As I was saying, however, we have one more piece of news to discuss before we begin setting any new course of action."

She turned to Allie Feder.

"You're up, professor."

Nervously, Allie stood up.

"I'm not sure I can follow that, but I'll try," she said, eliciting laugher that helped clear the air.

She then proceeded to explain her breakthrough.

That she could do it all now.

She could create gates anywhere, shut off and reconnect Star Drive engines from source to source. She still needed to test it on a skimmer to be sure she got the physical parameters right, but the full plan could go on now without problem.

"I'm almost certain we can change *Defender*'s source, and then shut down Alpha Centauri A to system-lock the UG," she said.

"That's it, then," Yamada said. "If that's true, it solves everything. And once Alpha Centauri A is disconnected, we could jump there to run forensics on the *Icarus* mission without having to worry about any ambush."

Deidra smiled. She loved it when her team came to the right conclusion on their own.

An audible tone came to the communications system built into the seat beside Martin Scalese. That tone, combined with the obvious importance of the session, meant the call was highest priority.

All eyes turned to him as he toggled his personal feed.

"Martin," Deidra said as the communications director took in the missive. The man's expression was hard to read. "What's happening?"

"Thomas Kitchell," Scalese said.

"He's returned?" Deidra was almost embarrassed at the hope she felt on the question. *Please,* she thought, *let this be that he's returned.*

"Yes," Scalese replied. "And he's got friends."

Chapter 57

Apogee: 37 Gem System
Local Date: C27/D43
Local Time: 2/04:55

A squad of Universe Three guards surrounded Torrance, Kitchell, and the quadars as they emerged from the skimmer.

"What the hell is that?" one of the guards said, leveling a weapon at Ezi first, then moving it to Baraq, then finally Pella.

"Calm down, Theo," the commander of the squad said as she stepped forward, plasma gun also drawn. She eyed the quadars, then glanced to Kitchell. "What gives?"

"They're quadars," Kitchell said. "They live on a planet in the Alpha Centauri A system. They're unarmed, as are we. No one is here to get hurt."

The commander gave them all another glance, then relaxed a notch. "You'll need to come with us," she said, using her weapon to be clear she wasn't going to take anything for granted. While their guns were of technology beyond anything the Tegra Family could have concocted, all three quadars seemed to get the idea.

"Where are we going?" Kitchell said.

"Leadership center," she snapped. "The staff is meeting there now."

Kitchell gave what could have been a sly grin, glancing at Torrance. "Probably deciding who gets to draw and quarter me."

"I suppose they do that to skimmer wranglers, don't they?" Torrance replied. He took in the quadars. "How far will it be?"

He was tired, and the air — while blissfully cool — was thicker than he was prepared for. Baraq, Ezi, and Pella were unprepared for this kind of humidity. Baraq, in particular, was already breathing heavily. His six fingers clutched his robe against his chest.

"A ways," Kitchell said, catching on. He turned to the guard. "Any chance we can catch a ride? Our guests might have difficulty with that kind of exertion here."

The guard assessed the situation.

"Get a hover cart here now," she said to a subordinate.

They waited.

"What is happening, Torranze?" Ezi said.

"We are going to be taken to a gathering of this group's leadership," Torrance replied in their shared qualish, drawing interest, if not action, from the guards. "They are bringing a vehicle. When it comes, follow me."

A moment later, a large hover cart arrived.

Torrance lifted his robes to keep from tripping over them as he entered the vehicle first. Baraq, then Pella, and Ezi followed. Kitchell entered last, escorted by two guards and the commander.

The cart jolted forward, engine whining.

"Are you all right, LC?" Kitchell asked, holding his arm out to Torrance.

"I'm fine," he said — though he wasn't certain. His legs burned, and his back hurt, too. Just this little exertion left him panting in the thick air. "Take care of the quadars."

Baraq was still struggling, but the other two seemed more able to deal with whatever distress the planet was putting on their bodies. Their demeanors were more worried than fatigued.

The hover cart, open to the air, moved through the city, passing buildings and people and areas of open construction. In the distance to their left, a line of mountains rose — green, unlike the harsher lands of Esgarat, and smaller, with peaks rounded and hill-like rather than jagged and angular like the lands that had birthed the quadars.

Movement of the hover cart created a cooling breeze.

Torrance was intrigued with the progress Universe Three had made here, but took more interest in watching the quadars—and specifically Pella—as they took in this new culture. He had tried to brief them on the way here, but time had been short, and the expressions on their faces now was proof that hearing about something like this was dramatically different from experiencing it.

Their eye were filled with a mix of awe and fear that Torrance didn't know how to deal with.

They were going to experience so much now.

The overload could be intense.

"What's going to happen now, Thomas?" Torrance said as the hover cart moved through the city.

As an ambassador, he had walked into uncertain rooms before. He wanted to center himself.

Kitchell raised an eyebrow. "Hard to predict. There are at least two strong camps at play here — one that wants to drop the black hole on the Solar System and be done with it, and one that doesn't. But there are schisms in each."

Torrance pressed his chapped lips together. "Factions among factions."

"Yes."

"I suppose your little jaunt isn't going to help anything."

Kitchell shrugged, then smiled and ran a sheepish hand through his hair. "It made sense at the time."

Torrance couldn't argue against that. However, he thought he could read the future well enough. Given the room would already be unsettled, inserting a trio of quadars — especially a trio of quadars who were growing more anxious as time progressed — was the definition of unpredictable.

Maybe ten minutes later, they arrived at the leadership center.

The four-story off-white building was larger than any they'd passed so far. It was made of what looked like local brick, with a series of wide windows and segments of walls designed to accordion open.

"Let's go," said the commander of the guards.

Kitchell exited first, then helped the rest.

The entrance was a double door.

Their footsteps echoed on the stonework floor, and then again as they climbed a wide stairway up to the third floor.

Through his labor, Torrance watched the quadars.

Ezi held a protective arm over Pella's shoulders, and the young whelp's eyes were less defiant than they'd been on Esgarat. Ezi appeared pensive and uncertain now. Only Baraq — while laboring — seemed something close to unfazed as they walked.

He, too, lifted his robes as he walked.

His gaze went left and right, his central cracking open and closed in various patterns.

"It's a lot to take in," Torrance said as they climbed.

Baraq clicked the affirmative.

They came to another guard and another set of double doors, smooth and broad, made of a local wood polished to a soft, almost golden glow. The frames bowed gently away from them, suggesting a rounded room inside.

With a nod from the commander, the guard stepped aside.

"Are you ready, LC?" Kitchell asked.

Torrance braced himself.

On the opposite side of those doors were the leadership of Universe Three, a body Torrance had fought against his entire life.

The idea would have startled him at one point.

Now Torrance simply wished he'd had time to clean up.

He pulled his dingy robes tighter and stood taller as the doorway opened.

"Let's do it."

Chapter 58

Apogee: 37 Gem System
Local Date: C27/D43
Local Time: 2/05:10

Kitchell stepped into the assembly room first, followed by Ezi, Pella, and Baraq, then, finally, Torrance.

Expectant faces and curious gazes met his, then slid back to the quadars. He watched the humans take them in, absorbing the oddity of their bodies and the sharp essence of their odors. From their positions around the table, Torrance saw them each shuffling in their seats, some giving audible exhalations of breath, others simply stunned. Word had surely come of the quadars' existence, but their arrival was still startling.

Torrance, Kitchell, and the three quadars filed into a row of seats along the wall opposite the director's station.

Torrance recognized Deidra Francis from holos of years past. She was older now, but her face held the classic cut of Francis sharpness, and her eyes were searing when her gaze landed on his. He could see her father in her.

"Welcome back, Thomas," said Deidra Francis. "Who have you brought us?"

"Let me introduce you to United Government Science Ambassador Torrance Black," Kitchell replied, motioning to Torrance, who stood.

"Ambassador Black," Francis said.

"Simply Torrance will do, Director." Torrance tried to stand taller, but glanced down at his mountain-worn garments, and saw the gnarled nature of his hands. "I'm sorry for my shoddy appearance before this gathering. I feel out of place. Especially after Thomas's grandiose use of my title."

"It's not a problem at all, Torrance," the director responded. "And your friends?"

"What are they saying?" Baraq asked.

"Be calm," Torrance replied, turning to the three quadars to explain what was happening. His use of their language — or what passed for it over human tongues — seemed to surprise the Universe Three staff. He'd almost forgotten how foreign its multitonal, almost jazzlike sound might be.

He had explained what he expected to happen while they were jumping, and at that time, each of the three understood they would be on display.

Torrance felt for them now, though.

They stood before these humans as exposed as anyone had ever been.

And he'd seen what human leadership was capable of. If it weren't for Kitchell's reassurances, he'd be terrified of what Universe Three might do to him now, better yet an alien species.

"I ask you to trust me," Torrance said.

He turned back to the collective.

"These are quadars," he said.

Speaking in his own language felt strange, and he was surprised to have to concentrate harder to avoid using the qualish he'd begun to think in.

"They are an intelligent, sentient species who live on a planet we know as Eden. There are thousands more there now." He put his hand on Baraq's shoulder. "This is Baraq Waganat. He is — among other things — an engineer and an inventor." He stepped down one spot. "Ezi Waganat leads a group of quadars trying to scrape out an existence in a rugged set of mountains as the land around them is dying. She is also what we would know as Baraq's daughter-in-law. Her pair-mate was killed by violence among quadarti Families."

Torrance put his hand over Pella's thin shoulder.

"And this is Pella, who has no other name. She is child still, a survivor with bright, beating hearts that will carry the future of her people. If you will help her."

"I see," the director said. "I assume you vouch for their behavior?"

"I've lived with them for a long time. They are my friends."

"Then please welcome them for us."

"I'd be careful about that," said a member of the staff, a woman sitting behind Francis. "We don't know anything about them. They could be contagious."

"Or armed," a man, sitting beside the woman, said.

Torrance stepped forward, filled with a sense of anger that grew as he spoke.

"As I've already said, I've lived among them for years. I promise you these quadars cannot hurt anything here."

"Perhaps, but you also just said they carry out war—"

"The quadars are a growing species," Torrance said. "Their society is complex. And, yes, there *is* war on their planet. Like us they are capable of destructive things. But I can guarantee you that these three pose no threat. And I should point out that the stresses we've put on their ecosystem have — at least in part — created the war this species is now suffering."

"Torrance is right," Kitchell said. "I've seen their technology. He has helped kickstart them, but these ... quadars ... don't have anything we need to be afraid of. And he's right to say we've destroyed their ecosystem, too. I've seen with my own eyes that the clouds that once covered the entire surface have died away."

"All right," Deidra Francis said. "I will take it as given for now that the quadars are not going to cause us harm."

"Good," Torrance said.

"So you see why your plans can't go on as you've been considering," Kitchell said. "If we destroy Alpha Centauri A, this whole population will die."

"Our other option is to destroy the Solar System," one of Deidra's staff spoke up.

Kitchell braced himself to speak, but Torrance motioned to him.

"This is mine, Thomas," he said in a soft voice.

As soon as he said it, he knew it was true. If he were a religious man, he'd say it was why he'd been born in the first place — but Torrance was not a religious man. Regardless, as he stood in front of the Universe Three leadership, he felt something bigger grow within him. God, random chance, or anything between, this was his purpose.

Kitchell let him go.

"Thomas has made me aware of your plans," Torrance said. "If everything goes well according to that plan, you'll finish the job I started years ago, and you'll kill Alpha Centauri A. I understand the reasoning behind that plan, too. Break Alpha Centauri A, and the United Government can't hurt you. But if you do that, the planet these three quadars are from will die — taking with it every member of their species and every other species who still survives there. I have spent a large part of my life trying to get human beings in the Solar System to see there could be life on that planet, and now these three — Baraq, Ezi, and little Pella — have come here to stand before you to show you that this story is true. I'm begging you not to do what you are planning to do. I'm telling you that you'll regret that decision."

"We have no choice," another member of the staff said. "If we don't shut down Alpha Centauri A, the United Government will still have jump capability."

"There's always a choice," Torrance replied.

"Says the man who wore UG stripes."

"I've not worn UG stripes for a very, very long time, young man," Torrance replied. The muscles between his shoulders ached now, as did his legs and back. He leaned forward against the back of an empty chair to stabilize himself. "If you had lived my life, you would know why I'll never wear stripes of any kind ever again. To be honest, given this conversation, I ponder whether any of you wear actual Universe Three stripes now."

"What do you mean by that?" Francis said.

The corners of Torrance's lips curled to a dry smile.

A distant look came across his gaze, then he looked directly at the director.

"I did not know your father," he said. "But I was there when he was killed. Or at least I was in the mix. I played my part, though to be fair I didn't know what was happening until it was too late. So, while it's true I didn't *know* Casmir Francis, I did learn about him, and I watched him. I've had time to look back on that time. I know he understood the risk he was taking. He was noble in his approach that day. My United Government was not particularly trustworthy, right? And yet he envisioned a universe that was big enough for all of us, and since he envisioned that world, he agreed to meet UG officials, and he stepped forward to shake the hand of a UG ambassador — which is the very action that got him killed."

"What are you saying, Ambassador?" Deidra Francis's voice had grown colder and quieter.

He'd gotten to her. Torrance saw it.

"Just Torrance, please."

"All right, what are you saying, Torrance?"

He smiled again.

"My philosophy is a bit rusty after years away, so my apologies if I get it wrong. But I believe your Universe Three doctrine calls for three spheres."

"Solar System, Galaxy, Universe," Francis said.

"Yes, that sounds like what I remember."

Torrance cleared his throat with a soft cough.

"Your father died because he wanted to bring the galaxy together. Or at least make it safer. It makes me wonder what he would do if faced with the quadars. Would he kill them all, simply to break the United Government?"

Francis pressed her lips together.

"I admit that, at the time, I did not agree with your father on much at all," Torrance said. "But there was a part of him I admire now. That part of him makes me wonder if my disagreement was simply because I did not understand what your Universe Three stood for, or if maybe I've just grown old.

"I don't know."

He shrugged.

"Perhaps it's the heat.

"But I *can* tell you that if you had spent the years I've spent on Eden with these quadars, you'd have a better idea of what this all means. They deserve a chance. A real chance. And there is every chance that humanity has already corrupted Esgarat — Eden — to the point it won't support life at all. I can't tell. But if that is true, we owe them our best efforts.

"There has to be a better way to solve your problems than to simply sacrifice my three friends and their entire civilization.

"If you had spent the years I've spent with this amazing species, you would know what I mean when I say there is always a choice."

The room was silent, and even the quadars seemed to be on edge.

The voice came firmly and clear from across the room.

"He's right, Director. There is another answer."

It was a woman, Torrance saw. Lithe, with red-bronze hair.

"What's that, Allie?" Director Francis said.

"There's another answer," the woman repeated. "Or at least there's something else to consider."

The room seemed to come to a halt then. Eyes turned completely toward the woman, and for an instant she glanced toward Torrance, and then the quadars.

Chapter 59

Apogee: 37 Gem System
Local Date: C27/D43
Local Time: 2/05:10

Allie Feder had grown familiar enough with attention by now that she did not wilt. There was that, at least.

She felt the pressure of everyone's eyes. She felt the presence of Thomas, who had indeed stolen her jump skimmer to find his friend.

After listening to the arguments and understanding the situation, after seeing the three quadars standing so boldly outside the ring of these Universe Three leaders, seeing them watch these leaders decide their fates, Allie knew what she should propose.

But when Torrance Black stood up and called them out on their beliefs, and when she stared into the eyes of the youngest of the quadars — Pella, Torrance had called her — she felt the connection there. Allie saw Pella's story in her posture and in her gaze of petrified defiance and realized the little quadar was alone in this world, just like Allie was alone in her own existence.

That was when she knew she was going to do it.

She stood firmly now.

Calmly.

"I can make the gate flow either way," Allie explained.

Thomas was first to catch the ramifications.

Of course he was.

"You're saying that we could replace the flow in Alpha Centauri A — essentially refill the star?"

"That's what I'm saying," Allie replied. "The system I've developed is flexible within our own universe. We could put a gate in another star, then set the flow gates to feed Alpha Centauri A — which would ensure it does not go dry. That would then modulate life there."

Thomas boggled for a moment.

"That's ... astonishing."

The admiration on Thomas's voice sent a bolt of electricity through her. Maybe he was beginning to understand the true power of the field she worked in.

"It wouldn't reverse anything completely," Allie said. "Entropy is entropy, and all the king's horses couldn't put Humpty Dumpty together again," she said, recalling a phrase her physics instructor had used when she was in school. "But it would at least stop the damage and give these people a chance to rebuild something."

"That would be amazing," Torrance said.

Kazima Yamada added, "Arguably, we could even regulate it so that the climate could be improved."

"One step at a time," Allie responded. "But yes."

Deego Larsi cleared his throat in that way that said he wanted the floor.

"Deego?" Deidra said.

"I hate to throw rain onto the idea now but doing that still leaves us with the original problem. If we don't shut down Alpha Centauri A, does that mean we drop the full force of the black hole onto the Solar System?"

"It does," Martin Scalese said with an audible sigh of frustration. "I can't see another way."

Chapter 60

Apogee: 37 Gem System
Local Date: C27/D43
Local Time: 2/05:15

As the dynamic shifted, Deidra Francis felt the room around her. She could almost taste the tension that had built from the moment she'd strode so forcefully into the assembly.

Keyes. Black. Yamada. Kitchell.

She still couldn't believe the presence of three alien creatures here in her center.

The idea stunned her.

For a moment she felt the presence of her father beside her, and then another essence, bold and pure, a sensation of freedom — a thrilling of something that might have been justice. An image of Ellyn Parker came over her — a holo she'd seen of the rebel leader, dancing at a party when she was very young.

Her gaze fell on Torrance Black then.

His body was bent. His skin creased and his face marred with cancers. Yet he stood with that air of nobility that came from living an honest life. Torrance Black had made her look in the mirror, had brought her back to her father, and in doing so had used a directness she hadn't had the courage to hold on to herself. She remembered the day her father died, stripping away the hurt and the anger that had always cloaked it.

Torrance Black was a good man.

He was right to say her father had walked onto a United Government ship because it was a chance for the universe to live in peace — for his people in U3 to live without fear.

She felt her father then.

Remembered his trials — thought back on the disease he'd carried, the last vestiges of cystic fibrosis that would set him back for weeks at a time.

The United Government had killed her father that day, but he'd been right to try.

And this time, Allie Feder had given *her* the leverage she needed to do the right thing.

Deidra Francis, director of Universe Three, now overcome with a sense of rightness that made the skin on her forearms sizzle, felt suddenly strong. She took in the room — wanting to remember this moment forever.

"I can think of another way," she said.

Conversation halted. Everyone turned to her.

"It's messy," Deidra said. "But I think it will work."

She turned to Martin Scalese.

"I want to talk to Supreme President Jihansen."

END GAME

CHAPTER 61

Alexandria, Virginia
Local Date: December 16, 2256
Local Time: 0115

The deputy director had not been wrong in her assessment of Marisa's capabilities when it came to the field of intelligence. Marisa understood that from the moment she started working for Zina Nichols.

Marisa was never going to be a great analyst. She wasn't blind to the fact that she'd also never be one who made certain decisions — nor even one who deeply influenced them. Not within the chain of command, anyway. She could think of other options, though. Other ways to make that kind of a difference. And from even her first day under Nichols's control, Marisa felt those other options lying silently in wait for her.

Sitting in her new apartment, Marisa felt a cold slice run down her spine as she considered her next move.

Zina Nichols had threatened her daughters.

And for the longest time Marisa had played Nichols's game.

Now, that same Zina Nichols wanted to meet with Ragnath Gavarian. And also now, Marisa had this new summons from Universe Three's leadership: Find a way to contact the supreme president — something she wasn't yet certain of how to do, but something she knew she could most definitely get done.

Well, all right then.

She'd told Deidra Francis there would be a price for her work. It was time to see if Universe Three would pay it.

She set her new security credentials — fully aware that her boss would certainly be able to access them — and contacted Nichols's dataclip directly.

Need session now, she sent through her connection. *Second party to join.*

Then she sat back and waited.

CHAPTER 62

Galopar
Local Date: Undefined
Local Time: Undefined

The modified Z-pad sat down in an open field covered by a patch of springlike grasses of green and gold. The engines disengaged, and the doorway opened. Deidra Francis stepped out, followed by Captain Timmon Keyes. A breeze redolent with a wild array of flavors picked at her hair.

She hoped it was a good sign.

They were on Galopar — the once secret outpost used by the United Government as a staging area for the surprise attack on Atropos back when Universe Three thought that had been a safe haven. She wasn't sure how to feel about the place. It wasn't the planet's fault that the Uglies had used it. Still, the aura of deceit lay heavy on the meadow of knee-high grass.

Galopar worked for this meeting because it was neutral ground, and because it was a location where deceit from either side was more difficult than in deep space.

That determination of location was the last domino of what had been a complex set of negotiations over the past three days of high-intensity, high-security conversations. Per their agreement, Supreme President Jihansen would land a distance away — a place of their own choosing just as Universe Three had chosen Deidra and Keyes's landing position. Both sides would monitor the zone where the session would happen.

One meeting.

One conversation.

Deidra's stomach roiled. Was this how her father felt in his last moments?

"Pretty place," Keyes said as he descended the ramp to come to her side.

"Yes, it is pretty. How much time do we have?"

"Fifteen minutes," Keyes replied. "Scans are clear."

"Then let's get going."

The two set off toward the agreed coordinates, a pair of armed guards trailing.

When she'd realized she couldn't go this one alone, Timmon Keyes was the obvious choice of escort. Deidra understood he would be the loudest voice against this meeting. To include him changed that dynamic.

It had also served to instill a change in Keyes himself.

She glanced at him as they trudged through the meadow, their boots whipping against the rough grasses. He had been professional about everything in the lead-up. If this succeeded, she had a place ready for him.

A few minutes later, they entered a tangle of dark woods and, after picking their way even further, came to a clearing.

Across the way, on the opposite side of a thin brook that split the ground between them, stood the supreme president of the United Government, flanked by his allotted pair of armed guards. He wore a light blue, long-sleeved business shirt that billowed at the wrist, his hair dark and pulled back, the corner of each eye marked with crow's feet.

A dark-clad agent stood beside him, Jihansen's version of Timmon Keyes.

Deidra checked upstream and down.

Her dataclip's scanners showed no other security. Martin Scalese's voice in her ear confirmed.

She fought a sudden pang of anxiety.

Perhaps something *could* come of this.

She stepped closer to the waterline, feeling tension in Captain Keyes's posture as he stepped beside her. Seeing her action, the supreme president made similar movement, stopping at a narrow part of the stream so they were barely an arm's length apart. The water gurgled with a sound pure and clear, smoothing over rocks below the surface. She was certain that if she were to scoop a handful, the current would be cool and taste sweet.

"Supreme President Jihansen," Deidra said, taking in the taller man.

"Director Francis," he replied. "You wanted to speak."

Keyes clenched his jaw, sending a direct message about his preferred approach to dealing with United Government executives, but he said nothing.

A moment of expectation crawled over Deidra's skin. Now or never.

"I have a proposal."

"This should be interesting."

"I suppose I should have expected condescension, but I would appreciate your full attention on the matter at hand."

"I apologize, Director. Please, let me hear your proposal."

The corner of her lips twitched upward for just an instant.

"I propose the United Government decommission every Star Drive spacecraft in your fleet, then turn them over to us. In return, I promise you that Universe Three will not destroy your system, and that your people — as well as mine — can live in peace."

His laughter was more expected than the condescension that had preceded it.

"That's quite a proposal, Deidra."

"I'm glad you think so, Ils."

The sound of the brook burbling rose in the space between their silence. A cool breeze picked up. Deidra kept her gaze focused on Jihansen's, her eyes direct, her jaw firm but not bold. After a moment, the set of his expression cracked.

"You're serious."

She looked at the dark-clad agent beside him. "Your intelligence office has certainly informed you that we ran an operation on your sun a while back."

"It didn't succeed."

She let her expression — a slight turn of the head and a thin smile that carried a hint of satisfaction — lead him to the next part of the conversation.

"But that's been fixed?" Jihansen said.

"The process is instantaneous now. Only a few days from my command to a fully drained star."

"I see," Jihansen said. "That's worrisome."

"You are a master of the understatement."

"Why should I believe you?"

"I don't know, Ils. Maybe you shouldn't. That's for you to decide. But I want to be as clear as I can be because I'm only going to say this one time: I don't believe that either of us are butchers at heart, but we would both do whatever we need to do if it meant protecting our people. You know we connected something into the sun. I'm here to tell you it's a black hole, and I'm here to tell you explicitly and without reservation that we now know how to turn it on full blast."

Jihansen took a breath of the open air.

His agent beside him seemed to grow even stiffer than he'd been before.

Jihansen didn't know what to do now, Deidra realized. He had been unprepared for this kind of revelation — a realization that set her opinion of him back a notch. She'd prepared herself for a series of different responses. Total surprise was not one of them.

"I could have you arrested right now, you know," he replied.

"You could. Maybe it would work. But I've learned my father's lesson, Ils," she said, admittedly taking too much personal pleasure in the use of his first name now. "If Captain Keyes and I don't return to our home base on schedule, the process will be enacted."

Jihansen's chest rose in a silent sigh, and his head drooped infinitesimally between his shoulders.

"I didn't come here to bargain, Ils," she continued. "I came here to confirm that there's a black hole attached to your sun. That we put it there, and that with the push of a button, we can now turn that connection on full blast."

A pained expression filled Jihansen's face, and she watched as calculations registered behind his gaze.

"And I came here to tell you that my cohort, Captain Keyes here, is going to oversee the process of Universe Three taking control of every ship in your fleet, and that Captain Keyes is not particularly inclined to give the United Government much in the way of wiggle room. If, during that process, he sees even a hint that the UG apparatus is going back on its commitment I will not hesitate to direct my science officers to destroy your sun."

She turned to Keyes. "Did I get it all?"

The muscles of his jaws rippled. "Yes, Director. I think you did."

Deidra turned back to Jihansen. It had grown warm now. She pushed hair from her forehead.

"That is my proposal, Supreme President."

He raised his gaze. "I'll need time to pull this off."

"You have a week."

"That's not enough."

"But it's what you have."

He nodded absently. "I see."

"And I want one more thing," Deidra said.

His look of resignation made her happier still. "What else could there be?"

Ten minutes later, after tramping back to the Z-pad, and after taking their seats for the shuttle to *Defender*, Deidra turned to Captain Keyes. He'd been remarkably silent during the return. "Did that go well?"

The corners of his lips skewed sideways. "As well as it could have."

"High praise," she said, sitting back as the pilot engaged the engines, and feeling the rumble come through her seatback.

He nodded. "Indeed."

The craft lifted off from Galopar's surface.

A moment later Keyes continued. "I'm not sure it will last."

"Maybe. But we've tried, and I think that's important."

He gave a soft hum of agreement.

"I think he'll make it stick," she said.

In that moment, she believed it. Jihansen had seen truth in her eyes. He'd agreed to both her requirements. He would find a way. Deidra sat back, feeling tension drain.

"If things can be worked out, perhaps this will even be the beginning of something bigger," she said.

She closed her eyes then and recalled the moment Torrance Black addressed the staff session. Deidra would remember the emotion in the old man's eyes when he mentioned her father.

She barely knew the man but already she had a lot to be grateful for when it came to Torrance Black. With that glance, the man had showed her a door back to who she wanted to be.

"I spent most of last night thinking about Ellyn Parker," she said.

"Perigee," Keyes replied.

"None of us had the chance to know her, but she changed everything for all of us."

"Mm-hmm."

"That's our problem today," she said, sitting forward and catching his attention. "We used to be agile because that's what rebellions are. But we're getting stodgy. Too cautious. We've been here long enough to forget how entire generations have sacrificed to get us here. When Thomas Kitchell stole that jumper, we were all so ... offended ... but last night I thought about how Gregor Anderson did the exact same thing when he stole *Defender* to save what he could of *Vengeance.*"

Deidra gave a soft laugh and a dismissive wave of a hand.

"Gregor's heroism was gaudy and audacious, but it was the right thing to do. If he hadn't been that bold, several of us wouldn't be here."

When Keyes gave a sullen nod, Deidra knew she didn't have to mention that the captain himself was one of those people.

"I spent time thinking about my father this morning, too.

"He taught me Perigee's original idea of the three spheres one day — the Solar System, the galaxy, and the universe — while we were sitting on Mars, outside a UG compound."

"I remember that story," Keyes said, flashing a sudden grin.

"That philosophy kept my father focused."

Deidra looked out the Z-pad's squared-off portal and was surprised she could already see the glint of *Defender* waiting for them.

The trip back had gone quickly.

She was looking forward to getting home. Her thoughts wandered to Matt Anderson, Gregor's boy, who had died in a mission against the UG, and to Katriana Martinez. A memory of Kel Melody came to her then, Kel Melody and Jamal, who had turned out to be the loves of her life. After they'd passed, she couldn't bring herself to be that close to anyone else ever again.

Thinking of them now felt different.

For the first time in longer than she could remember, Deidra Francis had begun to look into her own future.

"I have to apologize to you, Director," Timmon Keyes said.

"For what?"

"For being ... shortsighted."

"It's all right, Timmon."

"No, it's not."

"Yes, Captain, it is. I understand how you felt. I was on *Defender*. I gave the order to have the sun destroyed to begin with. You've served the people well. I'm glad you're coming back around."

Outside, *Defender*'s bay doors opened to receive them.

The Z-pad entered the air-lock systems, and the sound of atmosphere rushed over the smaller spacecraft.

"Thank you," he said.

CHAPTER 63

Free Space - Triton Station 12
Local Date: December 28, 2256
Local Time: 0213 (Earth Standard)

"Good morning," Captain Harthing said as Zina stepped into the skimmer and took her seat beside her.

"That remains to be seen," Zina replied, straightening the folds of her loose-fitting pants as she adjusted her position.

She didn't like traveling with companions, but it was the only way Ragnath Gavarian would accept her request for a session, so she'd agreed. Her subordinate's perkiness irked her.

The little ship smelled about as grungy as it looked, further irking her. The three hops she'd already taken to get here had been of varying quality, too, and her mood had grown fouler with each jaunt. She hadn't expected to jump first class, but she had limits and this one might well have crossed them. She'd altered identities at each step — the last including a digital cleansing so complete that she wouldn't need to hide her appearance from here on.

That part, at least, was good.

The skimmer's air lock irised closed with a mechanical whirr and then a solid *thunk*.

Harthing sat quietly, fidgeting her fingertips together in an absent way that said she was a nervous traveler. Zina stifled a scoff at that.

Some Interstellar Command asset she had here.

A moment later the pilot — a young man in a dark blue uniform sitting a short distance forward — toggled the engines. "Separation in a moment," he said. "Jump will come right after. Make sure you're properly affixed."

Zina took him in, noting the name on his uniform and the cut of his face. The man's hair was recently trimmed. The physicality of how he sat in the seat said he was eighty kilograms standard. She paid attention to the way his fingers moved across the controls, seeing how fluid they seemed, thinking about how usual or not that trait might be in the realm of spacecraft pilots, and wondering if he'd had musical or theatrical training.

She would look him up when she returned to the system.

Trace his lines.

The fact that he was here probably burned him as an agent for Gavarian, so that line would be a dead end. But she wanted to know where he had been working prior to coming to the job, wanted to know just *how* he'd come to connect with the journalist, and what he'd been doing just prior.

If she was going to enter into an agreement with Gavarian, she needed to learn everything about how he worked.

Examining the profile of the pilot's cheekbones, she wondered how he felt now that his life was being disrupted at a moment's notice. That's life in intelligence circles.

The engine rumbled through the compartment, and they were airborne.

"Are you ready?" Harthing asked.

Zina waved her hand as an agitated reply, then reviewed the conversation she had planned.

She needed a series of stories from Gavarian — one on each of her new boss's closest friends.

That would turn up the heat.

In the meantime, she would keep her finger on the pulse of numerous upheavals around the system to select the right one. She wanted the "beginning" of the scandal to start in an organic fashion

— a riot here, or an armed attack there. Her job was to tie things together. She could always find something useful happening.

When the whole thing went down, she would be there to pick up the pieces.

Again.

So, once again, she envisioned her conversations with Gavarian, tried on different entry points for size. Considered various answers he might give and the array of prices he might ask. She would pay them, of course. Whatever he asked would be worth it, and whatever he asked would be within her ability to pay once the plan cascaded down the system.

The skimmer disengaged with a resonate echo that cascaded through the fuselage.

"Prepare for jump," the pilot said.

Harthing triggered the controller that shut off the viewport.

Yes, nervous traveler.

The blank viewport was all right. Zina needed to focus.

A moment later, they were gone.

Chapter 64

Classified
Local Date: Classified
Local Time: Classified

The skimmer landed.

Marisa, calmer now, sat in her seat, watching Zina Nichols as her boss unbuckled herself in preparation for the door to open. Marisa wanted to see this.

"Are you coming?" Nichols asked, indicating Marisa's restraints. Nichols was standing now. The press of her palms down her hips was the only thing Marisa had seen to suggest her boss's anxiety.

"Yes," Marisa replied, reaching to disengage her restraints.

The door irised apart, and bright light slanted into the cabin.

"What is this?" Nichols raised a hand to shield her eyes.

She'd been told the session with Gavarian would happen in the "night" hours and in a cramped, dingy shipping bay on Ceres — a chunk of rock in the asteroid belt known for its wildcatting and its hosting of clandestine events such as Nichols had prepared for. This was most definitely not a loading bay on Ceres. The bay here echoed with activity across its expansive layout.

Nichols blinked and caught her bearings.

Lines of fighter spacecraft and autotechs ran out into the dark distance, and robotic service systems rolled across the bay floor.

The light was from a rack that lined the control room viewports — which was a short distance from where the craft had landed.

This was *Defender*, a U3 Star Drive cruiser.

"Welcome aboard, Deputy Director," a woman's voice called.

Deidra Frances stood there with a phalanx of armed guards on one side, and on the other side …

Supreme President Jihansen.

The supreme president seemed uncomfortable as he came to stand before Nichols.

The guards surrounded her.

"What is this?" Nichols said.

"I'm happy to say that you're under arrest for insubordination and treason against the United Government," Jihansen said. "You have tampered with official records and caused false accusations to be made against citizens of the Solar System — all of which carry extreme penalties."

Nichols's jaw fell. Her gaze, full of venom, swiveled to Marisa. "You?"

Marisa reveled in watching full realization cross Zina Nichols's expression.

Marisa stepped out of the shuttle and onto the loading bay. As her own eyes adjusted to the light, Marisa saw Thomas Kitchell standing behind Director Francis, and beside Kitchell was an older man who was familiar but didn't register.

Until suddenly he did.

Marisa went to him.

"Torrance," she said. The years had been hard on Torrance Black, but it was most definitely him. They embraced and she felt the fragility of his body in addition to the strength of his arms around her waist. "It's so good to have you home."

EPILOGUES

TORRANCE/DEIDRA

Torrance found Deidra Francis standing alone on a raised platform in *Defender's* observation dome. The small, retractable compartment built onto the surface of the ship allowed dignitaries a spectacular view of deep space: A wide expanse of velvet darkness filled with vast arrays of star fields whose light made the room glow that soft tone of violet he had always loved.

That light traced shadows on the director's face as she stood on the rounded platform, hands resting on raised rails. Torrance liked those shadows. The lines on her face, like those on his own face, and those on Baraq's and on Louratna's before him, revealed truths, dark and spidery under the paper-thin highlights of illumination.

He stepped into the compartment and took a padded seat.

After years of wearing billowing quadarti robes, his clothes — standard-issue slacks and a collared shirt — felt strange now. Comfortable, but tight. His legs ached as he crossed one over his knee. The shoes felt almost blocky.

"It's a beautiful thing, isn't it?" Deidra said, letting him know she was aware of his presence despite her gaze never leaving the stars. "How we all come from the stars?"

He nodded. "I'm sorry to interrupt you."

"I'm happy you did. I assume Deputy Director Nichols has been properly transferred?"

"The supreme president's guards left with her a moment ago."

"That's good."

Deidra's chest rose with a large, stress-filled inhale, and she let her gaze fall from the sky. "That's not why you came here, though, is it?"

"No, it isn't."

She stepped off the platform and sat next to him. Together, they stared into the depths.

"What you're trying to do," Torrance said. "It's a big task."

The UG leadership had capitulated and given them their Star Drives, but simply the raw coordination of the transition was overwhelming, and the politics of it all were even more so. U3 didn't have staffing to fly the entire UG fleet yet, which made it even more difficult to complete the overhaul that included disconnecting them from Alpha Centauri A quickly.

He'd been talking to Kitchell.

He understood she was going to direct her staff to work with UG resources, and that Timmon Keyes would be responsible for integrating their forces.

If that went well, perhaps this thing really could work.

If not, he didn't really want to think about that.

So much could go wrong.

The corner of Deidra's lip rose. She was tired, but strength showed in her eyes.

"I was too young," she said, suddenly turning to Torrance.

"When you took command of U3?"

She nodded. "I was too young, and I made decisions too rashly."

"You created a lot of problems for the United Government, that's for sure."

"But I was right, wasn't I?"

Torrance remained silent, waiting.

"Ellyn Parker was right," Deidra said, filling the silence. "My father was right. And me, too, even as dumb as I was, I was right. That's important, isn't it? Not to fool yourself, but to be actually right about what it means to have the people in your heart?"

She looked at him with a sense of expectation that seemed covered in starlight.

Torrance put his hand on her arm.

"I understand."

And he did understand. He thought about the quadar Families, and Louratna's commune in the mountains. Both systems worked in the sense that quadars could live under them. But one was right, and the other was not.

He thought about the UG and U3.

Both functioned.

One was right, the other wrong.

"The world needs structure to operate," he said. "I could live under a dictator, if it was the right dictator."

"I think that's going too far."

"Maybe," Torrance said, feeling suddenly closer to Louratna again. "But yes, you were right. In the end. And being right matters. Perhaps the galaxy will even be better for your attempts."

They sat in a long silence again.

"I need your help," she said.

"I don't think I have any help left to give."

"I think you're very much wrong about that."

His crooked smile registered doubt.

"I need you to manage the support efforts for the quadars of Eden." She looked at him, then. Took him in fully. "That's what you're here for, isn't it? You know that no one else here can do what you can do for them."

"I must be growing transparent in my old age."

"Not transparent," she said. "Focused. It's a quality we need right now." She turned her entire body to face him. "This is my life's work, Torrance. And from what I see, it's yours too. Our entire worldview is to see that people live freely and safely." Her gaze flickered to the star field and back. "*People* — and by that, I mean humans and quadars and any other species we find in the stars — all of us," she said. "We all need to be able to live good lives."

She paused before finishing. "We need your help."

Torrance smiled.

He uncrossed his leg and put both feet on the ground.

The ship's medical staff had already addressed the cancers that had been growing on his cheeks. They could do nothing to counteract the destruction years on Eden had done to his body, though. His bones and his muscles. Entropy is a bitch. Looking into the stars brought him the sense of Louratna so strongly he might smother in it.

He pictured himself bending over her covered body.

Remembered the edge of her bony shoulder against his fingertips as the desert sand blew over them. Remembered the smell of the desert and the force of Crissandr's arms wrapped around his waist as they mourned.

"Your father would be proud of you," he said.

"Thank you, but that doesn't answer my question."

"Yes," he said, his eyes shining. "Of course, I'll help you."

Kitchell/Allie

Thomas Kitchell decided to go to the science lab late at night, because he knew that's where Allie would be.

It was now or never. Her workload was intense, but between connecting another star to Alpha Centauri A, and reassigning *Defender* and then the entire UG fleet, it wasn't going to get better for a long time.

That didn't even consider the smaller machines.

The nighttime air was cold on his skin as he strode purposefully through the empty streets.

He found her just where he knew she'd be — hunched over her model and surrounded by five young student apprentices in a holo room where four was barely comfortable.

All of them looked at him as he burst through the doorway.

The air was warm from body heat and the hum of projectors.

The display showed a set of stars — each with hovering data boxes nearby, filled with parameters that described its star's construction. He didn't need a degree in astronomy to know that the inner workings of stars were no simple thing.

He shook his head to clear his brain's meanderings.

That wasn't what he was here for.

"Allie," he said.

"What are you doing, Thomas?"

"I apologize," he said, ignoring the apprentices. "I keep getting in your way, and I apologize."

"You're in my way now."

"No, I'm not," he said. "Well. Yes. I am. But I promise you that I'll never get in your way again — unless you want me to."

"What's that supposed to mean?"

The apprentices backed off, and Allie stood up from her chair. Suddenly Thomas felt awkward.

"I'm sorry," he said. "But I've spent too many years letting things slide by. We're good together. You know we are. At least I think I'm good for you if I can keep my fingers out of your work, anyway. No one else understands what this work really means to you, but I do. And I know without any reservation that you are good for me."

Her expression softened.

He saw just how tired she was.

"I miss you, Allie. I know I'm an idiot. And goofy. And I know I can get tied up into things no one else cares about. And everything else that I am. But you're the love of my life, and I'm hoping you'll give me a chance to prove I could be the one for you."

The room went silent except for the hum of the projectors.

"If you don't kiss him, I'm going to," one of the apprentices said.

Through her fatigue, Allie smiled. "That won't be necessary." Allie stepped through the model to stand before Thomas.

She kissed him, her lips soft at first.

He kissed her back.

A few moments later, he held her at arm's length.

"Get your work done. Well, at least get to a stopping place for tonight," he said. "Then come back to my place. I'll have dinner waiting. We can talk more then."

"You do have a way with a skillet," she said.

He kissed her again, then left her lab and strode back through the darkness, back to his quarters where, indeed, he did have a pasta dish ready to reheat.

The city around him filled the dark night, stars lighting the way, the sound of lizard-frogs croaking in the distance.

For what had to be the first time in his life, Thomas Kitchell felt such an extreme joy that he wept.

Torrance/Marisa

Three weeks of work and coordination passed before Torrance and Marisa could find a quiet night to have dinner together. When they did, it was in a private section of a community kitchen — at a small table on a deck that reached out into a wooded area. Torrance chuckled when he heard Kitchell calling the rolling hills here "mountains."

The place smelled heavenly, though, and Torrance was hungry. The aroma of green leaves and cool air added to the moment. The sounds of public conversation came as a low din in the background.

Meals here in the U3 community on Apogee were high on local vegetables and formulated proteins. Dinner would be sauteed and seasoned peppers and pasta. The wine was a deep red.

"I hear you're going back to the Solar System?" he said.

"I am," Marisa replied. "Director Francis asked me to take the position that oversees the process the UG will use to transition their Star Drive navigation systems to Universe Three."

"You've always been great at that kind of thing, and Deidra can be very convincing when she wants to be."

"I admit I wasn't a hard sell."

Torrance nodded and sipped wine. The essence of fruit was sharp.

Marisa smiled.

She looked amazing tonight. Still trim, her body athletic despite the years.

"I like managing processes, and this feels like an important one. More important than anything else I've ever done, really. Except raising Mercy and Ana."

"Mmm," Torrance said, nodding.

"I know I've done good work before, but I don't know. It seems like I've never felt…" She shrugged.

"It's all right," Torrance said. "Sometimes it takes a while to find out who you are supposed to be."

"I've always felt like there should be more to what I do."

He smiled. "I'm glad you'll be in the same system with the kids."

She smiled back. "They may not be so thrilled. I intend to be a bit more intrusive than I've been in the past."

They sat in silence as dinner came.

"What will you do?" Marisa said.

"Deidra asked me to help her with the quadars, so I'll do that for as long as I can." He speared lettuce with his fork, noting a dark moment cross her face. "What was that?" he said.

"You could come back with me."

He crunched the lettuce, then set the fork down, letting a feeling of comfort fall over him.

"Thank you," he said. "I appreciate the offer more than I can say. But we both know that's a bad idea."

She hesitated, then nodded. "I had to suggest it."

"It made me feel good to hear it."

"You're right, of course," Marisa finished. "We were great when we were great, but it's a bad idea."

He picked up his fork again, feeling the warmth of his smile filling his whole body. "I'm so happy we had that time together."

Her smile in return was both deep and heartbreaking, a hard pressing of her lips together as emotion spread over her face. She reached for her wineglass and raised it.

"To having been great," she said.

He raised his glass.

The wine was fantastic.

BARAQ/CRISSANDR

Baraq sat with Crissandr, his *kalla*, holding her hand and listening while Ezi spoke to the gathering of independent quadars.

After Torranze had arranged for Baraq, Ezi, and Pella to return to All of Esgarat, Ezi Waganat gathered the community together in the wide split in the mountain that was the grandest opening of Louratna's compound — the same place that earlier had witnessed the killing of their leader.

The Families will never change, Ezi said to them. *And the humans have made us an offer. If we want, we can start anew. We can go to another place.*

Baraq watched his whelp's pair-mate lay out the path that would have them leave Esgarat, cede this place to the Families, and lead the rest to a new planet, one suited to them. Dry, but fertile, a place with mountains, yes, but also with rivers of water that flowed on the surface. The humans had searched their systems, she said. It was a planet that could soon be lush with *havra* and *kado* root, and which had other plants and other animals, and other places where quadars could expand beyond any of their ability to comprehend.

The idea was worrisome, leaving the planet. But adventuresome.

Not everyone would go.

But as he listened to Ezi, he felt momentum turn.

His whelp had chosen well. The quadars trusted her as they had trusted Brada. His Brada.

Beside him, Crissandr took his hand.

Their Brada.

"It will be a hard life," she said.

"It will."

"But life is always hard."

Baraq's hearts beat more strongly as he realized what she was saying. "You want to go."

She raised a ridge over one primary and bent her central down in a way that said their departure was preordained.

"You don't think we are too old for that kind of adventure?"

She patted his hand. "Now you're being silly."

"Silly?"

"I know what is in you, Baraq."

He twisted his lips, recalling his deeds alone in the streets of Esgarat City. "I don't know if that is such a good idea."

She held his hand and turned her face to watch as Ezi continued to lay out the options.

There would be no pressure. All would make their own decisions, and Torranze will work to shuttle quadars back and forth as need be — over time, anyway. Any who joined would work to their capability, just as they did here. But any who decided coming was a mistake could return.

"You are a good quadar, Baraq. Fighting the Families was a good thing."

He breathed deeply.

"You are a dreamer. A quadar who invents. You know right and wrong. The new world will need you there."

"And you?"

Her smile was a light mix of humor and smugness that made him oddly happy.

"I see," he said. And he did. Crissandr would be who Crissandr always was. "You will be anything, and everything, and all the parts in between."

"Yes," she said, holding his hand tighter. "And I will be yours, too. Never forget that."

Crissandr put her head on his shoulder.

"I won't forget," he said. Her body beside his warmed him. He cupped his hand tighter to hers, and as he looked into the future, his hearts welled. "You are mine," he said. "And I am yours."

They sat together, watching as the gathering came around to Ezi's viewpoint.

Pella/Anko

"Come," Pella said, holding Anko Banit's hand as he made his way down a sheer cliff face.

The Banit had lived his whole life on the flatland fields of the desert plantations, which meant he was not familiar with climbing. It took him longer to get down than she wanted it to, but that was life right now. Wait, wait, wait.

She had returned from the place humans called Apogee so that she could be ready to join the next space shuttle to their new planet — a land the settlers, which turned out to be many, had decided collectively to name Louratna.

Pella had never met that quadar, but she had heard the wise quadar's teachings and understood instinctively that it had been a proper naming.

Excitement was nearly driving her insane.

She had spent another long heat of work with the refugees, so it was even later than she normally arrived, but she wanted to show Anko how her work had changed after learning from the humans. He'd been interested — asking her about it each time they were able to find moments together, which was not often enough for Pella's desires.

Anko was growing into a strong and supple quadar.

Pella tried to ignore his presence, but mostly failed.

Loose pebbles skittered down the cliff face as Anko grabbed

handholds. A moment later he was on stable ground, chest heaving but no worse for wear.

The garden's scent was fresh in the secluded chasm.

She felt close to him, then. They were both young, both on the precipice of being full quadars. He was as tall as she was. But she felt their differences just as strongly. Where he was strong in the way of field labor, she was tougher in the way of streets. He'd learned as much from his Family as Pella had from hers, but they were vastly different lessons. She was learning from the humans now, too. She wondered how he would take ideas from outside the Family.

"These are my rows," she said, suddenly anxious. She hoped Anko would find them good.

He bent to examine them, then moved from row to row, stopping at each to trace two long fingers from the plant's roots to stop just before each plant's sprouting leaf.

He bent to his hands and knees to sniff at the last plant.

"You've adjusted watering," he said.

"Yes. And some have different feeding than ground shells. I wanted to see what worked best."

"And?"

She scanned the rows. "The answer seems clear."

"It may seem that way," Anko said, standing fully upright. "But it depends on whether you are growing for food or fiber."

"How do you mean?" She crossed her arms.

"*Kado* root watered well gives sweet food stock. But if we want the best material for creating fiber cloth, we taper watering at the half point. When that happens, the plant reacts by pulling its water to the core."

"I see," Pella replied. "That makes sense. The far-down fibers become dry and coarse."

He clicked a delighted sound. "Right. They become tough like a free ranger."

They were silent for a moment.

All this knowledge mattered because the next mission would take quadarti seeds with them. So much of their life was going to be tied to these seeds, and early testing said that the hardier plants could take sustenance from the new lands of Louratna. It also mattered because Pella would be part of that mission. She wanted to make a life planting. She may be young, but her need to help her people thrive was no less fervent. Hearing her elders condescend to her youth simply drove her harder.

She hoped Anko would go, too.

"Can I ask why you are here?" she finally asked.

"I think you just did."

"You know what I mean. Your Family is still together."

"What is left of them, yes."

"What is left?"

He shrugged and avoided her gaze.

"The Tegra and Festia have taken control." He squinted as he craned his gaze up the wall. "For now, anyway."

"So," she said. "Why are you here?"

He shrugged. "I don't believe in that future."

"And you believe in this one?" She glanced at the rows.

He drew a breath, then bent to the closest row she'd planted. "I don't know what I believe in," he said, cupping a flower between two fingers again. "But I like it here."

The sight of him, caressing the plant, brought warmth to her hearts. Her tongue became stuck in her mouth. She didn't know what that feeling meant. Or, rather, she was embarrassed of what it meant. Finally, she managed to come to her real question.

"Will you go with me?"

His primaries glanced her way, then deflected back to the rows.

Anxiously, she touched his arm. "It will be very hard," she said.

"I came here to be with you," he said. "If you go, then I will, too."

He smiled and, when he put his hand on her arm, she felt a dazzling moment in which everything snapped into place.

She thought of her mother then.

And her father.

Scraping together simply to find food in Esgarat City.

She remembered sleeping while hungry, remembered heats and darktimes alone while her parents scurried to find labor.

The idea of a life with Anko swelled in her mind.

They were young.

It *would* be hard.

But she had seen the new world, and she had seen what human support could do. If they worked, they could make it.

"We will have so much to learn," she said.

"Maybe it will be less difficult to learn together," he replied.

Her smile turned so coy then that she was embarrassed. She wanted to ask him a hundred questions. Everything from what his favorite things were to how it felt to have a Family around him.

They would have time for that, though.

If it was true, anyway. If Anko had come to the compound for her.

"That would be nice," she said.

Anko's central opened.

"You can start by showing me your plans for the next row."

Together, they got to work.

CODA

Torrance/Baraq

Over the next several weeks, Torrance came to understand the immense complexity involved in moving half a population from one planet to the next, even if the population was small.

As time passed, he grew more worried about them.

Their sun wasn't going to die now. Did it really make sense for them to go? Even though the new planet had been selected to come close to matching Esgarat's climate, everything would still be different.

Could they adapt?

What if they couldn't?

Was he going to kill off the very species he'd fought so hard to save? He was too old for this. Wouldn't it just be better to bring the force of human technology down so hard on the Families that they capitulated?

That last was a danger that made him shudder to think he'd thought it.

Force could change behavior, but it could not change thought.

Someday, when the Families' reliance on their form of feudalistic capitalism ran its course, they might change. Now, though, the only goal was to keep them in the confined space of the Esgarat mountains until the rest of the quadars could leave if they so desired.

The work was hard, and confusing.

The Orange Ring was not so authoritative that they led to efficiency, and the communication barriers between human and quadar were immense.

He considered quitting a half dozen times, even once bringing his concerns to Ezi, who immediately berated him angrily.

"You have told me that humans moved from place to place many times," she said, shaking her hand at him. "You consider my quadars worse?"

Director Francis dedicated *Magellan* to the quadars, which was helpful — and which Torrance could not see as anything other than the fates of time casting their ironic glances his way. Before the UG repurposed it, *Magellan* was chartered to be the first Star Drive cruiser assigned to scientific missions. Torrance had spent many hours planning its arrival at Eden in those days.

Deego Larsi pitched in, and Kazima Yamada did, too — when she wasn't working on U3's own expansion plans, which was most of the time. But mostly it fell to Torrance, Ezi, Oast'el, Vareta, and the rest of the Orange Ring to make things happen.

Crissandr, too, was everywhere at once.

Baraq spent every moment he could with Universe Three construction teams to learn about their equipment. Young Pella seemed to live in the fields, returning each day covered in so much dirt the quadars took to calling her Dusty.

Still, the teams had to work together to complete the process in a series of intricate stages that felt excruciatingly slow.

The first phase was a scouting party led by Oast'el.

Then came surveying missions and other planning sessions.

Temporary housing was next, along with core necessities including foodstuff and power.

Two standard months passed before the first mission of quadars left for their new planet.

As the shuttle carrying that first mission left Esgarat, Torrance stood in the evening gloaming with Baraq, on the same viewing platform they'd stood on to watch their rockets fly.

The spacecraft carried Edart Kel and her partner Zvin Tek, which made Torrance's heart twist too many ways to be able to describe.

His heart contained a joy, of course. A feeling of anticipation that he knew he would never see play out. But that anticipation came with a sadness, too. He wanted to know.

"You have taught her well, Torranze," Baraq said to him. "She will be amazing."

Torrance worried that speaking would be too difficult, so instead he gave a quadarti grunt that meant something like *time will pass.*

When the launch had completed and the shuttle's contrails had dissipated into the darkening sky, Torrance paid good nights to Baraq and the other quadars there, then he turned to walk into the looming afterdark.

He was tired, but thoughts cluttered his mind with such rapid-fire speed that he knew sleep would be impossible. Feeling restless, he walked alone, a short but familiar distance around the mountain, feeling the stone hard under his feet as he ambled gingerly down a path and around a bend to arrive at a tall formation that rose into the sky.

Rocket Rock.

He arched his back to take in the whole formation.

He had loved this place from the moment he first found it.

The stone was still warm to the touch, its windswept grain rough under his hands. The sense of it against his fingertips brought back memories. A gentle breeze came, formed by falling temperatures and the curve of the mountain upslope. He put his other hand on the rock, and an essence of power come over him that seized his chest. The planet was talking to him, he thought. He put his ear against the warm rock and felt power in the stone. Closing his eyes felt good.

One fingertip lay in a low handhold.

Lifting his head, the breeze cooled his forehead.

Without a second thought, and forgetting the aches in his elbows and knees, Torrance reached into that handhold, and then another, climbing higher, digging his fingers into the formation's rough holes, and scraping his knees as he clung to ledges, feeling his belly slide over the rock, hearing blood ring in his ears.

He pulled himself to the top and rolled over to sit upright. His legs crossed, his chest heaved, his muscles burned with pain that suddenly felt good. How he would make it down, he didn't know. But for now, alone, he simply looked over the landscape.

Torrance had forgotten how beautiful the planet was. The land sprawled out before him in mottled patches of orange and brown, the purple dome of sky above it.

Dense clouds formed over the horizon tonight. Signs that the climate was already coming back.

Maybe.

Every climatologist Torrance talked to said it could take decades for Esgarat to recover, but Torrance was going to take what solace he could of tonight's images.

He took in as large of a breath as he could manage, and let it go slowly.

This was it.

He had come full circle.

The tenuous agreement between UG and U3 could collapse at any moment, of course. The quadars would go on, as would humanity. The future was always uncertain, and no matter what he or any other person in the galaxy did today, the worlds around them would change in ways they could never guess.

But, for him, this was the moment.

Sitting alone on Rocket Rock, he recalled standing likewise alone on a command platform on a spaceship riding the solar waves of Alpha Centauri A, feeling a sense of despair for his own life, and contemplating what he could do to save Eden.

Torrance had always known he was right.

He had always had a fervid belief that *someone* was here — even as far back as when he was a kid, lying back in green Wisconsin grass and looking up into the stars with his parents. The idea was in his bones someplace.

Undefinable. Impossible to specify. But there.

Looking back, he realized the data files he gathered on *Everguard* had simply confirmed that belief.

He gave a delighted smile then.

All along he'd thought it was the other way around.

He remembered Alexandir Romanov, the captain who had protected Torrance. He thought about his team on *Everguard*, even Karl Malloy, the U3 agent turned rogue. Malloy's hearty poundings on the back were legendary. Torrance could still see the plaque his team had given him. He wondered what Deidra Francis would say about Malloy and his mission. If Torrance had learned one thing in his life, it was to be wary of people in power. Deidra had been firm on her idea of right and wrong, and she was right to do that. Her frame could change, though. Over time it *would* change because that's what people and civilizations do.

"I thought I might find you here."

The voice startled Torrance enough he almost fell off the rock. He laughed, though, and peering into the darkness below he saw it was Baraq.

"I'm sorry to startle you," the quadar said. "Can I join?"

Torrance clicked affirmative, and a moment later, the quadar was beside him, barely fazed by the climb.

They sat in silence, both with legs pulled up and elbows over knees.

"What are you thinking, Torranze?"

"Oh," he replied in a tone drawn out long enough to give himself time to settle. "About everything and nothing, I guess."

"Those are good things to think about."

"To be honest, I was thinking about the mountains, and about something Director Francis said about the stars."

Baraq waited this time.

"She said we are all born from them." He looked to Baraq, realizing how deeply he appreciated the fact that even as she said it, Deidra Francis had included the quadars in her idea.

"I like that," Baraq said. "But I'm not sure how to think about it."

"It means we all return to them, too," Torrance said, feeling the connection between his thought and the quadarti view that the dead return to the land around them.

"I see," Baraq said with a contemplative tone. "Then that *is* good."

The skies were growing darker now, indigo heading toward black. Tiny Eterdane — Proxima to his human colleagues — had made its brilliant appearance.

"I need to give you gratitude," Baraq finally said.

Torrance gave a soft *hmm* to acknowledge Baraq's comment, but he wasn't sure how to feel about it.

"I have heard stories these past heats," Baraq said. "About what you did to send us the Light That Fell from the Sky when no one else would do anything. And about deciding to come to Esgarat on your own." He waited, but Torrance didn't respond. "They are true?"

Torrance clicked a begrudging affirmative and drew a deep breath of Esgarat air. "True enough."

Baraq said nothing, but he shifted his position to sit directly beside Torrance. The heat of Baraq's body pressed against Torrance's side. The sharpness of Baraq's backplate pressed firmly on Torrance's shoulder.

Both looked up into the darkness.

Above them, a pair of *jah* took wing for their evening hunt.

"I'm glad we have had this moment together," Baraq said. "Here on this little rock."

"I am, too," Torrance replied. "I am, too."

This is the end of

STARBORN

STEALING THE SUN: BOOK 9

If you enjoyed this story, please consider stopping by your favorite online booksellers' websites and leaving a review. Word of mouth is the most powerful force in the universe when it comes to the livelihood of your favorite authors. Even a few sentences can help!

If you haven't read the full series, you might be interested in:

STARFLIGHT

STARBURST

STARFALL

STARCLASH

STARBOUND

STARCRASH

STARGAMES

STARDUST

STARBORN

ACKNOWLEDGMENTS

I want to thank every person who has helped me through this series in any way. David Farland, who gave me the assignment in the first Writers of the Future class where I wrote the original story in. And Algis Budrys, who gave me courage. Amy Sterling Casil, whose pen holder became those wormhole pod launchers. Carla Montgomery, who provided that first title. The Fisher's Five — Charles Eckert, Kevin Shadle, Linda Dunn, John Bodin, and of course Lisa Silverthorne.

Stan Schmitt, the then-editor at *Analog*, who asked that simple question I noted in my dedication, "What comes next?" and who, after the third story said, "I think it's time to write the novel."

I want to thank my beautiful wife for supporting me through this whole journey, and for being the world-class copyeditor she is (all errors left in these books are most assuredly mine). And Brigid, my amazing daughter for early reads and lots of support.

I've been blessed with amazing Beta readers. I want to thank all of you. But especially John Bodin and Sharon Bass — both of whom stuck through to the end. My goodness, what a fantastic thing it's been to have you with me. Many, many thanks.

And, finally, let me thank everyone who reads the books.

I wouldn't be here without all of you.

ABOUT THE AUTHOR

Ron Collins is an Amazon best-selling Science Fiction and Dark Fantasy author who writes across the spectrum of fiction genres.

His fantasy series *Saga of the God-Touched Mage* reached Amazon's bestselling dark fantasy list several countries. His short story "The White Game" was nominated for the Short Mystery Fiction Society's Derringer Award.

He has contributed a couple hundred or so short stories to *Analog, Asimov's, Fiction River* Anthology Series, and several other professional magazines and anthologies.

He holds a degree in Mechanical Engineering, and has worked to develop avionics systems, electronics, and information technology before chucking it all to write full-time.

Ron's website is: www.typosphere.com
Follow Ron on Twitter: @roncollins13

Sign up for his newsletter to get free stuff!

http://www.typosphere.com/newsletter